HEROES ARE HARD TO FIND

by

Mike Looney

PUBLISH AMERICA

PublishAmerica

Baltimore

First printing

ISBN: 1-4137-1667-9
PUBLISHED BY PUBLISHAMERICA, LLLP
www.publishamerica.com
Baltimore

Printed in the United States of America

This story takes place before man's
most worthless invention—
the metal baseball bat.

ACKNOWLEDGEMENT

After originally drafting Heroes in a screenplay format and enduring a couple of false starts in the movie business, I decided to make the conversion to a novel. Quickly learning that my prose was weaker than a number nine batter, I sought help by reading some of the industry heavy weights—in particular, W. P. Kinsella and John Irving. Readers will find their influence in passages everywhere—Kinsella's metaphors from most any of his work and especially Irving's masterpiece, Prayer For Owen Meaney.

A special thanks also goes to Jon Anders, former writer for the now defunct Dallas Times Herald, and his column of over ten years ago on the very real W.C. Harrell and Harrell's Drugstore. Also consideration to Kevin Sherrington of the Dallas Morning News for his recent column on former University of Texas quarterback, Randy McEachern.

Finally, a tribute to Woodrow Wilson High School, the only high school with two Heisman trophy winners, Tim Brown and Davey O'Brien, for providing the story's back drop. After seventy-five years, Woodrow still sits proudly on Glasgow Avenue, ever durable to the demands and kinetic energy of a student body comprised of all races and color.

Chapter One
THE LAST GAME

It seemed inconceivable to Stormy Weathers that he might never play another game in Yankee Stadium or any other major league yard, for that matter. From Jaynie's front row seat, her transistor radio carried this bit of gloom above the crowd's noisy din.

A brief swell of anger made his chest sting when one of the announcers had the audacity to say: "Stormy's body has become like one of those subcompact cars with a couple of hundred thousand miles. Parts keep falling off."

Kneeling on his tattered and torn right knee, Stormy's brown eyes absorbed the site of sixty thousand plus jammed in their seats like peas in a can. In left field, the sun had already disappeared behind the third deck, leaving the orange sky no option but to dissolve into blue. As comforting as a World Series in October, the warm fall breeze whispered melodically through the stadium aisles and ushered the smoky aroma of ballpark food to Stormy in the on-deck circle.

"Oh, that brat looks good. Do you eat that with your hands?" Stormy heard an usher say to a spectator. "I'm sweatin' like hell and I have been since I got here," the usher added. True, it seemed awfully warm for the last day of September.

Younger players tended to stand in the on-deck circle, flailing away with a violent swing of the bat. Some would swing downward in an apparent mad effort to drive the invisible ball into the ground. Stormy always knelt beside the on-deck circle, preferring to relax, rest on one knee, swing gracefully, casually, preserving energy for the real battle. For reasons of superstition, Stormy would enter the heart of the on-deck circle only during his leisurely stroll to the plate.

Through wire-rimmed glasses, Stormy's glance met Jaynie's and both briefly smiled. The twenty-two-year-old bleached blond wore a brief cotton dress with absolutely nothing on underneath. Only spaghetti straps prevented the garment from falling; its fresh snow color served to exaggerate her deep bronze tan. Jaynie discreetly spread her perfectly shaped legs so Stormy could sneak a glance. Nice, real nice. After twenty years in the big leagues, he still appreciated the chance to look up a young woman's dress from on-deck.

Thankfully, Stormy's good looks hadn't faded as much as his baseball skills, but he figured these enticing young babes wouldn't give him the time to round the base paths if he weren't a famous ballplayer.

At the start of the season, Stormy considered announcing his retirement— doing one of those farewell tours, collecting expensive gifts in each city. But he couldn't quit on his own; they would have to kick him out of the game.

And now only two outs remained in his career unless, Jackie Runnels, who prepared to take the batter's box, or Stormy could drive in Reynolds or Blanchard. The Yankee runners stood on second and third base, respectively, stranded like penguins in the desert.

A victory and New York would make the play-offs. Pretty hairy situation, one that separated the men from the boys, but no problem for a stepper. Granted, his .274 average was his worst year in the bigs, but like the radio boys said, a good play-off and Stormy might land a contract for next year.

Runnels took a pitch for a ball. Stormy rubbed his right hand across the coarse dark stubbles on his face. He hated shaving and once wore a beard, but now it would grow salt and pepper. In a young man's game, no need to look older than necessary. Hell, recently he even spotted a gray nose hair.

With the arms of a blacksmith, Stormy took a few more gentle warmup swings. Though not a huge man, his teammates always said Stormy grew with each layer of his uniform that he dropped to the locker room floor.

Stormy's intense eyes traced Runnels's hissing line drive foul into the stands above first base. The aging ballplayer honed in on the glass dirt base paths and perfectly manicured grass of the playing field.

Would he ever again hear the applause of the home crowd when his team took the field? During today's national anthem, he had memorized the sight of his teammate's standing in their defensive positions, hats held snugly to their hearts. Stormy felt goose bumps erupt on his arm thinking about it. It never failed. Some rambunctious fan had yelled, "play ball" after the song's last note.

During the seventh inning stretch, the melody of the house organ had practically spelled the words to "Take me out to the Ball Game." The crowd merrily sang or hummed along, providing one last serenade to Stormy.

A distant roar pulled Stormy's eyes toward the sight of a commercial airliner; its jet stream painted a long white streak across the pale blue sky. The sound of an airplane even reminded him of a ballpark, he decided.

Runnels took another pitch outside for ball two. The vendors' solicitations carried above the crowd's anxious buzz. "Ice cold cokes, Dr. Pepper, Cracker Jacks here. Coors, Miller, Bud," the beer peddler offered loudly. For years, Stormy had wanted to do it. Today might be the last chance. Should he? Hell, yeah!

"Hey Sam," Stormy barked. "Let me have a Coors."

The startled vendor's head snapped toward the stone-faced Stormy. After a slight hesitation, the vendor leaned over the railing and prepared to hand Stormy the brew but Stormy's face took on the grin of the Cheshire cat and the vendor realized he'd chased a bad pitch.

Stormy knew from the crackling sound that Runnels hit the ball hard. A wicked line drive darted along the third base line.

The crowd roared and leapt to its feet in anticipation of a Yankee victory. Boston's third baseman dove to his right, his body stretched perfectly horizontal to the ground. He stabbed air to make the backhanded catch and then crashed on his side to the soft dirt, creating a small cloud of dust. While he scrambled to his feet, both base runners dove back safely to their respective bases, also stirring up countless specks of red dirt. The third sacker calmly tossed the ball back to his pitcher. Runnels, in disgust, heaved his batting helmet high in the air.

With the crowd now more deflated than a punctured tire, Stormy wrapped his hands around the thin end of the baseball bat. Muscles rippled along his forearms as he shoved the barrel end of the bat to the ground and propped his body upright. Stormy swung the bat gently during his slow hobble to the plate.

Oh, to hear the crisp sound of ash spanking cowhide and have the ball land safely in the outfield's sea of green. Or better yet, to send the ball crashing into the outfield stands like a downed sputnik and during his home run stroll, drink in the sight of a small mob scrambling for the home-run souvenir. He'd deliver the hit to keep his team alive and his career alive. That's what he'd do.

Stormy's name came over the PA and no crowd had ever cheered louder for him. "Stormy, Stormy," the crowd yelled, fully aware this could be the last hurrah. (On the road, it was usually "Weathers, you're gonna strike out!")

But wait. Here came Jackson, the lanky Red Sox reliever strolling in from the bullpen. Stormy hated batting off this guy. Jackson threw hard enough to dent steel. His sidearm delivery brought terror to right-handed batters, and he was so damn tall, he seemed to step off the mound and hand the ball to you.

Stormy walked halfway between the on-deck circle and home plate and studied Jackson on the mound. Rock n' roll blared across the stadium PA and, like speed with power, blended nicely with the pop of Jackson's pitches into the catcher's mitt. After seven warm-up-bb's, the ump cried, "Play ball!"

An old nemesis greeted Stormy the instant he stepped into the batter's box.

"Hey, no way we're gonna let a fossil like you beat us for the title. Just sit this one out; save yourself the embarrassment."

Stormy glared down at Josh Howard, a fourteen year veteran and no youngster himself. Josh's face bore the puffy flesh and sporadic lumps of a losing fighter. The burly catcher's tobacco juice oozed from his curled lip and down his sandpaper chin. Short sleeves exposed muscular arms covered with hair thick and dark enough to pass for fur. He was gross, but tough as the back end of a shooting gallery, and Stormy liked him for that alone.

A trace of Texas surfaced in Stormy's calm reply. "Bro, I appreciate your interest in my well-being, but I'll take my chances. Tell that six o'clock twerp to throw it straight down the middle."

"You got it, old-timer."

In the catcher's crouch, Josh skillfully concealed the signals between his legs. Stormy would try to sneak a peak but the odds of catching Josh asleep were less than hitting a ball over Yankee Stadium's third deck.

Jackson stared menacingly at Stormy, as if insulted by Stormy's audacity to assume the batter's box. The ball soon raced to home plate. Stormy swung and felt a warm sensation fill both arms. The crowd erupted as the ball, white against blue, sailed toward the safety of the left field bleachers.

Stormy remained in the batter's box, admiring the moon shot. No one would catch that ball, but damn, its trajectory angled left, like a failing rocket. Josh, now standing, leaned far left as if using body English to guide the ball foul.

Stormy leaned right, hoping the same technique would steer the ball in play.

"Shane come back!" Josh gasped.

Stormy's blast, weary from a near four hundred-foot journey, collapsed as harmlessly as it did foul into the left field stands. A disappointed hush smothered the crowd.

Stormy only shook his head. "Damn."

"Never a doubt. Foul all the way," Josh said matter-of-factly.

Stormy's eyes never strayed from the mound. "Shut up, wolf breath."

The umpire tossed a new ball to the mound.

"Maybe we'll put a little hook on this one," Josh chattered while flashing finger signals to his hurler.

Boston's young Turk had a wicked breaking ball—the nastiest one since Koufax. Stormy would need to stay in the box because the ball would seem on a path for his head but at the last second, break over the plate for a strike. No one had ever accused Stormy Weathers of bailing out on a curve. Stormy dug in ready for combat. He'd kick Josh and his teammates one last time.

Stormy hit the dirt so hard and fast, his helmet stayed behind, momentarily frozen in midair. His bare head exposed a thick growth of brown hair streaked with gray. Josh, the bastard, had crossed him; the missile narrowly missed caving in one side of his skull.

Amid the hometown boos, Stormy climbed to his feet, sporting the surprised look of someone who had just survived a car wreck. He dusted off his Yankee pinstripes, and while retrieving his helmet, stumbled in a manner that suggested some body parts were out of warranty.

"You worthless scumbag sack of shit. You said it was gonna be a curve."

"I said maybe. Now I'm confused myself."

"Hey bro, is that mound too close?" Stormy attempted to remain cool in an anything but a cool situation. He knew he'd shown weakness.

"That long drink of water gets it here pretty quick, huh? I love you, man, but this is survival of the fittest. Anyway, it's time to call it a career."

A wide grin divided Josh's leathery face; he spit tobacco juice to the ground, then fired the ball to his pitcher.

Boston's pitcher kicked his leg to the second deck and grunted audibly. A trail of white pitcher's resin followed the darting sphere to the plate.

"Fastball," said Stormy internally. Stormy swung hard enough to stir up a minor twister.

"Strike two!" declared the man in blue.

The crowd buzzed with an equal mix of disappointment and excitement. Stormy Weathers proved exciting to watch, even when fanning air. You didn't hit over six hundred career homers by swinging like a choirboy.

With hands large enough to hold four baseballs at once, Josh massaged the ball then tossed it back to his pitcher. "Who's going to show me around the Big Apple next year if you're not here? The night with those chicks at P.T.'s was one of my major league highlights," Josh said, spitting tobacco juice to the ground with such force, motes of dirt rose around home plate.

"Corkscrew brain, with your career, it was the highlight." Stormy had taken Josh out a few times when the Red Sox visited New York. He'd met Josh's wife once when the Yankees played in Boston and felt sorry for him. She was a real nag and ugly enough to wrinkle a shirt. Josh was no prize, but he'd married while still in the minors. Josh should have waited until he made it to the big show, where even slobs have their pick of pretty women.

As the ball shot toward home plate, an ugly thought hit Stormy's mind with the impact of a well-placed bean ball. His confidence was sinking, its depth charge accelerated by the weighted notion that Father Time had torpedoed his once unsinkable skills. Stormy whipped the bat across the plate, and the ball darted between the shortstop and third baseman. Boston's shortstop moved far to his right and roamed out of the infield dirt into shallow left field.

Stormy raced for first with all the speed his bad knee and forty-one years allowed. He slammed the pedal to the metal, but the once-upon-a-time sports car now turned sedan refused to accelerate. From the corner of his eye, Stormy saw the young Latin shortstop would get to the ball. The kid covered more ground than the infield tarpolium.

Boston's phenom bent to the ground and scooped the ball cleanly. With his momentum carrying him to the outfield, he leapt in the air and rifled a rocket toward first base. The ball sailed high right.

The first sacker leapt to his max; his left mitt hand reached to the sky and swallowed the ball. Airborne, the ballplayer lowered his glove in lightening fashion, swatting Stormy on his left shoulder. Stormy crossed first base and sixty thousand amateur umps screamed "safe" but only one person's opinion mattered on this day.

The first base umpire yelled the most dreaded two words Stormy had ever heard in his life. "You're out!"

A hush descended over Yankee Stadium as the Red Sox bench mobbed their teammates on the field. Stormy made his way toward the Yankee dugout; he briefly wondered why more people didn't get hurt in these insidious celebrations. He thought of an old Beatle's song; "How can you laugh when you know I'm down?" Red Sox players continued to flop on top of each other, forming a huge pile of flesh.

That's what he'd do. He'd go to the locker room and listen to some music; that's about all that remained of the world he cared for.

The crowd filed out of the old stadium as if on a death march. Josh took a break from the festivities and noticed Stormy, head down, limping out of sight to the Yankee locker room; the catcher almost felt sympathy for his long time foe.

Chapter Two
THE LAST LOCKER ROOM

Carpet thick as outfield grass covered the floor of the Yankee dressing room. Each player had an individual stall wide enough for a batting cage and his name inscribed at the top of his cubicle. Though a faint, pungent smell from a season of sweat-soiled uniforms still hung in the air, the lockers were bare, cleaned out for the winter. One last object remained in Stormy's bin: an old half-torn Playboy centerfold. Only bare legs and feet remained, taped inside the locker.

Stormy had long forgotten the identity of the centerfold picture. After his first year or so in the bigs, he discovered beautiful young women in every city, willing and able; the real thing dramatically reduced Stormy's interest in mere photographs.

Stormy sat alone in his rocking chair, packing his duffel bag and softly singing along with his nearby tape player. Most of the athletes had comfortable chairs for their cubicles, but Stormy's leather rocker was large enough to nap in, a symbol of his senior status.

The artist was J.J. Cale, a Southern white singer who sang black. Stormy had picked up on J.J. as a kid from the blacks at the orphanage. "Magnolia, you sweet dream, you're driving me mad. Magnolia you sweet dream, the best I ever had."

He wore his off the field uniform: blue jeans, T-shirt, Yankee hat and white tennis shoes. Stormy heard the sound of lockers slamming and abruptly stopped singing. A voice bellowed from another area of the clubhouse.

"Stormy, is that you in there?"

"Yeah."

It was Doc Rivers, the clubhouse manager. With the Yankees for over thirty years, Doc had seen enough ballplayers come and go to pack the bleachers at Yankee Stadium.

The short, balding man entered the room. He wore solid white and kept half a cigar buried in the corner of his mouth. Since Doc's cigar was never lit, no one ever understood what happened to the other half. He retrieved a nearby stool and sat beside Stormy.

"How'd you know it was me?" Stormy said somberly.

"I guess by now I'd know you're the first one here and the last one to leave. And your music. With every generation of players the music gets worse. The more money you fellas make the lousier the music. I ain't gonna make it through this hard rock."

"You're talking about that heavy metal crap."

"Whatever it is," Doc said, munching enthusiastically on his stogie.

Doc was always yelling for the players to turn the music down and often complained the racket was causing him to lose his sanity. Stormy usually just laughed at Doc's musical woes.

"You ever gonna find that girl?"

"Who?" Stormy appeared preoccupied with packing but it was more to disguise his interest in the question.

"Magnolia, the girl you been singing about all these years."

Stormy's eyes betrayed his indifferent shrug. A weighted silence overpowered the room. "It was my last game."

"Reckon so. The hell of it is I'm just gettin' used to your music. Son, you've done it all. Golden glove, M.V.P., All Star teams, championship teams, a cinch for the Hall of Fame. There ain't nothing else for you to accomplish anyway."

Stormy pondered, dragging his hand across his chin. "State championship."

"Huh?"

"It was the only year my high school made the state play-offs, much less the finals. My senior year, back in Dallas. We lost the state championship game 'cause I made the last out. Blew it with a pussy slide at home. I should have blasted that catcher to the Trinity River. I'd love the chance to go back and play that game again. Funny how some things stay with you your whole life."

Doc sprang to life like fire after a shot of lighter fluid. "That must have been your last soft slide. I fell off the bench in Cleveland when your bat broke and all those corks fell out and started bouncin' all around home plate. You didn't say a word, just turned around and walked back to the dugout."

Stormy tugged on the brim of his Yankee hat. "Well, I guess you could say I was looking for a little unfair advantage," he said through a sly conspiratorial grin. "That one generated a three-day vacation sipping margaritas on the beaches in Mexico."

"What about the time you rounded third against Detroit and headed straight into their dugout after Sturdivan?"

"The man had been throwin' at my head all season like it was a replaceable item."

"Yeah, but not many players attack an entire team's visiting dugout."

Both men snickered like schoolboys. J.J. Cale continued to moan softly behind them.

"My favorite was in California when you hit the third base ump in the back with a perfect strike from center field. Everybody in the stadium knew you did it on purpose."

"Blind ass Walker. Stevie Wonder would have been a better ump. He got the message. I never lost a close call to him again."

"Stormy, I believe you'd take a switch to a bear hunt or even tangle with Lucifer himself."

The men's laughter wound down like an unplugged turntable. Stormy exhaled with such force, he felt momentarily dizzy.

"Things are sure different than when I broke in, that's for sure. When I started playing, parents could drop their kids off at the ballpark and never give it a second thought. Even the new stadiums aren't the same. What about that damn ballpark in Houston with that god-awful roof and fake grass?"

"It's enough to make you puke your sunflower seeds," moaned Doc, nodding his head wistfully.

"Now Fenway, that's a green cathedral."

"The green monster," Doc said, awe in his tone. He referred to Boston's giant green wall in left field. "I heard when the Red Sox would change pitchers, Ted Williams would walk through the wall and go across the street to get some ice cream," Doc added, his awe greater than before.

"And what about the outfield in Cincinnati?"

"Crosley," Doc quickly replied. "You had to run up hill to catch a fly ball in left."

"I guess Wrigley is still my favorite with all the ivy covering the outfield walls." Stormy's brown eyes were dancing now. "You had the monuments right here in Yankee Stadium," Stormy said, referring to the monuments of past Yankee greats that once stood 457 feet from home plate in center field.

"Remember when Piersall hid behind Ruth's monument during a game?" Doc's smile went halfway between his ears.

Stormy returned the smile exposing perfect white teeth.

"They used to build ballparks like Rembrandt's."

"Huh?"

"Rembrandt's, you know one of a kind."

"Well Stormy, that's what you were—one of a kind."

With Stormy processing that, they sat in silence, the kind of silence long time friends share without undue discomfort.

Stormy finally said, "All I know is the ballpark has been my home for over twenty years and I ain't exactly ready to leave the nest." Stormy's mouth flinched with something related to a frown.

"Stormy, what ya gonna do?" Doc asked, his voice softening a bit.

"Autograph baseball cards at those card shows, I guess." Stormy sighed and raised his shoulders. His forehead creased into a deep furrow. "It's a scary feeling when you're forty and what you love most is over. What do you do for another forty years? A man can only paint his house so many times. I never thought I'd get old."

Doc began to wave his arms all over the place.

"Hell, son you ain't old! When you got more hair growin' out your nose and ears than the top of your head, that's old. When you have to get up in the night two or three times to use the john, that's old. And, most important, when you wake up in the morning and you can't piss clear across the room anymore, you know you're old. You ain't old for a human being, just for a ballplayer."

Stormy laughed so hard he started to cough, but both men knew it was laughter to conceal sorrow. His teammates had left over an hour ago, acting as if their senior member would return next year. Just the normal, "See you next spring." It would be different with Doc. They had experienced too much together.

"I remember you walking in here as a rookie over twenty years ago. I knew you were special right off the bat. You lived on the playing field like it was your last day. Some players go soft with age, but not you. If anything, you got crustier by the day." Doc took a deep drag of air as if remembering all these things stirred his emotions.

"Baseball is all I know. My life. Without baseball, I won't even know who the enemy is." Stormy stared at the floor, dragging Doc's eyes along for companionship.

A trace of a mist surfaced in Stormy's eyes. That never happened. Not after a big loss, a bad game: never. Not even the year a private plane crash killed Ralph Lema, Stormy's best friend on the team. He bit his cheek to scare away any teardrop's notion of making an appearance.

"Aw, Stormy, it won't be that bad," Doc said, nodding in sympathy. An overdose of sorrow sent an epidemic of lines across his high forehead.

"Doc, I'd walk thru hell in a gasoline suit to keep playin'. I'd give anything to do it over again. Absolutely anything," Stormy said, his voice dead. His packing complete, Stormy put the tape player in the bag. He and Doc stood, looking at each other awkwardly. Stormy extended his hand to Doc and the men shook. "See you around town, bro."

"Take care, Stormy."

Stormy tossed his bag over his shoulder and started for the door. Suddenly he stopped and turned to face his old friend one last time. Seeing the pain on Doc's face, Stormy spoke in a monotone: no emotion, just fact. "You know I spent a good chunk of my life holding a baseball. In the end, turns out it was the other way around all the time."

"Hey, Stormy, what about your rocking chair?"

Stormy never looked back.

"Give it to one of the young bucks." He was gone.

Chapter Three
MAC SWINDELL

Daylight continued its losing streak to nightfall as Stormy walked through the dimly lit players' parking area. The lot was empty except for Stormy's black Porsche convertible. In the background, Yankee Stadium, a triple-deck layer of steel and brick, rested quietly enough to pass for a massive painting of itself.

Stormy had made the walk to his car over a thousand times before, but tonight something seemed peculiar like maybe the planets were out of line. His tennis shoes squeaked eerily against the pavement. On this unseasonably warm night, he could feel his jeans pasting to his legs. Approaching his auto, the silhouette of a man standing in the dark startled him. The man stepped into a dim light thrown off by a nearby light pole.

Stormy immediately heaved a sigh of relief, his shoulders relaxed. He had seen plenty of these guys over the years. Jock sniffers, as the athletes liked to call them, a nuisance, but a harmless bore.

"Mr. Weathers. I realize I've startled you. Allow me to introduce myself. My name is Mac Swindell."

Mac, about forty, extended his hand. He shook Stormy's hand with enthusiasm, appearing happy to meet the legend himself. Though his nose pointed a bit and his sharp cheekbones blended into a narrow jaw, Mac had a friendly but ordinary face. The kind you could see a hundred times and still not recognize the next day. One could only describe his physical stature as frail. He wore casual, nondescript clothes and his affable tone left an impression of boyish innocence.

"Based on your comments in the locker room, I thought it was finally time we meet."

What the hell is he talking about? What comments? Stormy hadn't seen anyone in the dressing room but Doc.

Mac reached in his shirt pocket and removed a pack of cigarettes. He flipped a cigarette in his mouth and buried his hands deep in his pockets searching for a light.

"Terrible habit. I've been trying to quit for years. At least a hundred, in fact." Mac giggled like the goose nobody would sit by in the lunchroom at school.

A real comedian. No shit, Sherlock. It is a nasty habit. As a teenager, Stormy and his buddies at the orphanage had smoked pot a time or two, but never stockers and he couldn't stand someone that did.

Mac failed to locate a light. Suddenly, a flick of his thumb produced a flame. A mini-bonfire erupted and brightened the scene, showcasing Mac's shiny dark eyes which housed even darker shadows. Lighting his cigarette, he blew out his thumb and took a long, slow drag. His euphoric smile spread from ear to ear and easily betrayed his nicotine concern.

Great, Stormy thought. *Worst day of his life. Second worst, anyhow. Not every guy's mom would put him in an orphanage. That was the worst day, but this one ranked a close second. Already drenched in misery, and now some guy is trying to amuse him with magic tricks.*

"Nice trick. You're staying out here kinda late for an autograph, aren't you?"

That was one thing he wouldn't miss, signing autographs. When he died and went to heaven or hell or wherever, the first thing they'd probably make him do was sit in a corner and sign a couple of dozen baseballs.

"Say how did you get in the players area anyway?"

"I'm not here for an autograph. I wasn't in the locker room."

The man's voice was too smooth. It sent a shiver up Stormy's spine. And that damned grin of his looked more like a crack in the pavement.

"Magic tricks and good ears, huh?"

"Stormy, I'm going to get straight to the point. I have an extraordinary offer for you."

"Damn! I knew it. Another scumbag agent."

It was probably for those card shows. That's all the promoters want with the dinosaurs. Line them up and just keep signing. Like a hitter buried in a deep slump, accepting the anguish of it all, Stormy had already prepared himself to sign at card shows if he ever needed money. He had heard enough. Stormy moved to the driver's side of his car and opened the door.

"I know a lot about you, Stormy." Mac spoke quietly, no comment in his voice.

So what? Anybody can buy one of those baseball record books and learn a few stats. Stormy retrieved his keys from his jeans pocket and started to unlock the driver's door.

"Yeah? Like what, bro?"

"I know you're feeling bad about your contract not being renewed."

"Well, what jock wouldn't be?" A real rocket scientist. Stormy's patience grew thinner than a lousy pitching staff.

"I know about the night at P.T.'s that the catcher mentioned."

The man heard better than some of those rabbit eared umps. Stormy would give him that.

"I know your mother left you in an orphanage when you were six."

Whoops! No baseball encyclopedia contained that stat. Nobody but Whitey Virdon, the Yankee scout who signed him twenty-three years ago, knew that, and Whitey took that secret to his grave. Stormy shut the car door, turning abruptly to face Mac's thin smile.

"Your official press release states you were raised in an orphanage from birth. That's not true, is it, Stormy?"

This guy was throwing a knuckle change. How could he know? Stormy still remembered his mom. They were tight, often playing catch together. He was good even back then. Hell, *she* was good! With no dad, she filled the role of both parents and then, poof, one day she's gone. Suddenly he's living in an orphanage and never saw his mother again. Not the kind of story a man wanted spread around.

"Stormy," a female voice called.

Stormy spun around to see Jaynie moving rapidly toward him. Crap! He had forgotten all about her. He was so late getting to the car, she probably went looking for him.

"Stormy! Where've you been?"

Jaynie snuggled against him; while grasping his hand, she gently kissed him on the cheek.

"Uh, it took a little longer than usual to clear out my stuff. Jaynie, meet, uh, what did you say your name was?"

Mac politely extended his hand to Jaynie. "Mac Swindell. Nice to meet you, Jaynie."

After the two exchanged handshakes, Stormy faced Jaynie. "Get in the car. I'll be there in a minute."

She obeyed, and the two men walked far enough away to prevent her from hearing.

"What an attractive young woman. Certainly one advantage of a famous athlete," Mac said, admiring her crawl into the expensive sports car.

Stormy felt too anxious for any discussion concerning the fringe benefits of his recently completed occupation. "What's the offer?"

Mac handed him a business card.

"My organization would like to offer you the opportunity to become a high school senior again," Mac said, his composed manner official, yet courteous, his tone near paternal. "Your body will revert to eighteen, but your mind will remain intact. Just think, an adult in a strapping kid's body, youth combined with wisdom. You can play in the majors again, but first maybe win that state championship you missed."

Stormy sank to the curb. He removed his Yankee ball hat, rubbed his hand through his thick hair and stared at the business card. It read: "Swindell's Human Recycling Program." In the bottom left-hand corner, it stated, "Established a Long Time Ago."

"You don't go back in time or anything silly like that. You'll just reappear one day with a youthful body and all its advantages."

Stormy's eyes alternated from the card to Mac. Well, that was it. He had finally flipped, gone bonkers, lost his marbles, whatever. He'd heard it happened like this. One minute you're fine, the next you're on full tilt, listening to some nerd tell you he's going to give you a new body.

"Sorta like a new engine under the hood?" asked the bewildered ballplayer.

"Yes, sorta like a new engine under the hood. I like that."

Stormy gulped audibly and squinted his eyes. "I'm having a little trouble with all this, bro."

He stood to face Mac, studying him the way he would study a rookie pitcher on the mound. Mac continued to smile.

Stormy's voice dropped a few decibels. "Who are you?"

"Let's just say I'm a man of extraordinary resources."

Stormy digested Mac's answer for a bit then asked, "Why me?"

Mac leaned closer.

"Of course, you're puzzled by all this. Actually, I've had you in mind for our recycling program for years. We're a lot alike. We need a guy like you in circulation as long as possible. A guy that will take that unfair advantage."

Unfair advantage. A term Stormy used often over the years. This guy knew everything.

"If you've got these magic powers, make a lightening bolt appear in the sky."

Mac rolled his eyes. "Stormy, please, something more original."

Stormy gazed at the stars on this balmy night. His mind burst into a small fire. His first good idea of the day.

"Okay, put the old Pirates' stadium, Forbes Field, right up there in the sky."

That'd do it, send this guy packing. But first Stormy would discover how Mac knew so much. If Mac wouldn't tell, he'd beat the snot out of him.

"No problem," Mac said.

Mac closed his eyes and started to grunt and strain, as if afflicted with a bad case of constipation. He abruptly stopped and stared at Stormy.

Stormy knew it. It was all a joke. The guy couldn't do it. Josh probably was responsible for this. The Red Sox always stayed at the Hilton. He'd drive over there right now and bust Josh good. What a way to treat a guy his last day on the job!

"Could you give me the location and a year?"

"Huh?" Stormy in his elation at solving the mystery almost did not hear Mac's reply.

"What city and when?"

"Oh, uh, Pittsburgh, any time in the fifties."

"What century?"

"Twentieth," Stormy replied, exhaling heavily. This turkey was stalling, no doubt about it.

Once again Mac closed his eyes. The image of an old stadium gradually took shape in the sky.

With brown eyes the size of softballs, Stormy gawked at the ball yard. He gulped for air which suddenly seemed in short supply. "Shit! That's not Forbes Field, that's Crosley, the old stadium in Cincinnati."

At the corner of Findlay and Western Avenue, the park's image was so clear Stormy could read the distances on the outfield walls—three hundred twenty-eight feet to left, three hundred eighty-seven to center and three hundred sixty-six to right field. Painted in white at the base of the wall clear as day. Stormy immediately noticed the incline of the playing field at the base of the left field wall. He found small consolation in the geographic error.

"Sorry, Stormy, I don't follow sports anymore. After gladiators, it all seems anticlimactic to me," Mac said, genuinely apologetic. "So what do you think? You want to play in old-timers' games the rest of your life or take my offer?"

Stormy tugged on his cheeks with enough force to leave traces of red.

"What's the catch? There's gotta be a hook here somewhere."

"Nothing, simply continue in the same manner you have for the last twenty years."

22

"So," Stormy said after a deep pause. "What's next?"

"Carry on as if we've never met. You'll be contacted at the appropriate time and given your instructions how the recycling will occur. The transformation will be painless. All the necessary papers and identification will be provided for you at that time. Your appearance will be similar to your original age eighteen, but different enough to avoid arousing suspicions."

Without warning, Mac abruptly turned and vanished into midair. Stormy, dazed and confused, searched for the man but he was gone.

More confused than a nearsighted umpire, Stormy made his way to the car door and slid into the driver's seat. Jaynie was filing her nails.

"Are you okay?" she asked.

"Yeah, I'm fine."

"Who was that guy?"

"Mac? Beats me."

"He seemed sort of like your basic Joe fan to me."

"Yeah, maybe."

Stormy started the engine. He would go home and sleep; possibly, he'd suffered a breakdown. Maybe he'd wake up and tomorrow everything would be fine. Lesser men would crumble with what he'd been through today. The black Porsche drove off into the night.

Chapter Four

IT WAS CROSLEY

Stormy flashed his manufactured smile while signing autographs in assembly-line fashion. Four months had passed since that night in the players' parking lot of Yankee Stadium, and not a peep from one piss-ant Mac Swindell. After Stormy convinced himself it was just a dream, he wished otherwise. Anybody in his position would feel the same way. Mac did put in the sky a stadium that was torn down years ago. Who's to say he couldn't make a few repairs on an old model like Stormy?

Stormy would continue with his winter routine of golf and a few card shows as long as possible. Things would get tough in the next few weeks, when spring training started. A sharp pain surged through his stomach just thinking about it.

Stormy sat between Ralph Clendenon and Mickey Doby, two other ex-players. The ex-ballplayers offered the occasional "how are you" and "thanks for coming" to the fans. Both men wore outdated plaid sport coats over their open-collar golf shirts.

"Stormy, did you read in the paper where your old teammate Smith turned down a fat contract from the Yankees?" With his pug nose and flat top, Clendenon looked like an escapee from the fifties.

Doby, his bald head shiny enough to throw off light, leaned to Stormy's ear and whispered ferociously, "He's a sexual deviate, you know."

Clendenon knew more. "He claims on the night of your last game, he saw a stadium in the sky while driving out of the parking lot."

"What stadium?" Stormy replied faster and louder than he had intended.

"Polo Grounds, I think he said, but the crazy bastard thinks it's a religious experience so he's becoming a preacher. It won't be Catholic. No way is he going with a religion that don't let the pastor have sex."

"He's tryin' to bargain his way into heaven. He thinks there's gonna be harps and sixteen-year-old chicks at the pearly gates," Stormy said; his flippant tone masked his sudden interest.

All the men laughed before noticing a wide-eyed kid of about ten facing them. Obviously, the subject matter greatly interested the youngster.

"Finally we're through." Doby sighed. Only one person remained in the autograph line.

Stormy glanced up to see Mac! So it wasn't a dream. Stormy's hopes lifted like a high-speed elevator. Mac wore casual plaid pants and a striped sport shirt. Bad threads, but he looked more harmless than ever.

"Gentlemen, how are you? Stormy, so good to see you again."

Stormy's eyes locked on Mac who returned the stare.

"Stormy, I was wondering if I might have a word with you in private."

"Back in a second, guys. I need to talk a little bizness." Stormy was not smiling.

The two men left the main area and found a smaller, more intimate room. Mac hurried a cigarette to his mouth and started fumbling for a light.

Stormy retrieved a pack of matches from a nearby table and tossed them to Mac, keeping a modest distance.

"There. That trick of yours gives me the jeebies."

Mac lit his cigarette, inhaled deep enough to move paper, and then blew rising smoke signals. A razor-thin smile split his razor-thin lips.

"Stormy, your recycling has been set for February the seventh," Mac said pleasantly. "Arrive by car in Dallas, Texas, and that afternoon drive it into Lake Ray Hubbard. After the vehicle submerges completely, simply swim to the surface and your body will be eighteen again. I hope returning to your old high school agrees with you."

"You want me to drive a fifty thousand-dollar car to Texas and then dump it in some lake? Are you nuts?" Stormy asked, bewilderment in his tone.

Better to play hard to get, Stormy decided. He pinned Mac with a frosty stare.

"Do I just drive off the road and kinda creep in the water like a turtle?" Stormy wove his arm in a slow sweeping motion. "Or I could just fly that sucker into the water like a jet crashing?" Stormy's arms became airplane wings in flight.

Mac's Halloween smile didn't change.

"I know it sounds silly, but trust me on this." He handed a wallet to Stormy, who accepted it as if it were contaminated.

"All the necessary papers are enclosed. Home address, drivers license, school registration papers. You're in great shape, so we'll leave your body measurements the same. It'll save you buying new clothes. Take one suitcase and enough cash to last a year. You'll be back in the pro's eventually, collecting bigger pay checks than ever."

Stormy opened the wallet to see a teenager named Cal Lucas on the driver's license. The kid looked good—thick neck, high cheekbones, a strong square jaw; confident brown eyes matched his coarse brown hair. And Mac was right, the kids made incredible money these days.

From the day he signed his first contract, Stormy traveled to Texas only when the Yankees played the Rangers in Arlington, halfway between Dallas and Fort Worth. Visiting Dallas would have reminded him of his mother, and that was too painful.

Maybe now he should try to learn what happened. He could handle it now. If Mac possessed all these powers, maybe he could help.

"What's to lose, except a car? I'll try it on two conditions."

"I'll do my best. What are they?"

"I want you there when I drive in the water. If this is a trick, I'm gonna open up one large can of whip-ass on your hide."

"I'll be there cheering you on. What else?"

"I want my mother's address. She's still alive, isn't she?" Stormy asked, unsure if he really wanted an answer.

Mac paced about as if Stormy had requested the combination to the vault. A few seconds passed during which Mac pulled on his chin quizzically.

"How about your place being next door to hers?" he finally asked.

"Yeah, I guess," Stormy said after another brief silence. Next door, wow. That could be heavy.

"Oh, by the way, if you ever tell a soul, your body will revert to its natural age."

"How long before that happens?"

"Maybe a day, maybe a week but if you tell, the party is over."

Mac vanished. Stormy started toward the main room, shaking his head. Who was he kidding? None of this would ever happen. But, man, was Mac good with those magic tricks. Stormy found Clendenon and Dobey rehashing old battles.

"Hey, Stormy, what business is that guy in?" Dobey asked.

"Uh, recycling."

"I've got three kids. You think he could get me a deal on a couple of ten-speeds?"

No one had ever mistaken Dobey for a brain surgeon; the man was actually serious. Stormy rolled his eyes to the sky and headed for the door. He had a tee time to make but wheeled around to face the two old players.

"It was Crosley."

"What?" asked Clendenon.

"The stadium in the sky. It was Crosley." And Stormy was gone.

Chapter Five
I'M TAKING A LONG TRIP

Only a bit more spacious than a major league dugout, Stormy's Manhattan apartment was decorated in early American baseball. A thin coat of dust covered his American League Most Valuable Player award, which sat on the floor in one corner of his bedroom; in a similar sanitary state, his Rookie of the Year award occupied the opposite corner. Two ball gloves and a dozen bats littered the living area that took on the aroma of a messy sporting goods store.

In his cluttered closet, game jerseys from past years hung with his many pairs of Levis. He had already packed some of these Levis in the open suitcase that lay on his unmade bed. A few team pictures and an old *Sports Illustrated* cover that featured Stormy swinging from his heels, hung from the otherwise bare bedroom walls. Stormy would look at that picture and long for the game the way a parent would long for a long-lost child. Dozens of game baseballs autographed by past teammates and opponents also cluttered his sparsely decorated home.

Stormy placed a ball glove in his suitcase, and locked it tight. His eyes roamed the unique bachelor pad for anything he might have omitted. Satisfied, Stormy donned a Yankee windbreaker. Never one to concern himself with money or possessions, he exited the apartment no differently than if going to the grocery store.

A cold, sunny day, Stormy approached his car which was parked illegally by the curb in front of his apartment, another fringe extended to a Yankee ballplayer. Everyone in the neighborhood, including police, knew Stormy lived there. He spotted a local teenager named Rupert.

"Hey, Stormy, taking a trip?" Teeth white enough for a toothpaste commercial flashed in the kid's dark face.

Stormy felt a brisk breeze slice through his windbreaker as he slung the suitcase in the trunk. "Yeah, Rupe. I'm goin' to play some ball."

"Aw, man, that's great! I knew you could still cut it. Who you gonna play for? The Dodgers? Reds? The Angels need a veteran like you."

Stormy shoved a hundred dollar bill in Rupert's hand. "I can't tell you. I'm gonna be incognito. High school ball. Watch after the place while I'm gone."

He chuckled to himself. Even Stormy was pretending this escapade would play out as promised. Though he paid six months rent in advance, he'd probably return in a week or so and go about planning the rest of his life.

"Aw, man, you jivin' me again?" Rupert pushed the cash deep into his pockets and strolled away.

With his throbbing knee reminding him of the cold, Stormy carefully entered the sports car. Almost immediately, he slowly drew his face to the rear-view mirror. After an inspection of his face, he retrieved a pair of tweezers from the glove box. Stormy methodically plucked hair from one ear, then the other and placed the tweezers back in the compartment.

The hair growing from his ears, not to mention his nose, drove him crazy. He tried to control the invasion with persistent use of tweezers and tiny clippers. In a new development, his eyebrows were growing bushy like the brows of older men. A doctor friend once said: "When hair starts sprouting from the outside of your nose, that's when Mother Nature is really turned against you." Stormy curiously ran his finger across the top of his nose. The beak was as smooth as a baby's bottom; at least that biological trick hadn't started yet.

Stormy patronized a Manhattan bank and always used the same teller, Mrs. Bauer, a grandmother and Sunday school teacher type. Stormy approached the gray-haired lady.

"Hello, Mrs. Bauer." He searched both rear pockets for one of several passbooks in his possession.

"Oh, Stormy, I'm glad you're here. Could you autograph this for my granddaughter?"

Stormy obediently took the paper and began scribbling. "What was her name?"

"Michelle, you remember. She's in her first year of college."

"Yeah, how's that goin'?"

The elderly lady leaned forward. "Okay, I suppose. One of her roommates curses and that bothers her."

"The hell you say!" Stormy produced three small, dark blue books.

"Well, I see no reason to be serious with you today," Mrs. Bauer said like she'd said a hundred times before, her tone full of mock anger.

Stormy settled on the account that contained over fifty thousand dollars. He slid the passbook to the teller. *Boy, this ought to flip her out*, he thought.

"Let's cash this one in. Hundreds will do."

"Wow," the lady responded loudly, too loudly; in an attempt to recompose herself, she poofed her hair and tugged on her collar. She cleared her throat.

"I'm taking a long trip."

She leaned in close enough to take a headshot, almost whispering, "I'll say. Where are you going?"

"Back in time, Mrs. Jackson, back in time."

Stormy's smile simultaneous gladdened and confused the teller. Mrs. Bauer started to count the money, shaking her head. "Stormy Weathers, you're insane."

Jaynie dialed Stormy's number from memory. He'd been so depressed lately, she'd stopped kidding him about how many little Stormy's he wanted, if they should ever marry. His reputation as the toughest guy in baseball was a cover. Along the way, someone must have hurt him. Maybe tonight he would finally open up to her, finally decide to settle down.

After five rings of the phone, Stormy's flat voice rose from his answering machine: "At the beep, leave your message."

Jaynie sounded the way a sexy kitten would sound if a sexy kitten could talk. "Stormy, what time should I come over tonight? Maybe we could go to that great Spanish restaurant in the village. Give me a call. Bye."

Chapter Six
TRAVELIN' LIGHT

A road sign informed Stormy he was leaving New York. J.J. Cale's "Travelin' Light" practically rattled the Porsche's stereo speakers. Stormy loved the mystical, pulsating, yet gentle rhythms of J.J.'s music. J.J.'s music made no concessions to the real world, his exact sentiment. He tapped his left foot to the upbeat tempo and smiled to himself; the words soared from J.J. and Stormy's duet.

"Travelin' light is the only way to fly.
Travelin' light, just you and I."

Per Mac's instructions, Stormy brought one suitcase and cash. It was as perfect as Larson's fifty-six World Series shutout. He'd always stayed light on his feet. No need to get rooted anywhere. The last time that happened was with his mother and look how that turned out.

"One way ticket to ecstasy. We are bound you and me.
Travelin' light, we can go beyond
Travelin' light, we can catch the wind
Travelin' light, let your mind pretend."

Stormy's car zoomed along the interstate. He closed his eyes for a few beats. That's exactly what he'd do; he would pretend he was eighteen again. It would be ecstasy. Stormy's shades remained intact, but his thick hair blew wildly in the windstorm generated by the speeding convertible. He was grinning broadly now.

"We can go to paradise
Maybe once, maybe twice
Travelin' light is the only way to fly."

Lake Ray Hubbard was as quiet and still as algae. Only a few broken trees poked through the water's brown glass surface and their branches seemed to

31

touch the low gray sky. A peculiar musky smell filled the air. Only Stormy's car traveled on the nearby highway. The flat Texas terrain stretched into infinity.

Mac suddenly was standing between the highway and the water. His Houdini like appearance startled Stormy only slightly more than his clothes. Mac's orange bell-bottomed pants clashed magnificently with his yellow and blue paisley shirt, white buck shoes and red socks. Stormy slammed on the brakes; with his rear tires howling loud enough for an echo, the car skidded within inches of Mac. Stormy eyed Mac's attire, whose grin stretched across the lake.

"Nice threads."

"Thanks. I wanted to make sure you saw me." In the manner of a model posing, he twirled about.

"I was wondering if you'd show."

"And I was sure that you would."

Stormy noticed that the world looked like a giant postcard. "Where is everybody?"

"Activity will return to normal when we're finished."

"You can do that?"

"Don't sell me short."

"Hey, bro, at this point in the ball game, you and I are on the same team. Hey, do I live in one of those foster homes or something? I mean, can a high school senior live by himself?"

"You'll have a legal guardian. If he's needed for a school function or social occasion, I'll play the role. The papers are in order. Is that okay?"

"Sure." Yeah, right, look at this guy, dressed like a Halloween ornament. Hopefully no reason would arise for the little twerp to come around.

Mac pointed to the water. "How about here?"

Stormy exited the car, his stride to the lake charged with purpose. He knelt, dabbled his hand in the murky water, and noticed his rippling reflection: a forty-one-year-old man in need of a shave, wearing Levis and a white T-shirt. No change yet.

His stomach felt hollow. The adrenaline buzz. Bases loaded, two outs, and a couple of runs behind, with Stormy at bat. Just the way he liked it.

"Damn, that water's chilly," Stormy heard himself say.

Mac lowered his chin and eyes. "Stormy, you're not going soft on me, are you?"

Stormy fired Mac his spaghetti-western stare. The nerve of that goofy ass

Eddie Haskell lookin' son-of-a-bitch to challenge his manhood!

Stormy stalked to his car, and after opening the trunk, grabbed the suitcase and tossed it to the ground. He slid back into the driver's seat and slowly drove the car off the highway into the soft mud. The Porsche crept closer to the water but then the wheels sunk into the wet dirt just short of the lake. Stormy revved the engine; a combination of flying mud and exhaust filled the air. He shifted the car into reverse and it suddenly darted back on the main road. Thick engine smoke obscured his vision.

"The hell with this!" Stormy's veins coiled in his muscular forearms like tiny cable. He was higher than a cheap bleacher seat from anticipation.

As if in a backward race, Stormy stomped the accelerator to the floorboard and drove his automobile in reverse about a hundred yards, then brought it to a screeching halt. If he was going down, he would do so with a flair. No half-ass swings with two strikes for Stormy. With the engine's purr the only sound, the black sports car sized up the target the way a bull would a matador. Mac suddenly stood beside the car, smiling from ear to ear.

"Stormy, I certainly haven't misjudged you."

Stormy's eyes had never focused on road stripes for so long. Tension hung like a bad curve ball. After a few seconds, he punished the accelerator harder than before; wheels spun and smoke exploded from the exhaust pipe. The sound of tires squealing echoed across the lake. Like a plane racing down the runway, the car lunged forward and became airborne the instant it left the road. From the soaring cockpit came a loud, long kamikaze yell. On touch down, giant waves of lake water splashed the shore and murky brown water slowly swallowed the car whole.

"Show off!" Mac yelled.

The lake's cold water sent a chill surging up Stormy's spine. Floating around him in underwater slow motion were a pen, stereo cassettes, coins, even his prescription lenses. His car drifted downward until it rested on the lake's muddy bottom. Stormy briefly considered the humor of driving his car out of the water as if commandeering a U-boat with wheels.

Time for the trek to the top and call this douche bag's bluff. Except his seat belt was stuck! Stormy frantically tugged on the buckle but no luck. What a sucker—no new body and the old one would expire soon! Stormy could feel his fear spreading faster than a fatal disease.

Ouch! He felt a sharp pain around his right cheekbone but due to the dark water, he was nearly blind. Ouch! He felt it again. With both hands he grabbed a solid rigid something.

Holy shit! A snapping turtle larger than a manhole cover stared Stormy directly in the eyes. After a flurry of punches and jabs, the turtle vanished.

In a matter of seconds, a snake thicker and longer than two baseball bats circled close enough to kiss Stormy on the cheek. Fearing that the nasty reptile relished the rare opportunity for a carnivorous meal over mere fish food, Stormy flailed away until the snake disappeared into the water's darkness. Any second Stormy figured the grandest catfish of Lake Ray Hubbard would swallow him whole, then digest him to the lake's bottom. How inappropriate— or perhaps fitting—that he would wind up kin to whale shit, since big leaguers often referred to a lousy pitcher as such. Stormy, fueled with terror, ripped the seat belt to shreds and shot upward through the murk.

The dark water gradually lightened, and then his head burst through the surface. Stormy positioned himself on his back and floated while he caught his breath, watching the sun penetrate the clouds and land on the lake's surface. His adrenaline was throwing off enough heat to prevent hypothermia, he supposed. A good thing no one had seen him afraid. *Bad for his image,* he thought.

After a short rest, he swam toward shore until his feet touched bottom. With water at his kneecaps, he noticed a blurry reflection of himself on the water's surface. His glasses lay in the bottom of the lake, but he'd take a third strike before going back in the water.

A nasty thought struck: *a new body wouldn't accompany old vision.* Stormy stooped further for a closer look.

His heart returned to the bottom of the lake when he saw the same crusty face as before. It was a face overflowing with disappointment. Blood trickled down his cheek. He immediately dabbed his fingers in the water to break up the disappointing image of himself. With vision as blurred as his thoughts, Stormy searched all around for Mac, but to no avail. Officially, this was a bad day. Not only was he unemployed, he was also a fool.

Stormy could never remember one man treating another so cold. He had spiked men while running the bases, barreled catchers over at home plate and stolen other players' women. Once he accidentally bit off part of an opponent's ear in a fight but he'd never done anything as cruel as this. His face gradually settled into an expression of forced acceptance.

Drenched, Stormy sloshed to shore, retrieved his suitcase, and walked to the highway. He sat on the suitcase burying his wet head into the palms of both hands. Stormy's head started to throb; he was shivering from the cold. If he knew how to cry, he would. Stormy decided to deal with this setback the way he dealt with any tough loss: ten minutes of mourning then move on to the next game.

About thirty minutes later, a large moving van rumbled over the horizon. Stormy stood in the middle of the road, waving his hands. The van chugged to a halt twenty-five feet from Stormy.

A grizzly bear of a man poked his head from the driver's window. An unlit cigarette drooped from the right corner of his mouth.

"You need a ride?"

Stormy nodded, and the driver leaned over to open the passenger door.

"Hop in."

"Thanks."

Stormy crawled into the big van. His host had a full, dark beard, shoulder-length hair in a ponytail and a full, round belly. His smile revealed a genuine need to visit a dentist.

"My name's Turk. Turk Hand." Instead of shaking hands, however, Turk shoved both beefy paws in front of Stormy's face. "Get it, hand," Turk said, clearly amused at his own cleverness. "What in the hell happened to you?"

"I had a little mishap. Put my car in the lake."

"There's a truck stop a few miles up the road. They've got a big tow truck. Maybe they can get it out."

"I appreciate it."

The van inched forward until picking up speed. Birds were now singing sonnets. Other cars zipped by. A stray mutt chased a jackrabbit that darted across the road.

"What kind of car?"

"Porsche."

"Porsche!" Turk's eyes grew with delight. "How fast were you going?"

"As fast as it would go," Stormy explained in a voice void of interest. He forced a smile of tolerance.

The burly man howled with laughter, but then he stopped and stared at Stormy through suspicious eyes.

"Hey, kid, you look familiar."

How nice. Someone still recognized him. "You probably saw me play, uh…"

Did he say kid? Stormy's eyes and ears shot rigidly upward.

"You all right, kid?"

Maybe he's one of those people that calls everybody kid like an ex-teammate, "Kid" Hughes. With an underwater slowness, Stormy leaned forward, pulled down the passenger visor, noticing a mirror. He inched closer to inspect his face. Only it was not his face anymore. In the mirror, the handsome youthful face on his new driver's license stared back. The same driver's license currently in the wallet of his soaked Levis. Stormy swallowed so hard, his gulp startled Turk.

"Kid, are you okay? You look like you seen the devil himself."

"Yeah, I'm fine." Stormy's voice somehow passed for nonchalance. "Can you take me to town? I'll mess with the car later."

"Sure, kid, I lend a hand whenever possible. Get it, hand," the trucker said through hearty laughter.

The commercial vehicle chugged along the highway. A road sign reminded Stormy that they traveled on U.S. Interstate Thirty; another sign proclaimed Dallas only eighteen miles away. Stormy read both perfectly. Flawless vision accompanied the new engine under the hood.

Stormy's heart started pumping so rapidly, he thought he was having a heart attack. Hell, one year when the Yankees clinched a pennant, a coach, Sam McGinty suffered a heart attack in the excitement and dropped dead right in the dugout.

Cool it, man! Cool it! You get your wish and stroke out. A deep relieved breath rose and then settled in his chest. How foolish. Eighteen-year-olds don't suffer heart attacks.

Chapter Seven

CRAZY MAMA, WHERE YOU BEEN SO LONG?

Utilizing fingers as bony as piano keys, the apartment manager mechanically counted the crisp one hundred dollar bills.

She had requested first and last month's rent, oblivious to his youthfulness or scruffy appearance. Two plaques that hung on one wall in the small office caught Stormy's eye. "Jesus Saves" hung directly above "Gun control allows only the criminals to have guns." Gee, it's good to be back home.

"We've been expecting you. Your legal guardian…" The woman locked the cash in the desk she currently sat behind; she looked down at some papers with eyes as narrow as her face and then peered out at Stormy over her long beak. "I believe, yes, it was Mr. Swindell that reserved this apartment. I remember, because he was so specific about renting the unit next to Norma Weathers."

The mention of Norma's name caused a twinge in Stormy's gut. Still, Stormy admitted internally, ole Mac had sure come through like a good hitter with the sacks full.

"I pride myself in my memory and it was last August. We don't usually hold one that long, but he paid the deposit in advance. Said you'd be here after that and both of you would move in. Mr. Swindell said he traveled a lot but you could take care of yourself."

She stood and handed the key to Stormy. "Walk straight out the front door and make an immediate left. Your place is down the hill."

As Stormy walked toward his new home, he noticed the rural landscape of hilly terrain and well planned trees. The buzz of urban traffic and feint smell of exhaust pipes reminded Stormy he now lived only a few miles from downtown Dallas. He stopped abruptly as if he had bumped into an invisible outfield wall. His left hand held his suitcase while he tugged on his jaw with his right. Did the apartment manager mention August? He didn't know Mac last August. How could Mac have known to rent a place next to his mother's? He decided to figure that out later. He'd just survived one crisis and now he prepared to face another. Time to meet one Norma Ivette Weathers.

Stormy hummed J.J.'s "Crazy Mama." J.J. had a tune for every occasion. "Crazy mama, where you been so long." It was a slow, sad, tune. It made no sense, his big day and now melancholy set in.

"You been hidin' out, you know that's true
Crazy Mama, I sure need you
Crazy Mama, you been gone so long."

His saliva suddenly turned bitter, and he felt like he might vomit. What would he say? What would he do?

"Down on the corner lookin' for you, babe
Down on the corner lookin' for you, babe"

Stormy stood at the corner of the two-story building that contained his apartment and the one supposedly housing Norma Weathers. No big deal; he had only wondered for over three decades why his mother dumped him. A significant day for sure, but he'd be damned glad when it was history.

"Lawdy mercy, can't I see
Crazy Mama, comin' back to me
Crazy Mama, where you been so long."

He located his place first. After unlocking the front door, he opened it and scanned his new home. Cheap rented furniture occupied a combination kitchen/den area and two bedrooms. Cheaper lime-colored carpet covered the floors. There were no pictures on the shiny white walls. Stormy's nostrils quickly filled with the scent of fresh wall paint and carpet detergent. It would do; he'd never needed anything fancy.

Stormy approached his lost mother's home, his heart doing double time. With the frenetic energy of a nervous animal, he stood close enough to touch the front door. He turned as if to leave, hesitated, spun back around and rang the doorbell.

Eternity passed before the door opened. His eyes could not believe what they saw. It really was his mother, and he even recognized her. She looked older, of course; her once brown hair had turned more gray, but it still softly touched her shoulders. She was still gracefully thin and wore a predominantly blue cotton dress that stopped just short of touching the ground; she was bare footed. His thoughts retreated to the attic of his memory bank: men had always liked the way she dressed.

His mother could pass for a dozen years younger. Her soft face, however, reflected troubled thoughts and sadness consumed her hazel eyes. Norma Weathers had survived in a tough world, but it showed.

As if stranded too long without water, Stormy could only gulp in the features of his mother. Heat flashes traveled his entire body, hauling confusion along for no charge.

"May I help you?" she asked kindly.

Can you help me? I'll say you can. You can start by explaining how you could dump your only child in Buckner Orphans Home—that's what you can do. The words did not tumble forth quickly nor as harshly.

"Uh, I, uh, just moved next door and I was, uh, wondering if I, uh, could use the phone?"

"I think that'd be okay," she replied.

The lady showed Stormy in. Her place had the same floor plan as Stormy's, but a jungle of plants surrounded the antique furniture. No Formica here. He wondered where she got the money? Did she have a job?

He stood in the middle of the living room with Norma beside him. "I really appreciate your letting me…"

One wall pulled his eyeballs out of their sockets. Framed pages from old newspapers touted his heroics. Trance-like, he walked closer for a better look. Stormy saw himself on the covers of several magazines. Countless ticket stubs framed from New York Yankee—Texas Ranger games adorned the wall. The wall was a campaign ad for Stormy's induction to the Baseball Hall of Fame. Twenty years of history covered on one sixty-year-old lady's apartment wall.

Under different circumstances, Stormy would have received enormous pleasure from the exhibit, but presently he thought only of leaving the apartment before he fainted. The storm rumbling in his brain told him he had a better shot at breaking DiMaggio's hitting streak.

Norma talked while approaching Stormy. "Most people do find that wall a strange way of decorating your home. I'm a big baseball fan and Stormy Weathers was my favorite player. He's retired now and I'm lost, not being able to watch him play. We have the same last names so I always followed his career. Do you like baseball?"

His legs felt as soft as margarine in the Texas heat. Through glassy eyes, he saw concern on Norma's face. Stormy barely acknowledged her previous question with a nod. His eyes rolled to the back of his head and he dropped to the living room carpet. A hundred-mile-an-hour Nolan Ryan bean ball could not have hit him harder.

Stormy's eyes followed the circular motion of the ceiling fan operating above his head. Where was he? Fog smothered his brain. Flat on his back, with his head resting comfortably on a pillow, he struggled to focus as Norma knelt beside him.

"Young man?"

For a long moment, Stormy could not find his vocal chords. "Yes." Collect your thoughts. Don't say anything stupid until the cobwebs clear from your brain.

"You went down like the Titanic."

"How long was I out?" Stormy moved only his lips.

"Only a few minutes. I was going to call a doctor. Are you okay?"

"Yeah, I'm fine. I've just had a weird day."

"My name is Norma Weathers. What's yours?"

Panic. What was his new name?

"Uhh, Lucas. Cal Lucas." Stormy said after too long a pause.

"Are you sure you're all right? I never saw anybody forget his own name before."

Stormy sat up with Norma still kneeling beside him. She smelled good, sweet as red clover. It was probably a tad premature to ask if he could stay the night. At least he still had a sense of humor.

"You're my new neighbor?"

"Yes." That's not all, lady.

"Where are you from?"

"New York City."

"Really! Did you ever go to Yankee Stadium?"

"Once in a while."

"Did you ever see Stormy Weathers play?"

"A few times."

"How exciting!" Norma said. "The boy could play some ball. I hated to see him get old."

No kiddin' Ms. Weathers.

"Where are your folks?"

"My, uh, legal guardian travels. He won't be home much."

"Do you have a father or mother?"

40

"I...I'm not sure," Stormy said, his voice dropping away. He stared at the floor.

Norma's voice lowered a decibel. "Oh, I see." Her glance followed Stormy's downward as if searching for lost parents.

"Hey, Stormy Weathers was my favorite player too," Stormy said honestly.

"Really!"

"Sure, I'm gonna play for Woodrow Wilson this year myself. We'll make a run at the state championship."

"Outstanding. Woodrow must have some good players this year."

"I wouldn't know. Haven't seen any of them play."

"Woodrow never won state even when Stormy was there, and, goodness knows, he was their best player ever," she said crisply.

You've got that right! "I know." Oops, how would he know that? Maybe she missed the slip. "Say, will your husband let you come to some games?"

"I'm not married." Her face hardened briefly, though her voice stayed even. "But I might come to a game. Let me know your schedule."

It pleased Stormy to stand so easily. In recent years, standing up had become a struggle. He walked to the door with Norma following behind.

"Do you still need to use the phone?"

"Nah. I'll grab one later. I'm sorry about scaring you like that. Passing out and all."

"You can pass out in my place anytime you want. Seriously, I just hope you're all right." She opened the door.

Standing in the doorway, Stormy faced his mother.

"Hey, Cal, how did you know Stormy Weathers went to Woodrow Wilson?"

Darn, she caught his goof, after all! Stormy smiled conspiratorially.

"How did you know?" Stormy asked.

And Stormy was gone. He still performed well under pressure.

41

Chapter Eight
IT'S TOUGH BREAKING OLD HABITS

Swollen paws held enough cash to fill a vault; gaudy gold jewelry loosely shackled both of the car salesman's wrists. A wide, obnoxious diamond ring sparkled on his meaty left hand. Stormy stood near the fat man, who finished counting the money for the third time—a green assault of Ben Franklin's with a few Grants and Washingtons for change.

An afternoon bright sun dissected the adjacent indoor showroom, spotlighting a handful of new Porsches shiny enough to throw off human reflections. Stormy briefly considered buying something less flashy like a Chevrolet or a Buick but it's tough breaking old habits.

"The money's all here." The salesman managed to speak with an unlit cigarette dangling from the corner of his mouth. He tossed a set of keys to Stormy. "We see a lot of high rollers here, Bub, but not many teenagers pay cash for one of these babies. Years ago, I sold a whole fleet of Cadillacs to the King himself, Elvis Presley, but, man, I don't remember him carrying cash like that. Course, a Cadillac back then was twelve grand." Fatso stopped to rearrange the cigarette in his mouth then said, "You bought yourself a fine car, son."

Stormy left without saying a word. He felt relieved to get that over with. He slid into the new black, low-slung convertible and peeled out of the dealership.

Although it was early February, Stormy drove with the top down in the sixty-degree temperature. He would stay on LBJ Freeway, then go south on Central Expressway to Mockingbird, swing east on Mockingbird and then south again on Abrams. A left on Glasgow would take him to Woodrow Wilson High School. He had never returned since graduation; it surprised him to remember the way so easily. He needed to enroll in school, go about the business of winning a state championship, and then reclaim the lofty status of a big league player.

The razor-thin man raised the wooden gate to allow the sports car passage to the school parking lot. Smiley had worked at Woodrow when Elvis was skinny and appeared to wear the same pair of overalls as before. The old fella had aged remarkably well; he looked seventy over twenty years ago—now, not a day over seventy-five. Then and now Stormy thought that Smiley resembled a character in a John Wayne movie seeking refuge from the desert.

Smiley, who smiled less than a presidential portrait, rose mechanically from the metal chair in his small covered cubicle. Well over a hundred cars filled the student parking lot and few were late models. Woodrow was not a rich school. It was nestled in a modest but well manicured residential neighborhood of homes and apartments.

Smiley approached Stormy's car so slowly, it seemed every step might be his last. Stormy had forgotten that the old man's ears stuck out so drastically. He knew his fancy car would carry no stroke with Smiley. Smiley slowly leaned down to Stormy's car window, assessing the potential trespasser. Stormy handed the leather-faced man his school registration papers. The old man's breath smelled of nicotine. Probably non-filtered Camels, thought Stormy.

Smiley inspected the forms from underneath a red ball cap that looked as worn as its owner.

"You gettin' here kinda late, ain't you? School be out in 'bout an hour," he drawled.

Stormy only shrugged, wisely remaining quiet as Smiley returned the forms.

"If you're late tomorrow, I ain't lettin' you through. I don't care if you got a letter from the gov'nor."

Nothing seemed to have changed at the Woodrow Wilson Wildcats parking lot. After leaving his car, Stormy walked to the main entrance of the three-story building. Woodrow looked exactly as before except for the more mature shrubs that lined the building's front. A triple-deck layer of windows, rimmed in white stone, evenly interrupted the massive red brick wall. Beside the front door, an American flag piggybacked the state flag of Texas, a lone white star set against red, white and blue; both flags drooped as wet noodles in the still air. It was High School, USA. He heard the sounds of a school day inside— the school bell, shuffling feet, teenage chatter and lockers slamming—and felt paralyzed by the weight of his nostalgia.

Woodrow was still surrounded by the practice football field to the south, school parking to the north and the junior high to the east. Woodrow's baseball field rested quietly across the street from the school's main entrance.

The dirt infield appeared in decent shape, but the outfield grass was still brown from winter, ditto the grass on the school's front lawn. Six idle tennis courts were to the north of the baseball facility.

As Stormy studied the high school's front entrance, he wondered if study hall remained on the third floor overlooking the front lawn below. Once, other classmates had distracted an elderly substitute teacher by throwing paper airplanes at her. During the attack, Stormy, undetected, left the study hall and raced down the three flights of stairs; he lay on the front lawn and closed his eyes to the sky, as if he had fallen three stories.

The other study hall students immediately showed the substitute their fallen comrade who promptly fainted dead away. Stormy smiled to himself as he remembered the paddling, sans pants, he and his buddies had received for the trick.

As Stormy entered the front door, he took in Woodrow's interior with one long nostalgic gaze. Teenage energy, hopeful and innocent, zigzagged through the air. With so many students between class, the halls seemed stiflingly narrow. Small black dots still decorated the marble beige floors. Bright red lockers lined both sides of the hallway and smelled of worn metal. Chocolate-colored wooden railings spiraled to the second and third floor. No change there. The students were casually dressed, and that was okay with him. He wore a collared pink knit shirt with his Levi's.

Stormy stopped in the front hallway to gaze into a large wooden trophy case which housed a multitude of tiny statues, all staring back as mum as sports cards. Batters stood coiled at the plate. Sprinters knelt on the blocks while hoopsters shot hoops. Football players struck a dashing pose, a football protected under their arms. After locating his team's runner-up state championship trophy, he moved on. The steady clanging of lockers opening and closing echoed throughout the halls. Stormy turned down another busy hallway; fueled by familiarity, his stride was now more rapid.

At first he went undetected by his new classmates, who were too absorbed with the intricacies of teenage adolescence. Finally a scrawny, pimply faced kid spotted Stormy and punched a large, round-faced buddy wearing a band jacket several sizes too small. Probably the clarinet and tuba player, decided Stormy.

"Hey, we must have some new blood," acne face said.

Stormy kept moving until he saw female twins practically the size of the tuba player. Side by side, they cleared a path like a snowplow. The two girls drifted apart the way military planes leave formation and she appeared in their path. Bam! Just like that, when you expected it the least. Throwing off light brighter than the brightest light on any Christmas tree, she was the most gorgeous female he had ever seen in his four plus decades.

Tall, but not too tall. Slender, but not skinny. Neatly pressed, perfectly fitting blue jeans covered long thin legs which carried her with thoughtless elegance. A red and gray Wildcats cheerleading jacket, along with schoolbooks nestled to her chest, concealed her bosom. He slowed to prolong his look. The girl's straight brown hair framed high-rise cheekbones and bounced gently off her shoulders. She chattered with two of her classmates. The instant their paths crossed, the air briefly filled with a sweet scent. Her large green eyes met his and she brushed a brown lock of hair from her cheeks.

What a face! She wore no makeup, but needed less than that. She reminded Stormy of the young models in New York on the way to their go-sees, the sort of girls that men would line the Manhattan sidewalks to admire.

With the girl now past him, Stormy stopped and turned to look at her shapely rump. Suddenly, the girl glanced over her shoulder and smiled at Stormy. Stormy could not remember more perfect white teeth. Caught in the act of gawking at the teenager, Stormy's head snapped the other way. A male student standing close by witnessed the exchange.

Stormy practically growled at the kid, "Who's Ms. America?"

"Parker's daughter," the kid said, as if everyone in the school must know that.

Stormy continued toward the school's office. He felt time peeling away and the reduced layers exposed conflicting emotions. Was he a middle-aged man or a teenager? Even Stormy had made it a practice to date women within two decades of his age. He shrugged internally. Over a thousand students attended Woodrow. He'd probably never even talk with the girl. Besides, more important things occupied his mind.

Team pictures from past years decorated the coach's modest office. Sports equipment and balls from multiple sports littered its concrete floor. Plaques on the wall directly behind the desk informed visitors that Coach Cotton Parker had lettered in football and baseball at Texas Tech University.

Cotton Parker's thick legs were crossed and propped on the single old wooden desk in Woodrow's athletic office. The newspaper that preoccupied him concealed his face from a hard-bodied woman of about thirty, who filed forms in a nearby metal cabinet. His left leg re-shifted to rest on top of the right and the newspaper made the familiar crackling sound.

"This could be nasty," Cotton said, his tone edgy.

Red sweats clung like paint to the woman's athletic body. White letters spelled "Wildcats" across the front of her sweatshirt. She ignored Cotton's remark.

"I don't like the sounds of this at all," the coach said from behind the newspaper.

She remained silent.

Cotton's feet crossed again amid more crackling newspaper. He wore black coach's shoes, the kind with the rubber nubs on the bottom.

"Crap!" Cotton said more to himself than the woman.

The female gym instructor, still tending to the file cabinet, remained uninterested.

"I can't believe it."

The lady could ignore Cotton no longer, but she sounded bored. "Something in the paper doesn't agree with you?"

As she spoke, Stormy appeared in the doorway. The familiar smell of the past came to him in the aroma of worn leather and A-Balm and musty towels. Neither coach noticed him.

The tone behind The Dallas Times Herald sounded distinctly Texan. "It says right here in the sports page that Stormy Weathers has been missing for four days. If that isn't bad enough, he made a large cash withdrawal from his bank right before he disappeared. Doesn't sound good to me."

The woman, unaffected, kept her head buried in the file cabinet. "Who's Stormy Weathers?"

Stormy remained undetected in the entranceway. *So I'm missing huh,* he thought. Stormy struggled to contain a grin yet also wondered who reported him missing? But how could this woman, obviously a coach of some kind, not know of Stormy Weathers? Come on! No other Woodrow kid had ever made it to the bigs much less became a star.

"Heck, he's one of this high school's most famous graduates," said the invisible man. "Just retired last season, after playing for the Yankees probably twenty years."

Stormy beamed inside. That was more like it.

"Some lady friend reported him missing. He didn't show up for a date," the voice continued from behind the paper.

Stormy grimaced involuntarily. "Jaynie!" He'd forgotten about Jaynie. He should have at least called to say he was leaving on business for a while.

Arms that looked capable of fifty pushups on command jerked the paper away to expose a rugged, square face of about forty. The coach's neck looked strong enough to stop live ammo. Cotton Parker's thick frame and crew cut reminded Stormy of a drill sergeant.

"What's up, big un?" Cotton spoke loudly and with enthusiasm.

Stormy approached the desk. "I'm lookin' for the baseball coach. My name is…"

Stormy hesitated, having forgotten his new name again; thankfully, the name soon flashed in his mind. "Uh, Cal Lucas."

"Hope that wasn't a hard question, son."

Stormy smiled uncomfortably.

"You found him and the sociology teacher all in one. Cotton Parker, Coach Parker to you. That's Miss Johnson, the girls' PE teacher."

Cotton leaned across the desk and shook hands with Stormy. He had a good, firm handshake. A good beginning; Stormy could not stand a soft, mushy grip. Stormy nodded to Miss Johnson.

"I'm here to play baseball."

"And go to school, I hope," the coach responded.

Stormy handed the registration papers to his new coach. While Cotton scanned the papers, Stormy searched the room. Possibly he'd find a picture from his previous tenure, but he saw none that old. Stormy's eyes barely scanned a plaque hanging below the coach's two college letters. It read: "'An athlete who runs in a race cannot win the prize unless he obeys the rules.' 2 Timothy 2:5."

"So you want to play ball," Cotton said. "We've been working out since January. First game's next week."

"I'd like a shot, Coach. I don't think you'd be disappointed."

Cotton scratched his head in a pondering way. "This is our best baseball team in my sixteen years at Woodrow; and you're behind." Cotton's eyes alternated between Stormy's registration papers and his potential new player.

"Ah, why not, big 'un? Practice is in an hour. You've got enough time to register for school and dress out." The coach's tone turned from serious to more serious. "By the way, class attendance and passing your school work is mandatory if you want to play ball."

"Thanks, Coach." He turned to leave but heard his new coach.

"Hey, Lucas! What position do you play?"

"Center field," he replied, and was gone.

Cotton mumbled in the direction of Miss Johnson. "He probably won't be able to play a lick. The last kid we had looked that good was Tony Lovitto.

Remember him? You know, one of those kids who would trip over a termite in the woods." Cotton ran his hands across the top of his crew cut and sighed. "Of course, after we found out he was staying higher than an infield fly, it made a little more sense."

Cotton focused on Stormy's registration forms. "His papers say he's from New York City. How's anybody gonna learn to play baseball on asphalt?"

The lady smiled warmly at Cotton. "Coach, maybe this kid's the missing ingredient to that championship you've wanted for so long."

"I hope so, Carol, you don't know how bad I hope so," Coach Parker said wistfully.

"Oh, yes, I do, and so does everybody else around here."

Chapter Nine
PUT ME IN, COACH,
I'M READY TO PLAY TODAY

With a bounce in his step, Coach Parker marched among his fifteen high school baseball players. He wore gray sweatpants and matching shirt. A gray W split the crown of his red baseball hat; his black shoes glistened from a fresh coat of shoe polish. A five star general could not have made a greater impression on his young troops.

A bright afternoon sun reflected off the school that sat still as a giant postcard across the street on Glasgow Avenue. Most of the players dressed like their coach, although a few had on gray baseball pants. The players chattered among themselves while playing catch. Cotton seemed oblivious, but he heard it all. He knew who had girl problems, slipping grades, or even troubles at home. He missed nothing.

A couple of years ago, from eavesdropping during this pre-practice game of catch, Cotton learned of a bully step dad who physically and verbally abused one of his players. Cotton informed the proper authorities, but not before he paid a surprise visit to the man's place of business, a mortuary. When the child welfare people arrived, they found the belligerent stepfather sporting a shiner under one eye, locked in one of his coffins, screaming for help. Police suspected Cotton was the culprit, but never even issued a warning.

The citizens of Lakewood, the area nearest Woodrow, respected Coach Parker as much as any man in their community. "If Coach Parker locked a man up in a coffin, he by-God deserved it," they'd said. The step dad never bothered the kid again.

Cotton drew in the cool afternoon air enjoying his best spirits since the day he lost his wife. Parker's daughter was also coping better than he could have hoped. Not to mention, this looked like his best club in his long tenure at Woodrow. With a team comprised of eight seniors and seven juniors, he could

avoid using sophomores—a rare luxury. Sure, he could use better pitching. His only decent starter would never draw comparisons to Drysdale. Still, Woodrow might go a long way this season if only a leader would step to the plate, that one stud to lead by example.

Coach Cotton Parker continued to mingle, clapping his hands, "Okay guys, let's get loose. No wasted time! No wasted energy! This is the year, all the way! Let's show some life." Who would fill the leadership role he longed for? Surely someone would step forth.

Lawrence "Po Po" Bonkers and Thomas "Smitty" Pierce, both seniors, first spotted the lone figure approaching from the locker room across the street. Smitty was the team's best pitcher and Po Po the starting catcher. Two visible chords of muscle ran along each side of Po Po's neck. Smitty's lanky frame and herky-jerky pitching motion foreshadowed only modest athletic ability.

Po Po returned the ball back to Smitty faster than he had delivered it. Close friends since children, Po Po often spoke to Smitty in a peculiar language only the pitcher understood.

"Po Po, is that the new guy coach was talking about?"

"E," the catcher grunted.

"Man, he looks like a jock. Look at what he's wearing!"

"Nine-ninety-fifty-four-fifty."

White letters crossing the chest of Stormy's navy blue jersey stated: "Property of New York Yankees." He broke into a slow jog toward the backstop. A quick inventory of his new teammates surprised Stormy; they didn't look as young as he had expected.

Coach Parker stood militarily erect at home plate. He spit sunflower seeds to the ground, and then blew his whistle.

"Okay, big uns. Everybody here. Now!"

The Woodrow players sprinted to the infield with Stormy following, less enthusiastically, behind.

"Men, meet Cal Lucas, from New York City. Wants to try out for the team."

Stormy's new teammates offered a chorus of "welcome" and "glad to have you." Several patted him on the back. The freckle-faced redhead, the one that was pitching, shook his hand. From the gleam in their eyes, the kids appeared green but ready.

Cotton barked his orders, "All right, everybody, take your positions. Outfielders, play catch while I hit infield."

While the infielders took their places, Stormy jogged to center field. A stocky, short southpaw joined Stormy and extended his hand.

"Stan Henderson."

"Cal Lucas," Stormy said, returning the handshake. The sound of Coach Parker hitting ground balls and yelling instructions to the infielders soothed Stormy's ears.

"I'm the returning starter in center. In left field you got a couple of juniors trying to win a spot. Might be an easier place to break in," Henderson said, not rudely, but with great confidence.

Henderson's remark went past Stormy like an errant toss for his attention had shifted to the infield. The white ball zipped around the infield with more efficiency and skill than he remembered from high school kids.

"I don't want to brag, but I'm penciled in for center field," Stanley reiterated, slight irritation in his tone.

"Oh, yeah, thanks, I'll consider that. How about a little catch?"

Both retreated a few steps and started lobbing the ball back and forth. Stormy's arm felt fine, but what could he tell from a few soft tosses. Suddenly Stormy could feel tension rising from him like smoke billowing. He hadn't tested anything but his new vision. In the excitement of meeting Norma, Stormy had arrived unprepared for his first practice. He looked for Mac, but a quick search of the grounds revealed only his new teammates and Coach Parker.

What if his new body took on the spastic movements of Tony Perkins in that baseball movie about Jimmy Piersall, the one-time Indian's center fielder? Better a has-been than a never-was. He'd probably flunk out considering he barely graduated the first time. Imagining a life of flipping burgers and wearing one of those funny paper hats caused a rapid morale dive. This new body better work. Who wanted an unknown high school dropout at an autograph show?

Coach Parker skillfully slapped a crisp ground ball to his shortstop, who smoothly threw out the imaginary runner at first base.

"Let's go, toss it around the horn!" Parker bellowed.

The ball raced crisply around the diamond until it returned to Po Po, the catcher. The wide-eyed receiver calmly flipped the baseball to his coach.

"Get two!" Parker demanded loudly.

He hit a shot to his third baseman who scooped the ball cleanly and rifled it to second. Woodrow's second baseman made a good pivot and completed the double play to the first baseman.

"Awright! Awright! Way to go, big uns! Okay, outfielders, let's throw a few to the bases."

Uncertainty written in headlines on Stormy's face, he tentatively began running in place. With each step, his knees elevated higher until they churned like pistons, practically touching his chest. Unable to move his legs in such a fashion for years, Stormy felt cautiously satisfied while watching the nearby left fielder field the balls hit from Coach Parker.

"Damn thing doesn't hurt," Stormy muttered.

"What doesn't hurt?" Stanley stared curiously at Stormy.

"Oh, my knee's been bothering me." Stormy continued running in place.

"Really? When did you hurt it?"

"About twelve years ago."

"When you were six?" Henderson's eyes narrowed.

No, kid, I was thirty, but I can't really explain right now.

"Okay, center field!" Cotton's voice roared. "Henderson! Second, third and home in that order. Lucas, give him some room!"

Stormy quickly stepped aside to allow Stanley sole occupancy of center field, gladly avoiding an explanation of his first grade knee injury. The truth was this: while playing golf on an off day in California, a temper tantrum got the best of him and he accidentally clubbed himself in the knee with a four iron. Yankee management protected his image and reported to the media he suffered from shin splints—whatever that was. At any rate, the so-called shin splints had vanished in his recycled anatomy.

Henderson moved with only mediocre speed, but caught the lazy fly ball cleanly. His rainbow toss bounced three times before crawling to second base. In one play, Stormy knew Stanley would never play beyond high school. Stormy nervously shuffled his weight from side to side. Henderson's subsequent pegs to the infield fared no better.

Parker took the toss from his catcher and nodded to center field. "Well, Lawrence, let's see what our new man can do. Lucas! Second, third and home in that order!"

Show time. Stormy replaced Henderson in center field. Butterflies cluttered his stomach. Palms down on both knees, Stormy resembled a panther prepared to strike. All eyes locked on the new kid.

A crack of Cotton Parker's Fungo bat brought a lazy fly ball to center field. Stormy barely moved and the ball disappeared in his oversized outfielder's glove. The pretty girl at school could have made the catch, Stormy said silently. Stormy's perfect no arc missile arrived on the fly to the startled second baseman. The second sacker threw his glove to the ground and attended to his stinging hand.

Cotton motioned for Lawrence to toss him a baseball. "My, my Lawrence. Looks like the new kid can throw but can he get on his horse?"

Stormy, cautiously relieved at his brief performance, knew from the sound that the towering fly ball would sail far over his head. With hurried grace, Stormy turned and broke into a sprint. With his backside now to home plate, Stormy followed the ball with deft serenity. He altered his course toward left center and fully extended his left glove hand. The ball dropped gently from the sky and into his outstretched glove. Stormy abruptly applied the brakes, did a three-sixty and fired a rocket toward third base. Stormy's throw seemed to whistle and dance on its path to the infield. A one-hop throw arrived perfectly to the third baseman.

Stormy heaved a complete sigh of relief. He felt good, really good. He once possessed an arm so powerful opposing base runners didn't dare take that extra base, and it was back. Furthermore, he'd once run fast enough to stir a buzz saw of a wind, but had never run faster than today. And with vision so pure, he could practically read the writing on the baseball while it soared in flight.

For the first time, Stormy admitted to himself that the most difficult part of aging was the loss of confidence. Not knowing whether he really could cut it anymore had eaten at his soul. To spend a lifetime perfecting a craft and then discover that Father Time had robbed him of his skills, it was as if all those years were a waste. But now his confidence soared. How wonderful to feel cocky again.

Cotton turned to face his catcher. "Who is this guy?" he asked, awe in his tone. Before Po Po could answer, Cotton shouted instructions to his prospective star. "Son! Stay in center. I want you to field a few more! Make the throws here to Lawrence," the coach instructed, tapping home plate with his bat.

Stormy began to strut slightly and softly sing a few bars of his favorite baseball tune: "Put me in, Coach, I'm ready to play today. Put me in, Coach. Look at me! I can be center field."

For the next few minutes Stormy put on a startling display of defensive brilliance. He caught low line drives on his shoe tops, the type many major leaguers allowed to fall in for base hits. He cleanly fielded ground balls and fired strikes from the outfield to Po Po Bonkers at home plate. Stormy snagged balls hit shallow and deep. All eyes stayed on the spectacular performance, as if they had paid top dollar for admission.

"Lucas! Come in here and grab a bat!" Cotton yelled after a few minutes of Stormy's fielding clinic.

Stormy jogged to the infield. After inspecting a few of the wooden Louisville Sluggers in the dugout arc, he selected a weapon. While walking to the plate, he took a few practice swings; it was the picture perfect swing from an instructional video. Smitty stood at the pitcher's mound, tossing warmup pitches to Po Po.

Coach Parker moved from home plate to stand behind Smitty at the mound. He stoically observed Stormy as he stepped into the batter's box.

"Smitty, if this guy hits the way he plays defense we got a chance to…" Cotton said, his voice trailing away.

"Finally, win state," Smitty said respectfully.

The rest of the players were strangely quiet. They waited to retrieve the balls hit by the newest addition to their team.

"Yea, maybe so," Cotton said after a brief silence, his hard stare breaking into a warm grin.

Stormy assumed the batters box and looked at Po Po crouched behind home plate. With stringy blond hair thinning on top, Po Po appeared older than other high school seniors. Bigger and stronger too: one solid muscle ran from his neck to his toes. A sweet smell drifted up to Stormy. No coincidence, since a massive wad of bubble gum bloated the big catcher's mouth.

Stormy broke the silence. "How's it going, bro?"

Po Po glared at Stormy as if to say, "Who the hell are you?" before speaking through the wad of bubble gum. "Coach says baseball is a game of tradition; no short cuts. Coach is really big on doing things the right way. Course he and I don't always agree on what's the right way, but then Coach doesn't know that we occasionally have a difference in opinion. And while we're getting to know each other, I'm here for fun and more fun. Any new guy that comes in here and jacks with that and I might have to break their talented right arm. Got it, fifty?"

An outrageous grin divided Po Po's strong face.

"Lawrence quit jabbering and get on with the practice," demanded Cotton from the mound.

"Nine-ninety," the catcher grumbled. Po Po extended his glove hand toward the mound. "Okay, let's see your stick. Smitty's one of the best pitchers in the district, you know."

"Tell him to bring it on."

Smitty delivered a fat batting practice pitch that Stormy promptly smashed directly at third base. Woodrow's third baseman, Twiggy Hoak, wisely dove to his left to avoid the missile.

"Darn it, Hoak! If you're gonna dive out of the way every time someone hits a ball your way, we'll find someone else to play third!" Cotton said to his third baseman.

From behind his mask, Po Po peered up at his new teammate out of the top of his eyes. "My, my! Four-hundred-ninety-fifty-two-fifty! That ball's gone ballistic. If Twig hadn't moved, I do believe it would have gone through his chest and come out his back."

Po Po's smile exposed not only his stash of gum but also big broad teeth. His neck jerked gently three times. The kid's obviously from Mars, speaking in some foreign tongue but Stormy liked him already. One thing Stormy feared about retirement was losing the camaraderie with the guys. Maybe he had already found a new pal.

"Tell him to throw something with a little heat on it," said Stormy evenly.

"Tita, put some smoke on it! New man says you're a wuss."

"Aw, pipe down, Po Po," Smitty answered in a way that said he had heard his buddy's jabs often before. Still, he spoke in a more peaceful tone than his volatile friend.

"Po Po? Did he say Po Po?" Stormy asked, struggling to contain his laughter.

"Yep, friends can call me shit for short," quipped Po Po, his chest protector briefly inflating with pride.

Smitty's grunt on release plainly indicated the magnitude of his effort. The ball jumped from Stormy's bat and shot straight at the pitcher's mound. Smitty and his coach dove to the dirt like soldiers avoiding gunfire. Twiggy turned to conceal his smirk from Cotton.

Cotton slowly lifted his head as if to make sure the bullets had ceased. "Who is this guy?" Cotton repeated with more volume than before.

"Hey, fifty, you're not showing much respect for our honorable class president's best pitch," said Po Po, admiration in his tone.

"If that's his best pitch, we're in for a long season."

"Can you hit the long ball?"

"Longer than a whore's dream."

"Is that long?"

"You'll see."

Smitty, regaining his composure from the mortar attack, prepared for the next offering. Cotton, his arms folded, stood behind Smitty; the coach wore a look that could only be described as hopeful. He leaned in close to his pitcher and spoke in too low a voice for Stormy to hear.

Smitty's offering initially seemed inside. But wait! The ball was breaking across the plate slow enough for Stormy to count the stitches. The son-of-a-bitches tried to cross him with a curve! Lots of luck, bro. Wood met squarely with cowhide.

While leaping to his feet, Po Po threw his catcher's mask to the ground. Initially, the ball shot off into the sky but soon seemed suspended in space, as if painted into the sky. Stormy's blast eventually landed close to the tennis courts over four hundred feet away.

The veins in Po Po's neck began to bulge. His head cocked to one side. "My, my, my! There's gonna be reentry marks on that ball! You fifty-five fifty!" Po Po practically shouted, gesturing wildly. He looked to the mound. "Hey, Smitty that's the way to fool him!"

Stormy's display of power left Coach Parker speechless. Only Woodrow's ex-center fielder, Stanley Henderson spoke. "I'll play left field."

Chapter Ten
OUR FAVORITE PLAYER IS MISSING

It comforted Stormy that the boys' dressing room had changed little during the last two decades: the same drab concrete floors and plaster walls, the same plain brown lockers, the familiar mildew smell. He doubted the school had upgraded the plumbing; the water pressure during his shower barely washed the soap from his hair.

With only a few pictures on the walls, his eyes didn't search long until he found a picture of Stormy Weathers. His first baseball card picture, the ballplayer posed in a Yankee uniform, his bat cocked above his head. With thick brown hair, sturdy frame, and square jaw, the younger Stormy bore a brotherly resemblance to Cal Lucas.

Stormy sat on a wooden bench as he packed his duffel bag, inhaling the toasty aroma of shower steam that permeated the air. His teammates milled about the locker room in various stages of dress and undress. Stormy had combed his wet hair back like NBA coaches of future generations. Coach Parker approached; dressed in a T-shirt and black coach's shorts, the man looked powerful enough to lift one of those small French cars.

"Lucas, that was a decent first workout. We can probably find a spot for you," the coach said through a chuckle. "If I can't locate some eligibility forms you need to sign, I'll bring them to your place tonight. Okay?"

"Sure."

"Crescent Apartments, right?"

Stormy nodded, easily stifling any outward celebration. He was on schedule. First he'd win that state championship, then return to his rightful place in the big show. Somewhere along the way, he'd find out the truth from Norma Weathers. Life was good again.

The night sky was clear and looked out of reach for the highest of major league pop-ups. Under a full moon bright enough to eliminate the need for ballpark lights, the black Porsche darted into the Crescent Apartments' parking area and ground to a screeching halt. Stormy bolted from his new wheels, cradling a large, steamy pizza from Campisi's. The fresh scent of pepperoni and bell peppers penetrated Stormy's nostrils, the hot aroma contrasting nicely with the cool night air.

Stormy approached Norma's door with a high-energy gait. Hopefully, Norma would help him celebrate today's success by sharing Dallas' most famous pizza.

Stormy rang the doorbell and waited, but there was no answer. After a couple of minutes, he rang again and the door finally opened. Norma appeared in the doorway but since his previous visit, her face had stored up a lot of gloom. Red rimmed her swollen eyes; her matted hair looked slept on, creating an excess of cowlicks. Under less awkward circumstances, Norma's attire would have amused Stormy; with her gray wool pants, she wore a navy blue sweatshirt that looked kin to his own Yankee windbreaker.

"Oh, hi, Cal." She sounded as if she'd been asleep...or crying.

"Uh, Ms. Weathers, I was wondering if you wanted some pizza?"

"It's a bad time, but thanks, anyway."

The door shut gently; Stormy stood alone in stunned silence. He hesitated before ringing the bell again. After a shorter wait than before, Norma reappeared in the doorway.

Stormy could think of nothing better to say, "What's wrong?"

Norma left the door open and slowly returned inside, oblivious to whether Stormy followed or not. Stormy pursued, pizza in hand, until he stood beside her. She looked straight ahead but pointed to a newspaper lying on the round glass coffee table.

"Haven't you heard the news? Our favorite player is missing," she said softly.

He walked to the paper and stared at the front page. "Ex-Yankee Star Missing." The story wasn't the headline but it darn sure made the front page. Where was Mac when he needed him? Norma appeared on the verge of a meltdown because of his disappearance. What a mess. For the first time since the recycling, Stormy wondered if Mac had fully thought through the game plan. And why would she care?

"His girlfriend called the police. He didn't show for a date," Norma murmured.

"Yeah, I know. The coach was reading the article when I checked in at his office."

Stormy dropped heavily to the olive green couch and faced Norma. He spoke in a monotone. "Jaynie wasn't his girlfriend. She's getting carried away." It bothered Stormy when women behaved like he belonged to them. "He's all right. Take my word."

Norma wearily lowered herself beside Stormy. She stared a tunnel into his eyes.

"The paper says he made a large cash withdrawal right before he disappeared. A teller at the bank claims he never carried cash like that. Maybe he was being blackmailed and needed cash. What if someone knew that he had the money and they robbed him and you know…?" Norma's voice trailed off. "What makes you think he's okay?"

For reasons that Stormy could not understand, it hurt to see her so upset. "I know him, that's why."

Norma jerked militarily erect. "You know Stormy?"

"A little." Stormy shrugged, as if to say "No big deal". "You know us kids, we were always hanging around the stadium. He told us before I moved here that he was going to disappear for a while. Chill out. Take an extended vacation. That's all there is to it. Trust me. He's doing better than ever."

Norma's heavy expression lightened in an instant. "That's really true? He really told you that?"

"Yes ma'am."

"Why didn't you tell me you knew him before?"

"You didn't ask."

Norma leaned closer to Stormy.

"What was he like?" she asked intently.

Stormy reached for a piece of pizza and took a bite. The story was working. She'd started to relax.

"I'll tell you all I know if I can have a beer."

Norma managed a weak smile and playfully patted him on the knee. "I don't have any beer but if I did you couldn't have one. You're under age. How about a soda pop?"

Norma disappeared in the kitchen and immediately returned with a soft drink. "Now, tell me all about him."

Stormy took another bite of pizza; he propped his white canvas tennis shoes on the coffee table. This would be fun.

"Hell of a guy. Tad rambunctious at times but basically harmless. I think he had a soft spot for us kids cause he was always sneaking us into the stadium. Letting us hang around," Stormy said truthfully.

The pride in her eyes made him feel great. Should he go for it? Hell, yeah!

"He was raised in an orphanage. I think he related to kids who needed attention."

Norma looked like she'd just taken a laser beam to the heart. "He told you that, too?" she gasped.

"Hey, why are you so concerned about some ex-jock you never knew? It's not because you both have the same last name, is it?"

Norma's soft eyes narrowed and turned hard. She focused on the shrine behind him. Stormy's heart fluttered. Was she ready to come clean?

"You wouldn't believe it if I told you."

"Try me."

She faced Stormy, and a mist formed in her eyes.

"I can't. Believe me, you'd think I was nuts if I told you the whole story. I don't want to scare you away thinking I'm some crazy lady." Norma's look returned to the wall. "You really think he's okay?"

Damn! Close, but no cigar. The riddle remained intact. Still, her concern left a warm feeling in Stormy's gut. He flashed a wide grin.

"Yep, bet he's doing great."

She exhaled heavily and her shoulders lowered.

"Well, if you say so. How was practice today?"

Norma listened with great interest as Stormy informed her of his practice exploits. They went on to discuss many of Stormy Weathers most memorable days as a major leaguer. To his astonishment, she remembered more than he did. She knew the date of his three-homer game against the Tigers and the years of his MVP award, batting championship and gold glove awards.

Norma's mood darkened when discussing a paternity suit filed against him. "I knew that lady was just looking for publicity," she fumed.

Stormy grimaced inside; he'd never known whether he fathered the child or not. The woman miscarried during all the media hoopla. She'd dropped the charges after Stormy paid her medical bills; it remained one of the few bad memories from the good old days as a major league player.

After two hours of Norma providing most of the discussion, Stormy left for his apartment. How ironic. His first friend in his new life was the one that caused him so much grief before.

Chapter Eleven
SHE'S THE SENSITIVE KIND

The arms of the small plastic alarm clock on the mantle above the empty fireplace pointed to 7:15 PM. Stormy labored at his small Formica kitchen table, diligently oiling his baseball glove between sips of beer. He paid a wino at a local convenience store five bucks to buy him a six-pack. An old jock in a young jock's body still enjoyed a cold brew now and then.

Only a worn yellow cloth-covered couch and two matching chairs occupied the living area adjacent to the tiny kitchen area. The beige walls were barer than a baby's bottom. Through the jam box speakers on the table, J.J. practically whispered an achingly mellow ballad:
"Don't take her for granted
She's had a hard time
Don't misunderstand her
or play with her mind."

The doorbell rang. "Come in!" Stormy yelled, never taking his eyes off his ball glove.

The door opened. Stormy Weathers glanced up to see the beautiful young woman from school standing in his doorway.

J.J. continued to croon softly.
"Treat her so gently
It would pay you in time
You got to know
She's the sensitive kind."

As if shocked, Stormy leaped to his feet. "May I help you?" he asked, his tone registering an equal mix of admiration and surprise.

"Are you Cal?" Her voice was deep and hypnotically soft. It reminded Stormy of a young starlet from an old black and white movie.

"Uh, yes."

"I'm Susan Parker."

"Please come in. Have a seat."

After Stormy motioned to the couch, her runway model legs transported her across the floor and she lowered herself gracefully to the sofa. She tilted her knees sideways and folded her hands in her lap. Stormy tried to avoid staring. It wasn't easy.

She handed some papers to Stormy. Her hands were small and feminine, her short fingernails neatly manicured but without polish. She still smelled delicious.

"My dad's delayed at a PTA meeting at school; he asked me to drop some papers by. Fill these out and return them to him first thing in the morning. Dad can probably get you eligible for the first game."

After accepting the forms, Stormy dropped to the opposite end of the couch to inspect them. Name, address, social security number and other routine questions. No problem.

A light flashed inside Stormy's brain. So this is "Parker's daughter" the kid mentioned in the hallway.

"Uh, how about a beer?" Stormy motioned to the refrigerator with his eyes.

"No thanks." She glanced at the jam box. "What beautiful music. I've never heard it before. Who is it?"

"J.J. Cale."

"I've never heard of him, but then I listen to mostly classical."

J.J.'s melancholy wave continued on.

"Tell her you love her,
each and every night
You will discover,
She will treat you right."

"Most people your age think this is classical music," Stormy said, taking a drag on his beer.

"I'm eighteen. I suppose you're eighteen, too," she said through a soft giggle.

Oops. He stared at his beer and pushed his tongue firmly against the inside of his lower lip. How old was he? He hadn't studied his new date of birth.

"I guess I am," he finally answered.

"Dad says you were incredible in practice today. He said it would be just his luck you'll freeze in a real game."

63

Wolf shit! He wanted to say, "Just tell your old man to sit back and enjoy the ride," but only asked, "What do you think?"

She smiled coolly. "Guess we'll have to wait and see."

Susan suddenly stood and Stormy instinctively did the same. "You know, I don't know too many people here. Do you think I could talk you into a movie some night?" Stormy asked. He felt almost shy.

Stormy followed Susan to the door and opened it for her. The night air had a cool edge to it. She stared at Stormy, her face calm, and her look sure. Stormy wondered what she saw. What was she thinking? Some old ballplayer masquerading as a teenager? She smiled, and her eyes shone. She was as pretty as pretty gets.

"Yes, I think you might." Susan walked out the door, but turned to face him in the doorway. "By the way, don't let dad know about the beer. He doesn't think teenagers should drink, especially his players. That's a sure way to get on his bad side."

"Something tells me that's not a good place to be."

"Something tells you right. Bye, Cal."

Stormy watched Susan glide across the parking lot, sleek as an otter. Holy Roger Maris! A storm of confusion clouded his mind. Was he eighteen or forty-one? Stormy briefly thought of discussing this dilemma with Mac, but decided Mac wasn't who he wanted to share his romantic life with. Still, how could this high school senior—a virtual rookie—so unnerve an old veteran like Stormy?

J.J. softly spoke to Stormy.

"She is so lonely, waiting for you
You are the only one to help her through
Don't take her for granted. She's had
a hard time. You got to know. She's
the sensitive kind."

Susan entered the Ford sedan that once belonged to her mother. She liked this Cal Lucas, but what did she know?

Although Susan received countless requests for dates, she seldom went out. Everybody at school loved Lawrence for his outrageousness, his free spirit, but she thought of him as a big brother, a great protector. Besides he could be gross. Smitty had potential, but he simply didn't light any fires. And things got worse from there.

As a freshman, the kids gathered at the East Dallas YMCA for necking parties in the bushes after freshmen football games. Susan avoided the necking like she would a drunken party, but one night curiosity reeled her in. She'd handpicked Smitty but after two kisses, she burst out laughing and the experiment ended. A few months later, some crazy person murdered her mother and Susan lost interest in the pursuit of teenage love.

Tonight, however, while sitting beside Cal, she felt something new, a sort of slow heat radiating in his direction. He was strong, independent, sure of himself. Cal Lucas reminded Susan of her dad, only better looking.

Susan struggled to hold back tears. She longed to talk with her mother about this feeling. Mom could have offered some advice. Dad just wouldn't understand. One thing was certain: this new guy was different than the other guys at school. He acted older than eighteen.

Chapter Twelve
YOU AND I ARE A LOT ALIKE

Within minutes after Susan left, Stormy heard another slightly louder knock on his front door. Stormy's hopes rose like dust from a resin bag. Was she back?

"Door's open," Stormy said.

No such luck. Mac entered Stormy's new home. Despite Stormy's disappointment, Mac's wardrobe forced a grin. Mac wore a water-resistant Woodrow Wilson warmup outfit, with matching bright red top and pants.

"Dear old guardian, here."

"Where in the hell did you get that warmup suit?"

"I have my means. I wore them in celebration of your first day at school." Mac plopped on the couch and folded his arms across his chest; he crossed his black and white high-top Converse tennis shoes on the cheap coffee table. "You like them, huh?"

"I didn't say that."

"I thought I better check in and see how you're doing."

"Great, but I was a little worried back at the lake."

Mac shrugged. "Everything worked out okay, didn't it?"

Stormy returned the shrug. "Yeah, sure."

"Have you met your new neighbor?"

"Yeah, I did. Sure did."

"How did it go?" Mac leaned closer.

"Fine, but what do you care?"

"Your relationship with her—or should I say 'lack of'—plays a major role why we've chosen you for our recycling program." Mac became animated, waving his arms all about. "You and I are a lot alike. Take a victory any way we can, bend a rule or two, if necessary. Look for an unfair advantage. Traits of a winner. We like to keep your kind around as long as possible."

"I still don't understand what all that has to do with Norma."

"Her rejection of you as a child fostered a burning desire deep in your gut to succeed, belong, be recognized and respected, be the best at any cost. You turned a negative into a positive. I like that."

Stormy stopped oiling his glove and drug his right hand through his thick hair.

"You know, I went to her place to check her out. No way was I gonna like her. She did dump me; that's a fact. But she was so nice and caring, I couldn't help but like her. You know what's really weird?"

"What?"

"She followed every day of my career. Why would she do that if she didn't care about me?"

"Beats me," Mac replied, his tone bright and happy.

"She was really upset when she found out I'm missing. She thinks something bad has happened to me. We shouldn't have scared her like that."

"Sounds like everything's okay now."

"Yeah, but I bet she had a good reason for putting me in that orphanage."

"Why don't you ask her?" Mac asked nonchalantly.

Stormy leaned toward Mac with his shoulders hunched. He cupped his hands to his chin; his elbows rested in his knees. "Yeah, maybe I will."

Mac rose. "I'll stay in touch."

Mac walked through the door without bothering to open it and continued to the front sidewalk.

Norma stood by her window, observing Stormy's place from behind slightly cracked blinds. She dared not leave and possibly miss the exit of the man wearing the red warmups. Surely, she had mistaken his identity. His rapid entrance into Cal's place had prevented her from getting a good look.

Norma's mind ripped away the decades of time. At sixteen, she'd had the look of a centerfold. Older men pursued her. Her dad drove long-haul trucking and her mom was a waitress in a bar. Neither was around much, and Norma had to fend off the wolves alone. She became pregnant less than a year out of high school.

Norma planned to put the child up for adoption, but at the first sight of her son, she dropped the notion like dead weight. She supported them with a secretary's job. They didn't have much, only each other; mother and son lived happily together for six years. Then trouble arrived involving the man that Norma feared had entered the residence of Cal Lucas. There were no pitches down the middle when dealing with this man; Norma learned that the hard way.

Suddenly the man appeared in the walkway, his back facing Norma's apartment. As if he felt Norma's stare, he abruptly turned and glared fiercely at Norma through tiny, serpent eyes. The scowl on this man's face quickly transformed to a smile. Only the smile was as wicked as a wolf man's grin under a full moon. Norma retreated a step and then turned and ran to her bedroom. She dove into her queen-sized bed and pulled the dark green bedspread over her head.

Chapter Thirteen
REVERCHON PARK

The old man had marked the foul lines at Reverchon Park for over three decades. Before Francis Mack completed his day's work, the perfectly straight white chalk lines would clearly establish fair and foul territory for the first and third base sides.

Reverchon, nestled in a large, wooded park off Maple Avenue, served as a primary site of Dallas high school baseball. Within the ballpark, sparkling, rich, Bermuda grass covered the infield and outfield. Marble-smooth red dirt base paths surrounded the infield, its flawless condition the result of Francis' tender loving care. Wooden benches, six rows deep, extended down the foul lines. Behind home plate, a tin roof covered a section of about fifteen rows.

Remindful of Wrigley Field in Chicago, ivy smothered the wooden outfield fences. It was only two hundred ninety-six feet to left field and three hundred twenty-two feet to right but a twelve-foot-high fence prevented cheap home runs. A green, wooden scoreboard, in need of paint, stood on two legs directly below the three hundred seventy-nine-foot marker in center field. The scoreboard operator still used white portable letters and numbers to keep score.

Beyond the outfield fence, a creek divided the ball field from a dense wooded area. Across the creek, a playground contained slides, swings and a jungle gym, along with picnic tables and concrete barbecue pits. Mature trees provided shade from even the hottest Texas sun.

Under a high, pale blue sky and a bright afternoon sun, the trim, razor-jawed groundskeeper joyfully whistled while he prepared the field for play. In a couple of hours the sun would dip below the home plate grandstand, signaling the first inning of twilight. The soft breeze lifted his thin white hair as he eagerly awaited the first day of district competition.

Teenage energy thrown off by sixteen players, all wearing their new gray uniforms, crammed the bus. "Wildcats" inscribed in red script letters stretched across the front of the jerseys and matched the red in their stirrups; a gray "W" split the crown of each red cap.

On the back row of the driver's side, Stormy sat by himself. Smitty and Po Po occupied the seat directly in front. Smitty regarded his newest teammate curiously. More than Cal's talent intrigued Woodrow's pitcher; he could readily see that Cal Lucas walked his own walk.

Smitty, usually thinking, often concerned, always worried—about everything. Smitty worried his dad had tapped college funds to keep his sick grandmother in a decent rest home.

He wondered if he would ever marry, and, if so, would he divorce? So many of his friends came from broken homes. Though his parents seldom fought, what if they divorced? Or died? How would he take care of his little sister?

Smitty even worried about his death and especially if he died while still a virgin? It was one of two thoughts he and Po Po agreed upon. Smitty turned and addressed Woodrow's great hope as if something concerned him but he didn't want to stir up too big a ruckus about it.

"We've got to get to their pitcher," he said quietly. "He's their whole team. Best pitcher in our district."

Smitty oozed as much warmth and friendliness as his buddy farted outrageousness. To Stormy, his youthful naiveté made him seem trustworthy.

Stormy glanced Po Po's way, his brow briefly furrowed. "I thought you said Smitty was the best?"

Po Po grunted. His jaw, pregnant with bubble gum, appeared ready to explode.

Stormy nodded his head like a sage old pro. "So knock him out of the game and we can mark the season opener in the win column."

Po Po's neck snapped to the right, but he managed to stare straight ahead. He looked capable of eating his catcher's mitt. "E…"

Smitty interpreted. "That means yes."

Stormy smiled. "Thanks." Oh to travel with Po Po on the road trips in the old days. They would have cut a wide swath across any town, that's for sure.

"Tell me about Susan."

Po Po's eyes quickly cut toward Stormy. Emotion returned to his voice. "Un-nine-four-forty-touchable."

"Huh?"

"Me and Popehead have had a crush on Susan since first grade. So has every other boy in the school." Smitty tugged on the brim of his cap and shook his head regretfully. "She let us know a long time ago we were all just going to be friends. Po Po thinks she's got a college boyfriend. She doesn't hang out much after school. She always has to be some place."

"E." The catcher's eyes returned to the front of the bus. His mouth worked harder than before massaging the wad in his jaw.

"What do you think?" Stormy said, crossing his arms slowly.

Smitty shrugged and glanced at his best friend. "Would you really go against this man's opinion?"

Stormy studied the big, burly teenager. An internal rainstorm seemed to drown Po Po's normal, sunny disposition. His thick neck repeatedly twitched as if hooked by some invisible fishing line.

"Not me, bro."

"You'll have to pardon Po Po. He's getting ready for battle. Losing puts him in the worst mood."

"Don't tell me. Po Po played middle linebacker in football."

"Yep. For three years the coaches tried to stop him from tackling with his head." Smitty paused for dramatic effect. "It wasn't his head they were worried about. He kept cracking all the helmets," Smitty added through a grin.

Po Po's mouth turned upward at the corners. Stormy pursed his lips and, with absolutely no expression on his face, nodded approvingly. These guys were all right. They might have some good times together.

The old bus crept into the Reverchon parking area and slowly squeaked to a stop. Parker and his troops filed out of the bus, one by one, Stormy last. The team made its way to the front entrance on the third base side, near home plate. As his teammates entered, Stormy stopped short of the main gate and admired the old ballpark. Nothing had changed. He saw Francis Mack locking up his equipment in the storage bin by the front gate. It was all Stormy could do not to say hi.

Chapter Fourteen

THE FIRST GAME

Crouched behind home plate, Po Po dropped two fingers between his knees, signaling for a curve. Stormy, in center field, shaded toward left; with an off-speed pitch on the way, the batter would probably pull the ball. Playing shallow, he could read his catcher's signals, and position himself to make the play. Besides, with his reclaimed jackrabbit speed, few high school kids could drive a ball over his head anyway.

In the top of the first inning, Woodrow went three up and three down. Stormy would hit first the next inning. Fueled by adrenaline, internal juices surged through his body as he paced about center field.

Coach Parker, also wired, paced the dugout, constantly barking instructions. Susan sat among the crowd of two hundred or so, yelling encouragement. Stormy was surprised to find Norma sitting quietly in the stands by herself. Her floor-length, flower-patterned cotton dress and a wide-brim floppy brown hat made her easy to see.

No different than twenty years ago plus change, the Cougars still wore gray and dark green uniforms with green hats. Confirming Stormy's hunch, the batter blooped a pitch to shallow left field for the game's first base hit. Stan Henderson moved in, dropped to one knee, scooped the ball and delivered it to second base, holding the runner to a single. To his surprise, Stan found his center fielder beside him. Stormy winked and returned to center field.

Smitty's next offering, a lazy curve, split home plate. Norma could have hit the fat pitch; the Cougar batter rocked a high fly ball far over Stormy's head. Stormy turned his back to home plate and raced directly toward the center field wall. Reaching the barrier, he scaled halfway up the fence, clung to the vines, and watched helplessly as the ball disappeared on the other side.

Smitty gazed sheepishly toward center field. Stormy smiled reassuringly and said loud enough for Smitty to hear, "We'll get 'em."

Po Po bolted to the mound. The veins in the catcher's neck expanded to the size of construction cable, showing his rage. It was a brief heated discussion with Smitty on the listening end. With the uneven stride of a lumberjack, Po Po returned to home plate.

Stormy chuckled with delight. He loved playing with others who also wanted to win. In less than a year, life's journey had taken him from the shithouse to the penthouse. Things had never looked better.

Po Po's tough love worked. The batter popped up to the shortstop for the final out of the first inning.

After the teams exchanged sides, Stormy assumed the batters box and took the first pitch outside for ball one. The pitcher threw much slower than the heat from the big show. This "stud" on the mound would be a breeze.

Stormy's swing brought a loud crisp crack from his bat; the ball shot rapidly along the third baseline fair, but barely. He rounded first base as the left fielder retrieved the ball and delivered a looping throw to his second baseman. The faster Stormy ran, the closer his rear was to the ground; he looked like a roadrunner. He never slowed rounding second and headed for third. His headfirst dive stirred up a sandstorm and easily beat the throw from the Cougar's surprised second sacker.

Stormy stood, brushing the red dirt from the front of his jersey. He showed no emotion, but internally he was smiling from left to right field. His thoughts instantly focused on scoring. The Cougars stared at one another: where had this guy come from?

Susan, now on her feet, cheered wildly. Though Norma remained seated, an approving smile slid across her face. Coach Parker stood at the top of the dugout steps; he rubbed his left hand on his chin and then down his neck, displaying the brief grin of a man who had just found a wad of green money in his attic.

Po Po left the on-deck circle arriving at home plate with his predictable intensity. He pawed his cleats in the dirt of the batter's box and glared menacingly at the mound. A mighty swing at the first pitch produced a routine can of corn to shallow left field.

Stormy, still perched on third base, watched the outfielder camp under the fly ball. The instant the ball vanished in the opponent's glove, he steam-rolled toward home. Stormy expected a close play and plowed headfirst into the Cougar's catcher. Amid a loud belching grunt, the receiver and his glove flew in different directions. The ball sailed unattended all the way to the backstop.

Coach Parker somberly observed his center fielder leap to his feet and trot to the Woodrow dugout. Cal Lucas's new teammates greeted him with high fives and "way to go"; an especially approving smile covered Po Po's face.

The crowd became silent while the player stumbled awkwardly to his feet. His eyes looked glassy and out of focus, but then the player righted himself and appeared ready to play ball. Cotton released enough air to blow up a balloon.

After Twiggy Hoak slapped a weak grounder to the Cougars' pitcher for the third out, Stormy grabbed his glove and moved toward the dugout steps.

"Lucas!" came a crisp voice from behind.

Stormy wheeled to face Cotton Parker; the red in the coach's face and neck served to accentuate the intensity in his brown eyes. Cotton placed a large sincere hand on Stormy's shoulder.

"You arrived before the ball. There was no need to level the catcher like that. You would have been safe with a good hook slide," Cotton said with a fiery calm that matched the heat in his eyes.

"Yes sir, but this way he'll think twice before blocking home again." How could Stormy explain his lousy slide over twenty years ago had cost the Wildcats a championship?

As Stormy took a straight path toward center field, Cotton's past cut into his consciousness. Captain Cotton Parker, U.S.M.C., and his weary young troops, shuffled aimlessly along a dirt path in the dense jungle. They sweated rain as much from nervousness as the sweltering heat. The platoon of a dozen men arrived at a deserted crossroad. Captain Parker motioned for a volunteer but his eyes locked on a blonde, fuzzy-cheeked soldier who readily stepped forth.

Cotton Parker stoically watched the young private move down the road like a lonely child about to enter a haunted house at midnight. Cotton wore the same cold look on his face today as he watched Cal Lucas take his position in center field.

Maybe Cotton had acted too harshly with the new player, as he might have with the young private. Who's to say Lucas knew that the ball arrived late? Besides, Cotton wanted to finish on top, an experience foreign to him in high school, college or as a coach and certainly not in Vietnam. Cotton needed Lucas for a chance to win it all.

The Cougars still led two to one after four innings. Stormy was sandwiched between Smitty and Po Po in the Wildcat dugout. On the mound, the Cougar's pitcher sported a rooster's swagger. By this time, Stormy realized the southpaw intimidated his teammates. One of those guys without much stuff but who got the job done.

"Come on! This guy's nothin'. He couldn't get a lamb chop past a wolf!" Stormy declared.

Smitty wasn't so sure. "I don't know. Three innings left and you've got our only hit. Look at that asshole. Only guy I've seen that can strut while standing still."

Po Po popped another piece of gum in his mouth. "E, tita, not to mention, they're knocking the snot out of the ball. It's a miracle we're only down one."

Smitty turned up his nose at his best friend. "Thanks."

Stormy inspected the Wildcats' bench, taking note of the slumped shoulders and lowered heads.

"Well, maybe it's time for this prima donna pitcher to see my impression of Jackie Robinson."

"The Motown singer?" Po Po grunted.

"I think Popehead's thinking of Smokey Robinson," Smitty replied.

"Jackie Robinson was the first black player in the big leagues. He knew how to deal with arrogant pitchers."

Stormy stood and left the dugout. He grabbed a Hillerich and Bradsby from the bat rack and took his place in the on-deck circle. His Wildcat teammate promptly fanned on three pitches. He felt a sense of urgency to bring the advantage to his team. Stormy Weathers had a new engine under the hood but he operated the same as before.

The instant Stormy dropped the bunt just fair along the first base side he knew his plan would work to perfection. Darting from the mound, the Cougar hurler came too close to the speeding base runner.

At the precise moment the pitcher bent over to field the ball, Stormy ran up and down the opposing player's backside. The startled hurler crashed to the turf. After Stormy reached the bag safely, the Cougars' coach and players rushed to their fallen teammate. With the support of his coach and teammates, the pitcher managed to stand. His eye sockets were vacant and his head bobbed like a dashboard doll's.

The opposing coach, a big burly man, beamed an unmistakable look of contempt at Stormy while he complained passionately to the umpire, waving his big fingers in Stormy's direction. Stormy glared back, avoiding eye contact with his own coach; Stormy could feel the heat from Coach Parker's glare.

"Well tita's, I guess that's Cal's version of knocking a pitcher out of the game," Po Po cried from the bench. The entire team laughed a nervous laugh, except Smitty, who looked doubtful. Cheers erupted from the stands as the Cougar pitcher walked on his own to the sidelines. He was through for the day.

On the very first pitch from the new pitcher, Stormy raced for second base. The throw sailed high into center field. The Cougar center fielder backed up the play and fielded the ball cleanly after three hops. Since Stormy would easily make it to third, the outfielder made the throw to home plate.

Stormy had no intention of stopping at third. Po Po, who batted next, couldn't pick it up and hit it. Stormy would get home without him. He rounded third fast enough to generate a breeze in the coach's box. As inevitable as rainouts in April, Stormy thundered toward a violent collision at home plate.

The incoming throw skipped to the wide-eyed catcher's left but the approaching locomotive preoccupied him more than the ball. He didn't even get leather on the ball; it rolled past him to the backstop. Stormy scored standing up.

Cotton's broad shoulders relaxed and he exhaled heavily while clapping his hands. "Okay, tie game! Tie game! Let's go, guys!"

Woodrow led five to four in the last inning, thanks to Stormy's three run homer in the top half. Two outs meant a Woodrow victory.

The Cougar players had peppered the ball around from one foul line to the other all day but Stormy had roamed the outfield and held sure extra-base hits to singles or even outs. With the Yankees, Stormy had owned center field. "Where triples go to die," Doc had always said.

From the top step of his dugout, Cotton cupped both hands around his mouth and yelled. "Sharp defense guys! Two outs and we go to the house!"

Smitty offered a curve flat enough to sit on and the batter crushed the ball deep between Stormy and Henderson. Stormy beat Stanley to the ball and rifled it to Twiggy at third to hold the runner to a double. Smitty was spent, but no quit resided in the thin, lanky right-hander. Too bad Smitty didn't have a couple of good pitches to match his gutty attitude, Stormy mused.

With the fans for both teams standing and the air heavy with anticipation, the next Cougar batter sent a sinking line drive to right center field. After one step, Stormy reached warp speed; after several more, his body became horizontal as if lying on air and his gloved hand swallowed the ball.

Stormy slid on his belly, leaving a grass stain that stretched from his chest to his red stockings. Scrambling to his feet, he quickly delivered a frozen rope to second base; the perfect peg doubled up the runner for a double play and the final out. The Cougar base runner already approached home plate before the ashen look on his teammate's faces alerted him to the disaster.

Heads shook; eyes blinked. A disbelieving hush hung over the crowd—but not for long. Wildcat fans erupted like a flame in dry wood.

"I knew he had it all the time," Cotton uttered, shaking his head in admiration.

Woodrow's entire team rushed to center field. Stormy soon lay on the ground again, the result of a mauling by Po Po. The big catcher playfully continued to roughhouse, mumbling, "Cal Lucas is my hero" and "Heroes are hard to find."

While quietly leaving the ballpark, Norma watched the celebration with eyes long narrowed from life's unexpected change-ups. No doubt, Cal really had spent time watching Stormy play ball.

Chapter Fifteen
DROP BY MY PLACE TONIGHT

From his front row seat on the bus, Cotton heard his team chattering like a group of tipsy chipmunks, buzzed from a batch of spiked nuts. But was Cal Lucas magic or voodoo? After flattening the Cougar pitcher, Cal returned the malignant glare of the Cougar coach faster and harder than a high-speed tennis volley. Even Lawrence's balls weren't that big. In a Holy War, Lucas seemed the type to share a foxhole with, but this was not war.

Cotton continued to replay the game in his mind. On Cal's second mad dash to home, Cotton feared a train wreck but it never came. A troubling thought occurred to Cotton. Maybe Lucas knew more than he did. Maybe he should let the young man do his thing, and Cotton would win that elusive championship. Maybe Cal Lucas was a winner and Cotton Parker the loser. Cotton would call the Cougar coach tomorrow and apologize for Cal's aggressive play. He would explain that Cal was new and needed a little fine-tuning regarding Woodrow Wilson sportsmanship. Still, it might not be a bad idea to check out Cal's previous school history from New York.

The ride at the back of the bus was especially bumpy; heads bobbed; rears jostled on the rigid seats.

Po Po jabbed his pitcher in the side with his elbow. "Geez, fifty tita, they were knocking you around like a stepchild today. What's the scoop?"

Smitty seemed to study the question. He stared at the bus' dirty old flooring, as if addressing his baseball shoes. "I don't know."

Stormy quickly decided against coddling either of his new friends. They would be better off for it, he reasoned. "You're gonna get your tits lit all season if you don't get your breaking ball to move more."

Smitty stared hard at Po Po. "Maybe so, but Mr. Popehead slugger wasn't so hot today either. Molly Putz could hit the ball harder than he did," said Smitty, spunk returning to his voice.

Po Po's jaws dropped; his eyes bulged in mock horror.

"Get serious, Po Po; things don't look too good for either one of us."

"Wo, guys, no need to get down about one game. We did win you know," Stormy said.

Smitty's intelligent eyes showed concern. "We need scholarships. Our parents are strapped for cash. My grandmother's nursing home bill has left my parents too broke to pay attention."

"What about your folks?" Stormy asked Po Po.

"His dad's a TV repairman," Smitty said, answering for Po Po who was deeply engaged in the art of blowing a bubble. "His mom's a maid at the Hilton. They're hoping Po Po will be the first Bonkers to make it past high school."

"E," reluctantly grunted Po Po. His head nodded slowly in time with his chomps of gum.

Stormy had never considered college but Smitty and Po Po were not the next Ford/Berra battery; with a rising sense of duty. Stormy decided a college degree might not be a bad idea for his new pals.

"What do you guys want to study in college?"

"School administration," Smitty said.

Po Po mumbled through his gum, "What else? PE."

Stormy spoke in a voice that conveyed authority. "You guys drop by my place tonight. I have a couple of ideas that ought to help both of you."

Chapter Sixteen
HEROES ARE HARD TO FIND

Rays of moonlight sliced through Stormy's front window, spotlighting a kitchen table loaded with more goods than a hardware store. At the small table, Smitty and Po Po flanked Stormy. An old J.J. rocker blared from the stereo. Po Po and Cal sipped on bottles of Lone Star beer. Smitty lowered his half-empty bottle of Dr. Pepper to the table.

"I've never known anyone who lived with a guardian." Smitty's wide eyes matched the excitement in his tone.

"Yeah, especially one that never comes around," Po Po added through a mild burp. Po Po scanned the room as if searching for hidden adults. "It's like being older with no old people around," he reasoned.

"What's all this stuff on the kitchen table for?" Smitty asked.

Stormy's kitchen table contained a plastic baggie full of corks, another full of sawdust, a tube of Elmer's glue, a small electric drill, a can of lacquer spray, a shaving plane, and a tube of KY jelly. Stormy, lost in thought, was closely inspecting the wide barrel end of a wooden Louisville Slugger.

"Okay, look at this, guys—we're ready to go." Stormy proudly displayed the barrel end of the bat.

Both teenagers now looked more baffled than a rookie facing a Cy Young winner.

"Where did the inside of the bat go?" Po Po asked.

"The barrel's hollow—right? You know why it's hollow?" In unison, the two raised their shoulders.

"I made it that way with the drill before you got here." Stormy lightly tapped the drill with his bat.

After placing the bat on the table, Stormy held up the bag of corks as if showcasing precious jewels. "Now we're gonna take these corks and pack them nice and tight into our Louisville Slugger."

Smitty and Po Po closely watched their newest hero start the surgical procedure. He sprinkled the bag of sawdust on a newspaper that covered the table. Stormy used his fingers to distribute the dusty particles evenly. In silence, Stormy took the plastic bottle of Elmer's glue and poured it over the sawdust. Like stirring soup, he slowly stirred the concoction with a Popsicle stick.

"This gooey stuff is what will become the interior and end of our bat," Stormy explained. He scooped up the thick substance with the Popsicle stick and methodically poked the goop into the hollow fat end of the bat. In short order, Stormy had solidly packed the cork into the bat. "When it dries, we'll smooth the tip with sandpaper," he said, proudly displaying the tainted weapon.

"I don't get it," Smitty said.

Po Po looked more confused than during math class.

"If you make solid contact, the ball will explode off the bat like a shot out of a cannon. Po Po, your routine fly balls might turn into taters."

Po Po's expression remained blank.

"Tater, four bagger, round tripper, dinger, home run!" Stormy said, waving his hands like Woodrow's band conductor.

The lights came on. "Make me a star! Smitty, our new buddy is one fine cheater."

"That's not cheating, bro. Just looking for a little unfair advantage."

Everyone in the big leagues knew cheating existed, but few revealed their trade secrets. But these were high school players; Stormy saw no harm in sharing the best tricks he knew.

"Now we need to improve the odds that my bro Po Po's gonna make solid contact." Stormy raised the bat eye level for inspection. "Boys, the game of baseball involves trying to hit one round surface with another round surface. If one of these surfaces weren't quite so round, the game might be a little easier for the common man." Stormy placed the bat on the table and reached for the shaving plane. "We're gonna give our magic wand a flat side about six-inches long and about one half-inch wide right in the sweet spot of the bat."

Awestruck, the boys watched Stormy spend the next few minutes transforming a round surface to a flat one. Stormy knew if someone couldn't hit, it wouldn't matter if they took a sack full of bats or even a tree trunk to the plate. He always figured the true advantage of the tainted bat was mostly psychological.

Right now, Po Po needed any advantage possible. If one of Po Po's routine fly balls drifted beyond the outfield wall for a lazy homer, he might decide he could hit, and therefore win half the battle.

Wood shavings littered the table and floor below. With the skill of a master carpenter, Stormy used the plane to finish altering the bat. He held up the Hillerich and Bradsby, inspecting it as if he could see his major league future in the reflection of the shiny surface. Satisfied, he reached for the can of lacquer spray and started to spray the fresh wood. Woodrow's battery flinched from the harsh odor that invaded the room.

Stormy explained while he worked. "That'll keep our new section from sticking out like a sore thumb. Get this bat good and dirty in practice tomorrow and nobody can tell the difference."

"Cal," Po Po said. "You're the smartest person I know. Smitty, you might hit with this bat." Po Po now stood and fiercely whipped the bat through the air.

"I doubt it," Stormy said smiling. "Everybody knows pitchers can't hit. We're gonna do something else for Smitty's game." Stormy retrieved the jar of KY jelly. "Bro, you're gonna put a little of this across your forehead, eye brows, behind your ears, on your left wrist and most importantly your neck. A little dab of this on the ball and the hitters are going to start having trouble with that breaking ball."

Smitty stared hard at the jelly. "Does it work?"

"Oh man, the ball will dance like James Brown. The KY is a pitcher's best friend." In Stormy's playing days, quite a few pitchers tried the KY. Some had mastered the jelly while others achieved little or no success at all. Often the ball would move so much a pitcher would lose confidence in his ability to throw a strike, and thus lose the edge. Some couldn't make the ball dance and returned to traditional methods. Still, if Smitty would just think he maintained an edge on the competition…

"In the old days, pitchers would rub soap across their undershirt and the slime would sweat through the jersey. Guys would lather one up and let it fly. I swear I saw a bubble float off a ball once."

"No way fifty, no way," Po Po said.

Now Stormy was standing, animated with thoughts from his youth. "Oh man, the things pitchers would try. In the minors, I knew a pitcher who put pine tar on his pants. He'd take sliding practice before the games so the umps couldn't see it. I…" Stormy slammed on the verbal brakes. Damn! He'd lost it, rambling like some old-timer trying to relive glory days.

"In the minors?" Smitty asked meekly.

Silence. Think fast man…! "Oh, uh, I used to go see minor league games every now and then in Buffalo."

Stormy couldn't remember what minor league franchise was nearest New

York City. Maybe Newark or wherever, but Buffalo would do for now. All three sat around the table, staring at each other as if unsure who should speak.

"This is all very informative, but it goes against what Coach has been saying about winning the race fairly."

"The race?" Stormy asked.

"Something like that," Smitty said. "It doesn't feel right," he said. His red eyebrows furrowed with concern.

"Have you guys ever won a championship?"

Both boys' heads moved east to west.

"Nuff said."

The mantle clock ticking was the only sound until Po Po broke the thick silence.

"Tita, this unfair advantage, it might get us that scholarship."

"Count me out, Po Po. The right way or no way."

"Aw, Smitty, always the worry wart. Our whole lives, the worry wart." Po Po was irritated and it showed. "If I say it's hot, you say it's cold. Hell, if we somehow make it to college, you probably won't even go on those panty raids everybody talks about! I don't know how we ever became best friends."

"What are you talking about, me always the worry wart?" Smitty's face reddened, camouflaging the freckles on his cheeks and nose.

"What about when you made us quit riding our bikes on White Rock Lake, the only time it's even been frozen?"

"It was cracking. We would have died," Smitty said in exasperation.

Po Po seemed hell bent on pursuing the discussion with the mindset of someone determined to play every inning of a 162 game schedule.

"Yeah, well what about when you yelled at me for shootin' Suzanne Bailey in the leg with the BB gun. She had it comin'—you know she did."

"We were twelve; she didn't deserve to be shot just because she didn't want to French kiss you," cried Smitty, throwing up his hands in dismay. "Besides you ought to thank me; she's still ugly enough to stop traffic!"

The retorts now came rapid-fire, like a gunfight. Stormy, arms folded, pushed his chair away from the table as if to avoid the flying bullets.

"Or what about when you made me stop runnin' down Mick Lantos with the go cart. Everybody in the eighth grade hated that bugger-eatin' snot head."

Smitty's eyes shot upward in disgust. "You knew his family was in the Mafia, Popehead! They were going to have you snuffed out if you didn't leave him alone! You still ought to be thanking me."

The red veins on Po Po's neck rose visibly. "You got out of the car and walked home when I rammed Sandy Dew's car in the rear. Showed me up!"

"I don't care how stuck up Sandy Dew is; that was the fifth time you broke that girl's tail lights."

The boys shot to their feet. Only inches separated their faces.

"You wouldn't pick up those girls from BA that night at Charco's. They were ready for action."

"Po Po, they had zits all over their faces," Smitty said wearily.

"Not once have you ever cut school and gone to the movies with me."

"Because the only chance I have for a scholarship is for academics, not athletics," Smitty snapped.

Po Po moved rapidly toward the front door. "Well, I'm no Albert Bernstein; I'm going for it. Let's go home!"

"That's Einstein, and you're driving!" Smitty followed, slamming the door behind them.

Stormy sipped his beer. With the music stopped, he could hear his own gulp. The tires of Po Po's old blue GTO squealed so loudly that Stormy's hands darted to cover his ears. The engine's roar soon settled into a distant noise, like an airplane above the clouds. Stormy's eyes scanned his all but barren home. He didn't really care what the boys did. After Woodrow won state, he'd leave for the minors and in short order return to the big dance. Win state and go to the majors—that's all that really mattered.

A smile as substantial as Stormy's tenacity spread across his face. On the table, the rubble only partially covered the newspaper—a sports page, no less; he could still read the headlines. "Olympic Shot Putter Banned for Steroids." Stormy laughed. He'd forgotten to tell the boys: when applying the unfair advantage, don't get caught.

Mac stood hidden to one side of Stormy's apartment, reducing his cigarette in long intermittent drags. The nearby trees and shrubs took on menacing and foreboding shapes, like murky shadows ready to strike. He dressed in solid black with his pants legs stuffed inside his black cowboy boots. A black cowboy hat sat low on his head, its brim concealing his darting eyes. He enjoyed the boys' disagreement immensely and now could hear Stormy's hearty laugh from inside the apartment. Mac wore the look of the alley cat after discovering milk.

If only he had an associate to remind him of his brilliance. Stormy would continue to force Cotton Parker to compromise his principles. The Cotton Parkers of the world infuriated Mac. He could see through Parker's plastic, high-and-mighty self-righteousness. Parker would do anything to win that state championship. Mac's plan would prove that.

Mac could hardly contain his elation when thinking of Smitty Pierce and Do Do or Po Po or whatever they called the incredible hulk. Stormy's tactics had already divided Woodrow's battery regarding their feeble goal of a college education. Po Po's neck twitching and persistent gibberish irritated Mac, but the big catcher had potential. Maybe he and Po Po could conduct some business over the years.

Smitty was a wuss really, always trying to do the right thing. Smitty probably would become a principal some day, just like his dad. But Smitty would fall soon, and approach his new teammate for guidance—Mac would bet on that.

But, ah, Norma Weathers, what a sucker! Soon she would confess to Cal Lucas the whole story and receive her just reward. Norma was a loser, one of those gullible, pitiful people unable to round the bases in this game of life.

Stormy was Mac's kind of guy. Looking out for old number one and always willing to take an unfair advantage. Mac's long-term master plan had molded Stormy perfectly. Chuckling at his genius, Mac blew smoke rings in the air.

It was almost a shame the ordeal Stormy would shortly have to endure. The two really thought alike save one major difference. Stormy didn't realize he was a self-centered, win-at-all-cost, take-the-short-cut bastard.

Chapter Seventeen
YOU BETTER BRING THAT STUFF TO PRACTICE

With no more effort than reading his nightly Bible verse, Cotton Parker read the fatigue on Smitty's face. Cotton, his only respectable pitcher, and his rowdy catcher enclosed the pitcher's mound of Reverchon Park like a small closet. The ninety-degree heat from the spring Texas afternoon had drained the life from Smitty's right arm. Smitty's uniform was soiled; perspiration mixed with diamond dirt surrounded his tired face.

Cotton addressed Smitty. "Big un, one out—that's all we need."

Cotton gave both boys a reassuring pat on the rear and loped back to the dugout. Po Po rubbed the ball as if a good massage would force it to behave his command. "Well, fifty, we got 'em where we want 'em. Bases loaded, and they got nine runs."

Smitty jerked the ball from his catcher. "We've got ten, mastodon breath."

"Yeah, thanks to three home runs from Cal. Now bear down, Tita."

Po Po followed the worn brown path from the mound to his position. When would Smitty learn? Smitty should try Cal's advice. For title hopes, Smitty needed an out pitch worse than Po Po needed help in school. Nine runs by the opposition spelled an ass-kicking most of the time. As Po Po crouched into his position behind the plate, he shook his head in appreciation. Three home runs by his hero. No one could remember any player hitting three out of Reverchon in the same day.

Smitty's curve moved less than a tired glowworm. Crack! With his back to home plate, Stormy broke for the center field fence. He wheeled around to face home and pressed his butt against the fence. Like a lonely drop of hail, the ball fell gently from the high-blue sky. Stormy waited for the ball to land inside or outside the park. Finally, the ball vanished into his Heart-of-The-Hide leather for the game's last out.

While leaving the playing field, Stormy crossed the pitcher's mound and found Po Po and Smitty waiting for him. A few teammates were already boarding the bus.

86

"Hey, Cal, that single you got in the third inning sorta messed up your day, huh!" Po Po kidded, clearly energized by the close victory. He addressed Smitty, who looked as if someone had driven his head into his shoulders with a ball bat. "Smitty, don't sweat it, man. I knew you had 'em all the time. Just think of that last out as a three hundred ninety-foot pop-up." Abruptly, he darted toward the parking lot. "I gotta go check out one of their cheerleaders," Po Po said, the faint spring breeze carrying his words back toward Stormy and Smitty. Then he abruptly stopped and turned back around. "Hey what's a mastodon?"

"I'll tell you later," Smitty said, rolling his eyes to the sky.

After Po Po resumed his mad dash, the two started toward the bus.

"Nice game," Stormy said.

Smitty's internal lie detector sounded loud and clear. "Yeah, I held 'em to nine runs. That'll bring a lot of college scouts."

"Well, like you said, academics is your game."

Smitty stopped walking and Stormy did the same. Smitty glanced around quickly to make sure no one could hear.

"Hey, Cal, what other ideas have you got—you know—if I didn't want to use that jelly?"

"Put sandpaper inside the infielders' gloves. When they throw the ball around the horn, we'll have them scuff the ball a little." Stormy talked fast. "You see, if the ball's nicked, it moves more, it…"

Smitty raised his hand in a gesture of truce. "That's the last thing we need, any more people knowing what we're up to. Hell, Po Po would probably ask Coach Parker for the sandpaper." Smitty sighed with resignation. "You better bring that stuff to practice. I made a C in geometry."

Stormy had known Smitty wouldn't go for the sandpaper idea, though Stormy had seen it used successfully. But Smitty was smart; too many people would know. The jelly—it would be their secret.

"It's your call, Smitty. We'll start working in practice tomorrow on the wickedest breaking ball you've ever seen." Stormy placed a warm arm around his friend, and they continued toward the bus. "I'm sorry about the C, Smitty but things are gonna be all right."

The next day, Stormy and his two protégées sat huddled in the corner of the Woodrow dressing room. They dressed slowly to allow Coach Parker and their teammates time to leave for the practice field. Stormy held the tube of KY jelly in his hand and squeezed a portion the size of a quarter into Smitty's palms.

"Now wipe that all over your neck," Stormy ordered.

Smitty obeyed, but applied the slippery stuff as if it were poisonous.

"Do that before every game. Go to the neck right after you release the ball on your follow through."

Stormy stood and proceeded into a full pitcher's windup, swiping quickly at his neck with the fingers on his right hand as he finished his delivery.

"Nobody will see it; they never do. Don't apply your slimy fingers to the ball until you're in the wind up. Ump can't stop you if you're in your windup. Po Po, after you catch the ball, massage it good before sending it back to the mound. Even if the ump gets suspicious he won't find a thing. You two got it?"

Both nodded. Now Stormy squeezed a smaller amount on his fingers. He dabbed jelly on Smitty's forehead, eyebrow, left wrist and behind both ears. He backed away to inspect Smitty.

"There, that'll give you some reinforcement if the neck gets dry during the game. Po Po, you need to know when this pitch is coming or it might get by you. The ball will drop sharply, more like a sinker than a curve. One finger for the fastball, two for the curve and three for the super sinker. Okay?"

"Man, how do you know all this stuff?" Po Po said most agreeably.

"No kiddin', Cal." Smitty's face showed his concern at their doing something so clearly wrong.

"Like I said, boys, I hung out at the stadium a lot and learned from the big boys. Let's get to practice before Coach sends somebody lookin' for us."

Low gray clouds obscured the sun this warm afternoon. With the Woodrow players scattered about the practice diamond, Coach Parker studied his team while he mixed among them. Po Po refused Smitty's first batting practice pitch; it arrived low and in the dirt. Stormy, the batting practice catcher for the moment, blocked the offering and delivered the ball back to Smitty.

"Swing that sucker with confidence," Stormy said, peering up at Po Po from behind the catcher's mask. "Let the bat do the work."

Smitty lobbed one in waist high. Whack! The ball shot to attention and started its long distance flight. From the outfield, Cotton's head wrenched to the sound, and his eyes locked on the ball as it sailed far over his head.

"Lawrence?" Cotton mumbled.

The next pitch yielded similar results.

"Lawrence?" Cotton repeated, sounding like an echo.

Stormy flashed three fingers from his position behind the plate. "He's loading one up. You better stay loose until he gets a little practice with his new pitch."

"E."

Smitty quickly swiped his hand across his neck on the follow through. The ball sailed whiffle-ball wild toward Po Po's head. As if shot, Po Po flopped to the dirt landing flat on his back. Stormy lunged to catch the ball. Specs of dirt jitterbugged in the air around home plate.

"Too much," Stormy blurted a little too loudly. He immediately spit, rubbed his eyes and spoke through his laughter. "Smitty's got so much goop on the ball, it's about to drown me."

From the corner of his eye, Stormy noticed Coach Parker's radar eyes locking in on home plate.

"We better work on the wet one when Coach isn't looking," Stormy said slightly above a whisper.

From the mound, Smitty shrugged sheepishly with that, "What did you expect?" look. To be sure, the ball had dipped from midnight to daybreak. Maybe he would not be the anchor that dragged his team to the bottom. His latest grades ruined any chance for an academic scholarship but maybe he could earn that athletic scholarship. Maybe he could relieve his parents from any further financial hardship after all.

Chapter Eighteen
I'M GOING YOUR WAY

Rain pounded like angry fists on the hood and windshield of the black sports car. The windshield wipers worked overtime. A spring storm had prevented practice, leaving Stormy with a free afternoon for the first day since enrolling at Woodrow Wilson. His car left the school parking area with the others, the mass exit ushering his Porsche in a slow moving stream.

As the car turned onto Glasgow Avenue, he could not believe his eyes. Could it be? Susan Parker was walking in the rain, protected only by her umbrella. This mysterious older boyfriend must house shit for brains, allowing such a beauty to walk in the rain. College boys!

Stormy pulled up next to Susan, rolled down his window, and called, "I'm going your way."

A flash of recognition crossed Susan's face but she kept walking. Stormy's car poked along beside her.

"Climb in, you're getting wet. And so am I," Stormy said through his cool-as-December smile. His eyes motioned to the water invading the car's interior.

"That's okay. The bus stop is over there." She pointed across the street.

"Come on, Susan. No practice today. This may be my only chance to give you a ride all semester." He was practically begging. A man had his pride; he would not ask again.

As if pondering, Susan looked up to the rain that now pelted down hard enough to sting its target. To Stormy's relief, she turned toward the car; he leaned across his front seat and threw open the passenger door, and she hopped in the front seat. Stormy pressed the accelerator, sending great gobs of water out from behind the rear tires. As the car left Woodrow Wilson High, a cloud the same color as the rain clouds, spit from the exhaust.

J.J.'s slow, bluesy, muffled lyrics floated across the car's interior:
"Whippoorwill singing, soft summer breeze
Makes me think of my baby

I left down in New Orleans
I left down in New Orleans."

"What neat music," Susan said.
So she likes J.J., Stormy thought. *Not a bad start.*
"Where to?" he asked. Her perfume was driving him crazy.
"The corner of Swiss and Central. Just go to the stop sign and make a left."
"Who's singing?"
Their eyes met quickly and then darted back to the road.
"J.J. Cale."
"You can feel his pain," Susan said. "He misses her so much."
J.J. continued to mourn, his voice muffled and low.
"Magnolia, you sweet thing,
You're drivin' me mad.
Got to get back to you, babe,
You're the best I ever had."

Susan flinched a little with the verse then asked after a short pause. "Have you ever missed somebody so much that it hurt bad deep inside?"
Stormy could feel Susan's stare. God, she was beautiful. He struggled to keep his eyes straight ahead.
"No," he lied. "Have you?"
Pausing, her thoughts hung on something private before she replied evenly, "Yes."
Stormy heard the pain in her voice. Could some college punk really hurt her this way?
"What's the name of the song?"
"Magnolia."
"Makes sense."
"It's probably my favorite song of J.J.'s," Stormy said. "Funny, I always thought Magnolia was a corny name until I heard that song. Now I think of pure beauty." He chuckled. "I used to tell myself if I ever had a daughter, I'd name her Magnolia."
"Used to?" Susan asked, her eyebrows rising quizzically.
"I don't think much of getting married anymore."
"Aren't you kind of young to decide that?"
Stormy shrugged. "Yeah, I guess I am." Damn it to hell. Every time he relaxed, his age escaped like runaways from the orphanage.

"Did this college guy hurt you?"

"What?"

She looked bewildered, as if hit with a stun gun.

"Smitty and Po Po think you've got a boyfriend. Looks like he could at least pick you up when it's raining."

Stormy's goal was to flush out the truth but Susan looked closer to laughter than a heart felt confession.

"You've got to be kidding."

"They claim that's why you won't tell them where you go after school every day."

"They wouldn't understand." A hint of trouble streaked across her face.

"There's no older man?"

"No, my dad's the only older man in my life. Smitty should know better."

"And Po Po?" Stormy's tone showed delight in Susan's revelation.

"Po Po is a victim of the uncluttered mind," she said through a grin.

They laughed, and the lighter mood suited him fine. No reason to swap sad stories during his time alone with Woodrow's finest.

Susan lightly touched Stormy's right arm on the steering wheel. "Your first few games have been fantastic. Dad says the pro scouts are already showing up."

"That's what I've heard."

"Why did you run over the other team's players in the game the other day?"

"They were in the way."

"Do you run over everybody that's in the way?"

"Maybe so."

She seemed to digest his answer a bit before replying. "Are you afraid of anything?"

Tough question. He feared dying before learning why his mother put him in an orphanage. He also feared life without baseball but apparently he could bury that phobia for another twenty years or so.

"Winding up in an old folks home. Someone having to take care of me."

Boy was that true! The Yankees had made occasional goodwill visits to area rest homes. Stormy hated everything about those visits. He detested the sight of old geezers shuffling at a snail's pace with their four-legged crutches, and they were the lucky ones. Ugly aides pushed others around in wheel chairs with portable IV's hooked to their arms. Stormy grew to dread the sight of the listless, bedridden residents with tubes coming out their noses. Sometimes their eyes were closed; other times they stayed open, but blank, as if life had already left them. And the smell! Stormy always smelled urine and Lysol in the halls. Chill bumps rose on his arms just thinking about it. With no family, a rest home would prove even worse for him. He would jump out of Yankee Stadium's third deck before living in one of those places.

"Are you okay?"

Stormy snapped to. He smiled at his passenger, enjoying the pleasant view. "No old folks home for me. I'd rather go down on a ball field with a smile on my face."

"Cal! You're too young for that!" Her hand again shot to his right arm. "That's the second time in five minutes you've talked like you're older than you really are!"

She cared. It showed and Stormy Weathers loved it. A heat flash surged through his body and settled in his face.

"Aw, you know, maybe an old-timer's game, something like that," Stormy said more calmly than he felt.

"I will say this, Cal Lucas from New York City, you're sure confident. It's like you know exactly what it's going to take. Like you've been there before."

"Oh, really?" Stormy's eyebrows lifted.

"Yes. You're a leader—not many people have that quality. Actually, I think it's a gift. A responsibility not to be taken lightly."

Stormy's brain shook. She didn't talk like an eighteen-year-old. The downpour stopped, and the sun peeked through the clouds. A hint of a rainbow stretched across the downtown skyline.

"My dad has always had that same confidence, that same aggressiveness. He's a leader too."

She never mentioned her mother, only her dad, he thought. Better not ask. He didn't want to know.

"We're here," Susan announced.

Stormy maneuvered the car to the side of the road and stopped. His eyes swept the area but saw nothing of note in this old commercial section of town: a small, one-story paint store, a modest Mexican cafe, a string of used car lots; and beyond that, the hub of downtown Dallas. Across the street was a deserted softball field and public park. Multiple mini-ponds littered the clay infield.

"You don't want to tell me where you're going?"

"Not really."

"Uh, will you be okay?

Susan smiled. "I'll be fine."

"How do you get home?"

"I have my ways, Cal." She continued after a reflective pause, "I hope you're that special player dad needs for the championship. He deserves it." Suddenly she leaned over and quickly kissed Stormy on the mouth. She smelled sweet as cherry mints. Just as quickly she pulled away and the air that rushed into his mouth inflated his eyes to the size of a baseball. She jumped out of the car, and was gone. It's a fact that a highly aroused state can increase some senses and shut down others. Though she left behind the faint scent of her body and her perfume, Stormy didn't even hear the door close.

Stormy had previously considered the act of kissing more overrated then a twenty game winner with a high ERA. No more. He recovered just in time to see Susan walk briskly beyond the car lots and older one-story buildings. A burst of wind lifted her hair, revealing the back of her slender neck. At the end of the block, she disappeared out of sight.

Stormy's lips pressed together in thought. He whipped his car into the area of the paint store, locked it, and took off in Susan's direction, closing the gap quickly. He turned the corner and caught a glimpse of Susan's blue jean-clad long legs and shapely rear entered a dilapidated two-story brick building. As if it was booby trapped, Stormy tiptoed to the front door. The sign above the doorway read: "United Gospel Mission."

Slowly and curiously, he climbed the half-dozen entrance steps until he was looking through a shabby, antiquated, wooden front window. The sight inside shocked him. People of all shapes, sizes, ages and colors milled about a large, sparsely furnished room. The worn hardwood floors were uneven and split. Dirt had stained the cracked white plaster walls brown. Two-dozen or so sleeping cots and blankets lay on one side of the room. Like birds from a cage, heads poked forth from a few of the makeshift beds. A worn black and white picture of LBJ and a similar photograph of former Texas governor John Connally hung on the otherwise bare walls.

Stormy's bewildered eyes searched the entire room until he noticed a food line on the opposite side. The homeless stood quietly, wearing the same blank expressions. Where was Susan?

Large, steaming pots of hot food, several trays of sandwiches, and bowls of fresh fruits and vegetables weighted down two six-foot tables. A staff of six served the hungry from the opposite side of the table.

Stormy's eyes found Susan Parker as she offered a small black child an assortment of fruit. Her eyes were soft, her expression warm. The child took an apple and went on to the next station in line.

Susan's steady conversation with the other servers and the homeless, suggested she knew them all.

"I'll be damned," he muttered.

Well, if Susan wanted this part of her life private, so be it. He would not tell her or anyone else. Turbulent thoughts crowded his mind as he returned to the car. In the prime of her life, Susan should be having fun, not surrounding herself with the downtrodden.

Chapter Nineteen
THE RHUBARB

Stormy occupied a dugout seat between Po Po and Smitty as the crimson-and-blue uniformed Rebels took the field. From the top step of Woodrow's dugout, Coach Parker took his cue and walked faster than most people run to take his position in the third base coach's box. He cupped his hands to his mouth and called encouragement to his team.

Norma sat alone in the covered part of the Reverchon stands behind home plate. Stormy stood to wave and she returned the gesture but in a reserved way.

As he stood, cheers roared in his ears. Stormy spun around to find Susan and her friends sitting behind the dugout. Susan's skirt stopped short of her knees; no question, she owned the best set of legs this side of Heaven. Their eyes met, they smiled and Stormy assumed his seat between his new friends.

The exchange did not escape Po Po. "I'm telling you, tita, she's got her eyes on an older man. I feel it."

Stormy, his eyes loaded with secrets, shrugged.

"Let's worry about the women later, guys," Smitty said, pointing to first base with his eyes. "That gorilla led the city in homers last year—as a junior, no less. Name's Sammy Norton."

The big, burly first sacker tossed pre-game grounders to his fellow infielders. His size and thick five-o-clock shadow added a decade to his appearance.

Smitty thought so too. "Look at him. He's gotta be thirty years old."

"E," Po Po grunted.

Stormy had dealt with countless young phenoms in the majors and most could be intimidated in the early part of their careers. The Rebels' star player flipped the practice ball to his first base dugout and prepared for the initial pitch. Yep, intimidation would play a significant part of today's game.

Only a few minutes later, Stormy dug a tunnel in at the plate, the way hitters do when the guy on the mound is easy. On the second pitch, a curve ball in need of diet pills, floated Stormy's way. Stormy spanked a wicked drive past the hurler's ear into center field for a single.

Before the ball bounced its third time in the outfield, Stormy buzzed by first base and took a wide turn around the bag. The big first baseman fired Stormy an incredulous look as if wondering if he took a short cut. Woodrow supporters burst into modest cheers, clearly disappointed that Cal had only hit a single. Stormy returned to the bag, sporting the look of a successful thief. His stopover at first provided the opportunity to discuss things with Sammy Norton. A cold brooding look overcame Norton during the brief chat.

After taking two balls and fouling a pitch off, Po Po ripped at the pitch and delivered a high fly ball that barely cleared the fence in left for a home run.

Stormy failed miserably in his attempt to control his laughter as he rounded the bases. Po Po strutted like the Great Bambino while circling the diamond. He loped slowly, to prolong his glory; after reaching a bag he would stomp it like a pasty roach. Rounding third, he euphorically slapped his coach's extended hand. Finally, when he reached home, he bent down and kissed the plate. Woodrow's team rushed from the dugout and high-fived, back-slapped and hugged the big catcher.

Cotton's head shook in wonder but not before signaling for the celebration to stop. Stormy knew what Parker was thinking. Never show up the other team. Better to let a sleeping dog lie.

Twiggy grounded out to short, and the players changed sides. Woodrow led two to zip after a half-inning of play. Smitty stood on the mound when Stormy stopped for a visit on his way to center field.

Stormy's mischievous eyes motioned to the Rebels' dugout. "Throw Paul Bunyan a curve first pitch and then a fastball at his head the second pitch."

The intensity in his voice startled Smitty.

"Why?"

"I've already informed him you were gonna bean him if he so much as fouled one off today. I also told him the first pitch will be at his noggin, anyway—to show we mean business." Stormy stared hard at his confused friend; the two stood close enough to embrace. "Throw the curve first for a strike while he's hitting the dirt. Next pitch, he's looking for a curve and you brush him back. He'll be worthless the rest of the day."

"What if I hit him in the head?" Smitty's voice sounded anemic.

"Sorry, bro, it won't hurt him if you do."

"That big son of a buck might try to take my head off."

"No problem, bro—that's what your teammates are for."

97

The home plate umpire approached the mound.

"Do you guys mind if we resume play?"

Stormy tapped Smitty on the chest with his index finger. "Do it!"

Cotton missed the conversation because of his own powwow with Po Po while he donned his catcher equipment. The message: behave as if success comes along more often than Haley's comet.

As the Rebel first sacker stepped to the plate, sweat poured across Smitty's forehead; he shuddered inside and turned to face center field. Maybe Cal would smile, a signal that his instructions were a joke, or that he had changed his mind. No such luck. Cal, his eyes laser rays, leaned forward, hands on his knees, like a jungle cat prepared to attack. Smitty casually rubbed his right hand across his greasy neck and took his place on the rubber. What the hell, he had to face Cal daily. Norton, hopefully, just today.

The wet ball initially appeared to travel on a path for the batter's head; Norton dove to the dirt just in time to see the ball break across the plate. Smitty's shoulders stood erect. Smitty's confidence soared at the sight of the Rebel player sprawled on the ground.

Sammy Norton determinedly dug a trench with his spikes in the soft dirt around the plate. The next pitch seemed aimed at his head, and it narrowly missed. At the last instant, he dove to the ground a second time.

Cal was a genius, mused Smitty. He had this bozo in the palm of his hand. Smitty's next two super sinkers yielded a couple of the more tentative, futile swings Smitty could remember. Norton's face turned redder than the freckles on Smitty's face, and his glance locked on his shoes as he returned to his dugout.

Stormy treaded lightly into the batter's box. No reason to get comfortable. His hunch was immediately fact. A fastball honed in on his temples. He dropped to the dirt with ample time. Stormy knew of major league careers ruined by bean balls. Some players suffered physical damage that resulted in problems like blurred vision or constant headaches. Other players would bail out at the first sign of chin music. Their timidity produced a rapid plane trip home.

Stormy long ago had concluded that bean ball episodes had three distinct phases. Phase one was intimidation: the original knock down, its desired effect to scare the batter.

Phase two was retaliation. Returning to his feet, Stormy dusted the dirt off his gray and red uniform. He flashed an acknowledging grin to the first baseman who wore an unhappy scowl. The Rebels and Wildcats had advanced to the second stage.

Stormy called phase three the agitation stage. This usually happened after the assaulted team was victimized twice in one day.

The umpire abruptly squealed for time out and signaled to both dugouts for an impromptu meeting with the two coaches. Coach Parker and the Rebel coach arrived simultaneously at home plate. Stormy and the Rebel catcher stood within earshot of the conversation.

"Gentlemen! I don't know what's going on here, but this is not the World Series!" The umpire spoke rapidly, his eyes flaming with intensity. "This is a high school baseball game, and I will not tolerate any more knockdowns. Got it?"

"I agree one hundred percent," Cotton said.

"No problem here. I'm surprised at it myself," replied the Rebel skipper.

"Shape these kids up! Let's have a good clean game. Play ball!"

The umpire repositioned his mask on his face, bent over and swept home plate so feverishly, it looked like a West Texas dust storm. The coaches trotted to their respective dugouts.

Cotton immediately located Smitty, who squirmed nervously at the sight of his coach rapidly approaching.

"You hear the ump?" Cotton said, his demeanor stern and his eyes lively.

"Yes, sir!"

Smitty breathed a heavy sigh of relief as Coach Parker left the dugout and resumed his place in the coach's box. The turmoil was over and the game in hand.

From the batter's box, Stormy glanced at the catcher. "I'm sure glad we got that straight, aren't you?" he said loudly enough for both benches to hear.

The opposing player ignored Stormy and prepared for the next pitch. The ball arrived and Stormy took a monster swing, blasting the offering for a long home run high above the center field wall. While rounding first, he offered an affectionate mock smile to the frustrated Rebel first baseman. When he rounded third, Stormy received only a stoic glare from his good coach, who obviously failed to appreciate a little showmanship.

Amid cheers from the Wildcat supporters, Stormy accepted congratulations from his teammates and joined his two buddies on the bench.

Po Po slapped Stormy on the shoulder. "Way to go you, you, you fifty you! Seven run lead; that puts this game on ice."

"No kiddin!" Smitty chimed in.

"Throw at the big bopper next inning." Stormy's cold eyes fixed on the Rebel first sacker. He spoke in a no-nonsense monotone.

"What?" Smitty said, praying he misunderstood.

"You heard me," Stormy said, his eyes tightening.

Smitty removed his hat and rubbed his hand across his sweaty, matted hairline. A nauseating ache pierced his chest. "We've each had one knockdown. That's fair."

"That's exactly why we're not going to stop. We could meet later in the play-offs. No need for those boys to feel like equals."

"He's struck out every time and my man says we still put him down," Po Po said, his voice animated, his arms flailing about. "Fifty, you're bad to the bone."

After Woodrow took the field, Smitty easily retired the first two hitters; the big, cranky first baseman took the batter's box, his demeanor disturbing the surrounding air.

Parker bellowed from his dugout, "One more out and we go home!"

Swallowing hard enough to hear his gulp, Smitty eyed his opponent. His mind, searching for a comfortable hiding place, located Harrell's Drugstore at the corner of Abrams and Gaston. Smitty envisioned himself at the counter, sipping on a fountain coke, and digesting an old-fashioned hamburger.

Norton looked bigger since the beginning of the game. In only two hours, his gunmetal gray beard seemed thicker. And the hulk kept disgustedly spitting hard enough to punish the ground. The hitter stood primed at the plate, bat coiled. *What the hell,* Smitty thought. Cal's been right so far.

From the hollow sound, Smitty knew it was a direct hit. He felt a peculiar sense of accomplishment, but also concern. He had delivered his best fastball of the year exactly where intended. Yet, he wanted to harm no one.

Spectators and players alike grew silent; all eyes locked on Norton. Like a boxer stunned by a punch, he stumbled around while holding his injured head between both hands, eyes pointed to the ground. David had struck Goliath, but the big man refused to fall. Suddenly, the wounded player glared at the pitcher's mound. Norton's face was distorted in fury, his eyes the eyes of a vicious animal.

Smitty was relieved to know Norton wasn't badly hurt. Norton's speed in delivering the cargo of animosity to the mound proved that.

Spontaneously, both dugouts emptied and rushed to the middle of the diamond. Norton wrapped both hands around Smitty's neck and lifted him until his feet dangled helplessly in midair. Smitty's bulging eyes registered fear; his breath came in micro-gasps. Po Po flattened two Rebel players like bowling pins on his path to the mound.

Both sides were yelling and screaming, locked in hand-to-hand combat. The skirmish continued at fast-forward speed.

Stormy dove into a pile of human flesh only to find Po Po on the ground with Norton's ankle in his mouth, about to chomp. Norton, preoccupied removing Smitty's head from his body, was unaware of the danger from below. With a shriek, he released Smitty and fell to the earth, clutching his wounded ankle.

The coaches joined the melee, tossing bodies to both sides of the diamond in an effort to halt the donnybrook. Susan and Norma, mouths ajar, gasped in disbelief at the chaos on the field. Suddenly Norma's heart dipped faster than Smitty's super sinker. That terrible man sat alone on the hood of a car in the parking lot, watching the action.

An old New York Highlander jersey, with its thick wool fabric and faded white-with-dark pinstripes, covered Mac's scrawny chest. He took a bite of his hot dog through a sideburn to sideburn grin. Norma's stare pulled his eyes toward her. She rapidly looked away to the fracas on the field. With fearful eyes and thick saliva, she slowly peeked in Mac's direction. Their eyes met. Mac smiled and waved, as though addressing an old friend.

Chapter Twenty
WHAT ON EARTH WAS THE PROBLEM?

Smitty continued his ragged pace around Randall Park, the public park that contained the Woodrow practice field. Steam thrown off by the orange sun stretched across the pale blue sky. His luck was lousy; Texas has some cool spring days—but not today. But then the entire spring had seemed unseasonably warm. Drenched in sweat, he wondered how much longer his punishment would continue. If Cotton wasn't looking, his concerned teammates would glance Smitty's way to monitor his condition. Not well, was Smitty's personal conclusion.

After learning of Smitty's punishment, Stormy had insisted on informing Coach Parker that he ordered the beanings but Smitty objected vehemently. One more incident and Cal was history, leaving no chance for the state play-offs. The play-offs would bring college scouts and potential scholarships.

Smitty glanced over his shoulder. Po Po lumbered behind; with every step, he drew in air in god-awful gasps.

Parker had not punished Po Po for biting Norton, reluctantly admitting that without Po Po's rescue, Woodrow might need a new pitcher and class president. Po Po circled the jogging trail for his actions after the coaches had finally stopped the brawl. Norton was hobbling toward his team's dugout when Po Po, his face contorted, ran beside Norton, raised his right leg and made a loud hissing noise as if relieving himself. Cotton could only watch in horror as Norton served as Po Po's fire hydrant. Fortunately, the melee had left Norton and his teammates so exhausted that both teams filed onto their respective buses without further incident.

Cotton, arms folded, kept one cloudy eye on his practice and the other on his two inmates. He kicked diamond dust on the first base bag beside him and exhaled a faint tuneless whistle through lips rigid with disillusion. In one sense, Smitty's confession let Cotton off the hook; Cal was the real culprit but if he kicked Cal off the team, where would they be? Cotton closed his eyes so tight that specks of white flashed in his mind. Teaching young people the right way and raising his daughter were all that mattered now. Cotton longed for his wife's company and advice. His team remained undefeated and yet he felt more like a loser than ever. While pondering bad days, Cotton thought of the day his wife…his mind shut out the thought.

Stormy roamed center field, fielding balls hit his way during batting practice. Something clearly bothered his coach. Woodrow was winning more than ever. What on earth was the problem?

Later, while watching the Yankees on TV at Norma's place, Stormy learned of another problem. With his face twisted in agony, Stormy jumped to his feet when his former teammate, Clyde Daniel struck out. Sandwiched between Norma and Susan on Norma's living room couch, his actions startled both women.

"Come on, Clyde," Stormy said, dropping heavily to his seat. "I've told him not to chase that pitch," he mumbled in disgust.

"You know him?" Susan quizzed.

"Uh, yeah." Stormy hesitated again, exposed. "Like I said, my buddies and me were always at Yankee Stadium.

"The Yankee players listened to you?" Norma said. By now, she could believe it.

"Me? Nah, I was just talkin'. Those guys aren't gonna take any advice from some punk kid like me."

"Ms. Weathers, nothing would surprise me with Cal. My dad says he's the best baseball talent he's ever seen." Susan's hand rested on his knee, her face beamed with pride. "We're undefeated; one more win and we're city champs."

"Cal's doing just what he said he would do," Norma said. "And your dad's a heck of a coach. You must be very proud of him."

Susan nodded, her face still glowing.

"Does your mom work?" Norma asked.

Susan's exuberance quickly faded; the color drained from her face. She spoke in measured words. "My mother died a couple of years ago. It was an accident."

So that was the hurt she referred to that rainy day, Stormy thought. They both lost a mother, a tough common denominator. The room became silent as cobblestones.

Norma stood. "Susan, I'm terribly sorry. There's no hurt like losing a family member. I don't know what to say, other than we just have to carry on. From what I see, I'd say you've done that." Norma's eyes watered; she reached for the empty bowl of popcorn on the coffee table. "We need some more popcorn."

Susan stood; she attempted a smile but came up short. "Please, let me get it." She took the bowl and left for the kitchen.

Internally, Stormy repeated Norma's words, "There's no hurt like losing a family member." Maybe Norma had referred to the loss of her child. Maybe Norma had justifiable cause to place him in an orphanage. Soon he would muster the courage to ask.

"Cal." Stormy turned to face his mother. "I've been wanting to talk to you for weeks now, but you're always with Susan or your teammates."

"What's up?"

"There was a strange man standing outside your apartment one night a while back." Concern lined her face. "I hope you're not mixed up with him. I've even seen him lurking at some of the games. He's trouble—I feel it."

Stormy addressed the television, lifting his shoulders in a nonchalant shrug. "Beats me. It's probably a scout."

Stormy's eyes were noncommittal, but an echo pounded in his chest. Since the first Woodrow practice, everything had gone perfectly, but Norma's warning left him confused. So Mac was lurking about. What did Norma have to do with Mac? Stormy felt a chill enter the room, leaving goose bumps along both forearms.

Chapter Twenty-One
WHAT SIZE?

Smitty, his shoulders slumped with fatigue, stood on the pitcher's mound; the hurler removed his ball cap to reveal straw-colored strings of hair branded in sweat to his forehead. He ran his forearm sleeve across his face like a mop and returned his ball cap to its proper place. The unseasonably hot weather continued; the spring wind stirred an August breeze which was to say none at all. A late afternoon sunlight burned through the nearby trees of the adjacent park.

Smitty tugged the brim of his cap down snugly and leaned forward, searching for the signal from his oldest friend. Woodrow led four to one; a single out remained in the contest.

Smitty swiped the back of his right ear, went into his windup, and released the super sinker. The opponent lifted a high fly ball to center field. Stormy camped under the ball; finally, it disappeared in his oversized outfielder's mitt. Stormy, all business, strolled toward the infield but most of the team rushed to home plate to celebrate their city championship: no bodies flying, no piles of human flesh, but simply a combination of handshakes, back slaps, hugs and laughter. Cotton had reminded them before the game to save the real celebration until after claiming the big prize, the state championship.

Smitty stood alone, also avoiding the hoopla. From the stands, Norma and Susan cheered wildly and held a gray sign with red letters proclaiming: "Wildcats City Champs." Smitty smiled weakly and waved. His cheating had robbed him of any joy or right to celebrate. As he somberly observed the festivities, Smitty thought of the Bible verse in Parker's office: "An athlete who runs in a race cannot win the prize unless he obeys the rules." Since Coach Parker had never spoken of the passage, Smitty guessed he'd counted on osmosis to spread the word. It must have worked: Smitty dreaded telling Cal that he would quit using the unfair advantage.

It would take a ball bag stuffed full of miracles for Woodrow to win with the mediocre stuff he would serve up in the state play-offs. His grades hadn't improved either. Smitty would stress to his parents that he would rather work for a year or so, relieving them of guilt about family finances. What a lousy day this had turned out to be.

Po Po burped so loud he practically spit up. From Stormy's couch, he leaned over and placed an empty Lone Star long-neck on the glass coffee table. Stormy, who stood at his refrigerator door, retrieved another bottle for himself and Po Po. Smitty still nursed his first brew; strangely quiet, he sat alone at the kitchen table.

The aroma of recently inhaled burgers and fries cluttered the room. On the kitchen table, only a few tattered white sacks and depleted mini-ketchup packets remained.

Po Po looked up at Stormy with glassy eyes and accepted the beer. "Thanks, fifty." Po Po took a gulp so long, his Adam's apple looked alive; he raised his eyes to the ceiling and gargled as though using mouthwash. Finally he swallowed hard, and burped louder than before. "Smitty, isn't life grand?"

"If you say so."

Stormy plopped down at the table beside Smitty and raised his beer in a toast like manner. "Boys, in celebration of today's victory, let's go fight the wars of Greenville Avenue."

Po Po jumped to his feet the way he would volunteer to enter the girl's locker room. Greenville Avenue was the hottest street in Dallas, the location of the best nightspots, the most decadent women—and off limits to high school kids.

After they piled into Stormy's car, Stormy shoved a tape into the cassette player. The laid back rhythms of J.J. hung in midair as the Porsche roared from the parking lot, leaving behind the smell of burnt rubber.

J.J. always had something appropriate to say: "After midnight, we're gonna let it all hang out."

"Where we going?" Po Po asked, his big body cramped in the backseat of the Porsche like a giant oyster in a shell.

"To the land of peel and reveal. It's time you boys met some real women."

J.J. gently rocked in the background.

"We're gonna cause talk and suspicion
Give an exhibition; find out what's all about
After midnight, we're gonna let it all hang out."

"I was hoping Professor Lucas would teach us a little about the women. My batting average isn't too good with the ladies," Po Po confessed between beer-induced belches.

"I can't imagine why," Smitty chimed in deadpan from front seat shotgun. "You're such a gentleman and all."

"There are only two prerequisites to being successful with women. Spend a little money on them and be able to hold a fart in public," Stormy said with evangelical conviction.

Po Po howled, but Smitty barely smiled. Bright lights and shadows pierced the car's interior as the boys neared the heart of the Lakewood commercial district.

"Cal, you think you'll want to get married some day?" Smitty sounded like someone in thought but whose eyes saw nothing.

"I doubt it, bro. After women get married they usually adopt the theory that no sex will lengthen their life expectancy." Both boys giggled. "Most married couples need a strobe light in their bedroom. That way it seems like the woman's moving when they made love."

Po Po laughed louder than Smitty.

"Hey, fifty, are you a virgin?" Po Po asked.

"No, Po Po. I can't say that I am."

"Well, Tita and me are." Po Po motioned to Smitty, who feigned boredom with the subject matter. "Could you shed a little light on the subject?"

"Sex? Sex has a lot to do with dying. You can't be worrying about dying when making love. The younger the women, the further you feel from death. Why do you think so many old fossils hang out with young women?"

"Geez, Cal!" Smitty came alive. A frown formed a troubled expression across his face. "I've been looking forward to that first time, but you say it's about dying?" His head shook in despair.

"As long as I don't die before I get to do it. That's all I worry about," Po Po said. All three erupted in laughter loud enough to drown out J.J.

"Pull in quick," Po Po burst out spontaneously.

Stormy's black car abruptly stopped at the corner of Abrams and Gaston next to the ancient Harrell's Drugs. The one-story establishment occupied the northern tip of a block of longtime neighborhood establishments. The drugstore's blue spherical tower reminded passersby's of the days of hair wax, petticoats, and nickel soft drinks. Stormy quickly navigated the Porsche into one of the parking spots surrounding the strip center. The sudden stop almost threw Po Po into the front seat.

"Harrell's? What are we stopping here for?" Stormy asked.

"I was thinking," Po Po said hesitantly. "If you help us out with the women tonight, we might need to get some, uh, rubbers."

Stormy hunched forward so his hands rested on the steering wheel, stifling a grin.

"That's an optimistic attitude."

"What if we knock one of 'em up?" Po Po asked.

"Yeah, right. That's if we can figure out what to do," Smitty blurted.

"I can assure you, you're not going to get one of those girls pregnant. Besides I didn't say we were just gonna walk in and some lady's gonna immediately offer to take away your virginity. Sometimes these things take a little nurturing."

From his front seat, Smitty eyed the old drugstore. "I've read about a venereal disease called herpes; you get these little red bumps all over you and they never go away."

"Yuck!" Po Po turned up his nose, his face distorted in mock pain.

"Does Mr. Harrell still own the store?" Stormy asked, then tried to swallow his words back in.

"Yes," Po Po quickly replied. Stormy's slip went past Po Po like a wild pitch but Smitty's rust-colored brows raised dramatically.

Stormy opened his door, more concerned about his loose tongue than some disease. Besides, he knew exactly how E.C. Harrell would respond to the request for condoms.

His two teammates eagerly piled from the vehicle and entered the old drugstore. Stormy stopped short of the entrance and stared at the old building. "Some things never change," he mumbled.

Inside, a dark marble countertop serviced the row of round rotating stools. The fragrance of recently served old-fashioned hamburgers and malts came from the open grill behind the counter. An equally antique soda fountain offered the standard assortment of soft drinks. Almost quitting time, the grill was closed and no other customers were in the store.

Mr. Harrell was filling prescriptions in the back of the store. E.C. knew every kid at Woodrow; often parents called and asked about her son or daughter's whereabouts. "He's here," E.C. would tell the concerned parent over the phone.

Pre-high school kids would lie on their stomachs in the middle of the floor and read their favorite comic books. Harrell's Drugs was the Fenway Park or Wrigley Field of the drugstore world, a constant in changing times.

The unofficial mayor of Lakewood towered above Smitty and Po Po, who now stood across the back counter that displayed non-prescription items. Hesitance and self-doubt replaced the boy's eager gait of only a minute ago.

E.C.'s shiny bald head stared down at the boys; defying gravity, his tiny rectangular reading glasses nested on the tip of his nose. He spoke in a warm, paternal voice. "Smitty, Lawrence... what a pleasant surprise. What brings you here this late?"

Both stared at each other, swallowing hard as if thirsty, and smiled nervously. Smitty stepped forth, speaking slowly and deliberately. "We just need to pick up a pack of..." Smitty's mouth hung open but nothing came out; he froze with the last crucial word stuck inside. Smitty's breath erupted silently in his chest; he had choked with the game on the line.

E.C. thankfully broke the odd silence. "Well, while you're deciding why you're here, I'd like to congratulate both of you on winning city today. And you too, Mr. Lucas."

Both boys expunged a massive amount of air. Cal now stood beside them.

The years had treated the good man kindly. A little less hair, a few more lines on the round face, but the old guy had aged well.

"Cal, we've never met but I've enjoyed watching you play. Last ballplayer we had around here that could play like you was Stormy Weathers." Harrell's face darkened. "I sure hope he's okay. He's missing, you know."

Stormy beamed inside, resisted the urge to blurt: "Mr. Harrell, it's me!"

E.C. grinned. "I remember like it was yesterday. Stormy would come in here and shoplift."

Stormy's eyes widened at the speed of sound. It was true but the man had never said a thing to him.

"Nothing of real value. Just candy, combs, fingernail clippers, little necessities like that. He lived at the orphanage and didn't have any money." Mr. Harrell shook his head. "Just figured it was my way of supporting Woodrow." E.C. pointed a fatherly finger at the young men standing below him. "Don't get the wrong idea, boys; none of you live in an orphanage."

So E.C. had tried to help him all those years ago. How 'bout that! Gratitude was a strange feeling, but Stormy guessed he owed the old guy.

"At any rate, boys," Harrell said, "it's late and I'd like to close. What can I get you?"

Smitty and Po Po looked to their leader.

"I agree Mr. Harrell. Lawrence, tell Mr. Harrell what you need."

Po Po gulped loudly and his neck started to twitch. Stormy knew one thing. Po Po would not back down.

The big catcher's eyes frantically searched the counter separating the pharmacist from the boys. His desperate eyes saw only mouthwash, nose sprays, eardrops, decongestants, etc. Where were the damn rubbers?

Po Po grasped his hands together tightly; he grimaced, exposing clinched teeth and took a deep breath that swelled his broad chest. Po Po's jaws never moved but the words tumbled from his lips at warp speed. *"We need to buy some rubbers, uh, condoms."*

Silence reigned, as if Po Po had announced the end of all mankind. E.C.'s eyes tightened. Finally, after what seemed an eternity, old E.C. pressed his fingers together in a spiritual manner; he mechanically leaned forward and peered over his glasses. The words came out frigid as a mountain stream, his voice flat. "What size?"

The pitcher and catcher desperately looked to their hero for guidance but Stormy offered only an indifferent shrug. With faces red enough to stop traffic, both youngsters retreated wordlessly from the old drugstore. Stormy's smile met with a similar grin from E.C. Harrell.

"Same question I asked Stormy Weathers over twenty years ago." E.C. winked.

"I know." Stormy winked in return, then followed his teammates out the front door.

Chapter Twenty-Two
THE ELECTRIC CIRCUS

A huge, flashing neon sign practically blinded the boys on their arrival at The Electric Circus. Even from the parking lot, the boys heard the pulsating beat and could feel the energy from inside.

A muscular black man, well over seven feet tall and wearing a tuxedo, greeted them at the front door. Smitty and Po Po's eyebrows arched in anticipation.

Once inside, they were assaulted by a thick layer of tobacco-induced fog. The smell of alcohol dominated all other smells. Half-dozen small stages, positioned throughout a room nearly the size of an outfield, pulled in men like a giant round magnet. Dressed in micro-glitter costumes and looking barely older than their visitors from Woodrow, scores of topless dancers milled about the nightspot. Other strippers were gyrating like vertical snakes on the stages while steady streams of male admirers tucked folded bills under miniscule g-strings, forming money belts around the girls' tiny waists. With rock-n-roll at a deafening level, the drinks poured freely from bars at opposite ends of the crowded nightclub.

Woodrow's triumvirate took a seat at a circular table. Their eyes jumped to the stage in front of them only a tad quicker than they ordered a pitcher of beer. Stormy appreciatively studied a hard-bodied dancer that obviously belonged in a magazine—and not Better Homes and Gardens. He thought of the crazy feminists who argued that strippers degraded all women. Quite the opposite: women held the power here, not the men.

Stormy glanced at his two friends. Too paralyzed to drink, they clutched their beer mugs while gasping for air they could not find.

A club photographer arrived on the scene. In a temporary lapse into con-sciousness, Smitty and Po Po joined Stormy in a toast, raising their glasses. A bright camera flash temporarily blinded the boys and a few minutes later, the photographer returned with a black and white souvenir photo. Stormy, sandwiched between Smitty and Po Po, reached deep into his Levi's front pocket and handed a ten spot to the photographer.

He leaned close to Smitty and roared above the noisy din. "I'm afraid Po Po may yam on himself."

Po Po's wide eyes were pasted to the stage. With legs stretching all the way to her deep-cut belly button, the dancer moved with a pantherish grace to the edge of the stage; drawn by the youngster's lust, she knelt down to Po Po, the bangs of her long black hair dangling straight across her forehead. With her hungry eyes devouring Po Po's body, she dangled her top and gently dropped the garment on top of his head. Only the veins in Po Po's thick neck, which had taken on a spectacular shade of blue, exhibited signs of life.

When the music stopped, the dancer stepped off the stage and approached the players' table. She eyed the young men curiously. "Could a lady have her clothes back?" Her rich, sultry voice made her question sound like an invitation to something terribly wicked and exciting. She reached to the garment rack, which also served Po Po's head.

Stormy looked up to see high-rise bare breasts staring him in the face. He hoisted his beer mug and grinned.

"If you insist," Stormy said and took a gulp of beer.

To the dismay of all three, she deftly placed her upper garment to its rightful position. Her youthful features were betrayed by experienced eyes.

"My name's Candice. Would you gentlemen mind if I join you for a drink?" Stormy nodded. "We wouldn't mind."

Po Po squirmed in his chair, and buried ten fingers into his thighs in an apparent effort to stifle an unwanted ejaculation.

Candice took the vacant seat next to Smitty, surveying the three. She crossed her legs, exposing a magnificent contrast between her full thighs and slender ankles.

"Honey, would you bring me an ice cream cone?" she yelled to a nearby waitress who was one solid fishnet hose. After the waitress hurried away, Candice motioned to the empty pitcher of beer on the table.

"Say, you guys look a little young to be in here. I haven't seen you here before. Where are you from?"

"We go to school at SMU," Stormy replied without elaboration, the only one capable of a response.

"Ahh, college boys," she said slowly enough to digest the words. "You know, students are my favorites."

Candice placed a drink stir from the table in her mouth like a thermometer.

Gently, she inserted the stir until it disappeared and then pulled it completely out again. She repeated this several times before removing the stir and slowly licking her lips from corner to corner. A sly knowing smile slid across her face.

"I consider myself quite a teacher."

"I'll bet," Stormy said.

Candice glanced at Stormy's nervous friends. Sweat drenched their foreheads.

"Are your friends okay?"

Stormy inspected his buddies. Paralysis had overwhelmed both of them. He leaned across Smitty whose hands were locked in a death grip to the edge of the table.

"Yeah, first time to be in a place like this."

The sex goddess' beverage arrived, a creamy substance that rose above the oversized shooter glass and dripped down its sides.

"This will be a special little treat for your friends." She spoke loudly over Mick Jagger, who was wailing something about "Jumpin' Jack Flash."

Candice allowed both arms to dangle by her side and slowly inched her face close enough to bury her nose in the drink. Her tongue slowly began to massage the creamy substance. First the drink's white head vanished. Next, with repeated sensual, circular motions, her tongue focused on the interior of the shot glass.

Outwardly Stormy stayed calm, but inside he was shouting for the fire extinguisher. Smitty's eyes widened; his jaw slackened, and his stare became trance-like. Po Po's head jerked violently, the veins in his neck bulging like ball bats.

Candice lowered her head further, opened her mouth and totally engulfed the container with her generous lips. Holding the glass between her teeth, she abruptly jerked her head back until her closed eyes faced the ceiling. To the stunned attention of her small audience, the thick substance filtered slowly down her throat. Finished, the dancer swung her head down and gently dropped the shooter from her mouth to the table. Candice smiled wickedly at the boys and licked her lips with the exotic strokes of her tongue. The dancer's eyes were glazed over. Candice had succeeded in arousing herself.

A loud thud from Po Po's direction, startled the stripper. Dirty white tennis shoes now pointed to the ceiling. Po Po's chair had crashed to the floor. The night was still young.

Po Po wobbled into the crowded men's room as he would after riding an upchuck ride at the State Fair. His inexperience with alcohol showed like red socks with a tux. An old black man stoically sat in one corner, guarding the gum, mouthwash, mints, and hairbrushes that occupied the long lavatory counter.

Po Po assumed his place in line behind a man with a crew cut who wore a cheap dark suit and wrinkled white shirt. Startled, the man suddenly stretched to his tiptoes and quickly turned to see Po Po holding his tool in his hand; the outrageous one had accidentally rammed the man from behind. The man quickly moved aside and Po Po wobbled to the front of the line, closed one eye and relieved himself. Mission accomplished, the teenager weaved from the men's bathroom.

Stormy liked sitting beside Candice. He looked into eyes as dark as her past, he supposed. Stormy felt her muscular legs nudge against his. Her honey-rich perfume smelled of lust.

Candice took a sip of her bourbon on the rocks. With phone numbers already exchanged, she had promised to line up a couple of other dancers for a late night party—maybe even tonight. Stormy thought better of informing Po Po of this good news; the excitement might take him over the edge.

Stormy and Smitty, preoccupied with Candice, barely noticed Po Po stumbling to his seat. A firm meaty hand suddenly clamped on Po Po's shoulder, startling everyone at the table. Po Po glanced up through glazed eyes to see the man in the cheap suit flashing a police badge.

"Son, can I see an ID?" the man asked in a monotone as stern as his demeanor.

"Why does he need to show you an ID?" Smitty, the responsible one, uncharacteristically spoke at the wrong time.

The vice cop stared hard.

"He looks under age and drunk."

Po Po spoke defiantly through his thick tongue. "I ain't drunk—I'm just drinkin'."

Chapter Twenty-Three
STORMY'S VISITOR

A mood colder than the concrete jail floor permeated the room. Stormy and Smitty sat with their backs propped stiffly against the wall. Curled in the fetal position, Po Po snored so loud, he sounded on the verge of suffocating. The crown of his thin blond hair exposed the initial stages of a bald spot.

Though Stormy yawned with boredom, Smitty stared dejectedly at the floor, feeling anything but bored.

"Coach didn't sound too happy when I called," Smitty said.

Worry lines aged Smitty's face years in the last few hours. Going to jail was serious: a college education, or lack of, more serious; and cheating at baseball extremely serious. Too much serious for one red-haired, freckle-faced, skinny high school senior.

To make matters worse, he'd called Coach Parker to get them out of jail. With his mother spending a rough night with grandma at the rest home, and his dad attending a principal's convention in Austin, there had been no one else. Po Po's dad, the trucker, was on the road while his mom worked the late shift at the Hilton. For the next few minutes, Po Po's snore provided the only sound.

Stormy looked at the catcher. "How did Lawrence get such an endearing nickname?"

Smitty's eyes never left the floor. "A couple of years ago, neither one of us had ever had a drop to drink so we decided to try it at Po Po's house since his parent's are gone all the time. We polished off a bottle of bourbon and, man, were we history."

"So."

"Well, Goofus stumbled to the john; he must have missed the mark and crapped in his pants because he comes back smelling real bad. He's so out of it he doesn't know it and passes out on the couch." A smile busted through Smitty's somber mood. "I left and his parents found him asleep and stinking to high heaven. I gave him the name," Smitty said pridefully.

Other than his pursed lips, Stormy's expression remained deadpan.

"Man, I've never seen so many pro scouts. You gonna blow off college?" Smitty spoke softly, almost in awe.

"Yep. Winning state and going back, uh, I mean being in the big show is all that matters to me."

Po Po snorted loudly and rolled onto his back. The night was a downer anyway, a fitting night to drop the bomb on Cal. Angry little carpenters' invaded Smitty's chest, pounding non-stop. Butterflies fluttered recklessly in his stomach, as if fighting to break free. Smitty let out some air. His stomach never lied; he was nervous.

"I'm not gonna cheat in the play-offs," Smitty blurted. Fear shone like a spotlight from his eyes.

"Huh?"

"No stuff on the ball. I want to win straight up or not at all." Part of Smitty felt relief, another part hollow. Smitty felt selfish, but he couldn't live with the cheating.

"Oh, no! A born-again Christian!" Stormy's face distorted and a hard edge entered in his tone. "You're smart, a good learner. You've done better with the spitter than I could have ever hoped. And now you're going soft just at the wrong time!"

Smitty spoke barely above a whisper, a mix of uncertainly and newfound maturity coloring his voice. "I wish you'd get rid of that jacked-up bat, too. Po Po's no leader. He looks up to you. You could be a better example for him."

Stormy lowered his chin and stared straight ahead. He massaged his face with the palm of his hand. Any means that brought about the desired results made perfect sense to Stormy; how could Smitty not see that?

Smitty shattered the thick silence.

"How did you know about Mr. Harrell? You asked if he still owned the store, like you'd been there a long time ago."

Stormy's eyes shifted to face Smitty. The kid had figured something out. Smitty had challenged him and, to Stormy's surprise, he respected the kid for that.

"There's something you haven't told us, isn't there, Cal?"

"Maybe."

Smitty shrugged. "Yeah? I'd sure like to know what's going on."

Stormy's eyes softened. "Bro, I might tell you before I die; that's the best I can do."

Hearing keys rattle, the two looked up to see Coach Cotton Parker standing ramrod straight beside the jailer, his close-set eyes narrowed.

The noise aroused Po Po. His bloodshot eyes found his coach. "Aw, no, Coach! They got you, too!"

The Chevrolet sedan eased into Cotton Parker's driveway. Cotton wearily crawled from his car and looked at his watch. At two o'clock in the morning, fatigue had rendered his brain unresponsive. As he unlocked the front door to his one-story red brick home, a horrible thought returned like a recurring nightmare. Should he boot Cal Lucas from the team? Hopefully, he'd feel differently in the morning, after some rest, but he didn't think so. The joy of his first city championship had eroded into despair.

No doubt Cal provoked the bar escapade, but unfortunately there was more. Back at Woodrow after the game, Cotton prepared to lock up the dressing room, but noticed Smitty's warmup bag on the floor—with a tube of KY Jelly inside the open bag.

Parker walked down the hallway toward his bedroom. In a mirror at the end of the hall, his somber face stared back at him. Cotton stopped outside his daughter's room and opened the door. Susan slept soundly: the most important part of his life remained okay. He continued to his bedroom and began to undress.

Hell, it made perfect sense. Smitty had developed a big league breaking ball practically overnight. KY Jelly! Cotton shook his head. After allowing his pants and shirt to fall to the floor, he slid into bed and stared wistfully at the picture of his wife on the nightstand. It was easy to see where Susan inherited her looks. More than ever, Cotton missed his wife. A bitter taste stung Cotton's mouth. His head ached.

He pulled the top sheet to his chin, his troubled eyes searching for answers on the ceiling. Cotton hoped nightmares would not accompany his sleep. Cal was responsible for all that was good and bad about the team, but the bad was winning out. How could things be worse?

Aw, hell! Cotton's search of that elusive state title had caused him to deceive himself. The persistent hum of uneasiness about the boy had finally become a brain-vibrating roar. Cal Lucas had to go. Cotton Parker reached over and turned off the lamp.

He closed his eyes and started his nightly prayer. He prayed he would be a worthy parent but his mind drifted. Though often tempted, he had always avoided praying for a state title, doubtful it was a worthy reason to summon God's help. He felt thankful for that now. It all seemed sort of silly. It was his last conscious thought.

Susan had no idea why her father left the house over an hour ago, but he was back. With his bedroom now dark and silent, Susan knew he had fallen asleep. She kicked back the covers and rose from her bed. Fully clothed in jeans and a Woodrow Wilson sweatshirt, she silently opened her bedroom window and slipped outside. City champs, a time to celebrate—a time to enter the realm of womanhood.

Stormy had expected his visitor and opened the door. Only a brown terry-cloth bathrobe concealed a part of Stormy's anatomy that was rising faster than this body temperature. A recent shower left his thick hair wet, and the fresh scent of his cologne filled the air.

Candice's black leather outfit looked painted on. Her open-toed high heels elevated her to practically the same height as Stormy. With moist red lips and lust glowing in her jungle cat eyes, she entered his apartment with as confident a swagger as Stormy had ever seen on a woman. They stood in the middle of the small living area, saying nothing. Then their mouths came together and they went at each other like wild animals. Stormy's hands caressed and stroked her long hair. He drank in the aroma of her fertile sex. While the dancer's hands settled firmly on both cheeks of his buttocks, she raked her burning tongue across the inside of his mouth. What had he done to deserve this good fortune?

Susan parked her car, her thoughts overflowing with anxiety. It was late. What if Cal wouldn't wake up? She tried to leave home earlier, but her dad's strange departure had ruined that. What if Cal opened the door, took one look, and sent her home like a child? Susan walked slowly to Cal's door, her heart beating hard with anticipation and fear.

Through the blinds on Cal's front window, she saw the silhouette of two bodies embraced. Susan's heart pumped faster than she could think; she darted closer for a better look. Oh God! Cal and some woman were slobbering all over each other! With her eyes frozen on the pair, Susan felt her stomach rebel. The shock was heartbreaking: Cal Lucas was not the person she thought he was. He was a fraud, not like her father at all.

Susan ran to the car. Shuddering, she pitched forward, grabbed the door handle for support and began to vomit uncontrollably.

Chapter Twenty-Four
HAVE I DONE WELL OR ILL?

The sound of lockers slamming clamored throughout Woodrow Wilson's halls. The jammed hallways briefly brought back Stormy pleasant memories of strolling the Manhattan sidewalks. Many acknowledged Stormy with grins and positive nods; a few wished him luck in the play-offs. Stormy leaned against his locker holding his notebook to his chest. He felt ridiculous impersonating a student. His passing grades confirmed Smitty's theory: out of respect for Coach Parker, the teachers would not flunk Cal and leave him ineligible for post-season play. The hallways started to thin.

Seeing Smitty approach, Stormy could read the fatigue in his roadmap eyes. Stormy should feel worse, he decided. Candice had stayed all night, the topless dancer fulfilling all her promises as a teacher and throwing in a graduate course to boot.

"Hey, Cal." Smitty exhaled wearily, joining his teammate. "I'm beat; how about you?"

"I'll make it—deserve to feel worse, that's for sure. Did your parents find out?"

"No. My dad gets back from Austin today, and my mom was at the nursing home all night. I've got a good younger sister; she won't squeal about what time I got home." His expression turned serious. "I guess Coach will, though."

"Maybe not, bro. I don't think Coach will do anything to upset you or your parents for the play-offs. He wants that title as bad as we do."

"Then what do you think he's gonna do? Last night was pretty wild."

"Oh, I don't know. Make us run laps until our tongues fall out, I guess."

Susan appeared in the hallway sporting red-rimmed eyes and puffy, mussed hair. Her two girlfriends supported her.

"Susan!" Stormy called.

Her pain and his curiosity battled each other in their looks. Her companions shot him a glance loaded with fury and loathing. The two hurriedly guided Susan away.

"What's wrong with Susan? She looks worse than me," said Smitty.

"I don't know, bro. Don't you have a class with her now?"

"Yeah."

"See what you can find out."

"Sure."

Stormy, his eyes narrowed with concern, watched Smitty follow Susan to class.

That afternoon, while absorbing the sound of baseball cleats skating across concrete, Stormy sat beside his locker and laced his baseball shoes. He glanced up to see Smitty, who was already dressed for practice. Trouble filled Smitty's eyes.

"What's the deal with Susan?"

Smitty leaned down close and whispered, "Cal, she slipped out of her house last night and came over to your place. She snuck out after Coach got home from getting us out of jail. She saw you with some girl!"

"Oh, shit!" Stormy stiffened as tension raced through his body.

"I can't believe it. You're the first guy from Woodrow she's interested in, and you pull this! That's pretty low, Cal." Smitty paused to catch his breath. "This will break her heart, for sure. She was just getting over her mom getting killed by that homeless person."

Stormy stood, ironing the wrinkles out of his practice pants with the palms of his hands.

"I didn't know Susan was coming over. Hell, it was the middle of the night."

Stormy stopped short. What had Smitty said? Her mother killed by a homeless person?

"What are you talking about? I knew her mom had died suddenly—but murdered?"

"Yep, couple of years ago. She was a caterer and would take her extra food to where the homeless hang out. Some crazy freak went nuts and... Kinda makes you wonder about volunteer work."

Stormy lowered himself slowly to the bench. He buried his face in his hands, his mind on fire. Susan was helping the homeless, one of whom had killed her mother! And now he'd hurt her too.

"Who was the girl?"

"Candice. The girl from the club," Stormy said, his voice muffled, his look stuck to the floor.

"Wow!" Smitty's eyes suddenly expanded with envy. "Don't tell Po Po. He'll have a heart attack."

Stormy didn't move.

"Cal, I think you're in trouble. Coach was up when she got home. He knows everything. Susan said the last time she saw him this mad some guy got locked up in a coffin." Smitty laid his hand on Stormy's shoulder. "Let's get to practice before Coach finds us."

Too late, Smitty saw Coach Parker steam-rolling their direction. Parker's eyes simmered like charcoal briquettes about to erupt in flames. The coach zoomed past Smitty as if he were invisible and confronted Stormy.

"Big un! My office after practice!"

Stormy remained outwardly calm, but underneath he flinched at the sound of his coach's hostile voice. He raised his head to acknowledge the cold, angry face of Cotton Parker.

"Yes, sir."

The long day grew longer as Stormy made the slow walk from the dressing area to the coach's office. The punishment laps coupled with the lack of sleep, had taken its toll. Conflicting emotions tormented him. He had disappointed women before, but he'd never felt remorse like this.

So what if Parker tossed him from the squad? He'd go to the minors and rapidly move up to the big show. Who gives a wolf's shit about winning a high school state baseball championship? Besides, if Parker wanted to boot him off the team, he would have done so before practice. The truth quickly crushed deception. Damn, he didn't want to leave! More confusing, Stormy wanted the state title as much for Parker and the boys as he did for himself. He knocked on Parker's office door.

"Come in!"

Stormy entered to find the coach sitting at his desk, his face hidden behind a newspaper, remindful of their first meeting.

Without lowering the newspaper, Cotton issued a firm command, "Sit down."

Taking the lone chair directly in front of Parker's desk, Stormy quickly noticed another similarity to the day he'd met the coach: Coach Parker was reading about the missing baseball player, Stormy Weathers!

Stormy read The Dallas Morning News headlines from across Cotton's desk: "Missing Baseball Star's Car Found In Nearby Lake." Stormy dropped to his seat, free falling the last foot or so. He swallowed and discovered a void in his throat. Cotton lowered the newspaper to reveal a face filled with disgust.

Stormy squirmed uncomfortably, avoiding eye contact while trying to regain his composure.

"Big 'un," Cotton said, his posture now erect. His voice boomed with authority. "You're one of those fortunate few who's been handed the keys to the American dream; the least you could do is follow the roadmap."

"Sir?"

Against his better judgment, Stormy's eyes strayed to his coach. Though he feared Cotton's piercing eyes would tunnel a hole in his chest, he resisted the urge to duck.

"Let me tell you something. In our society we use sports to express and defend our values, as well as to teach them. Right or wrong, that's the case." Cotton's voice softened, but his eyes remained hard. "Unfortunately, so much of the sports world has become a world of shifting values, lack of commitment, and short cuts. Big 'un, that's you."

Beads of anxiety drenched the ballplayer's face. "If it's about last night, I…"

The coach leaned across the wooden desk. His voice carried his anger.

"Son, shut up and listen! You're the best talent I've ever had, and the worst leader. As a player or coach, I've never won the last game, that championship. Close, but never made it all the way." The coach relaxed in his chair and expunged air heavily. "Even felt like a loser at times but through it all, I've retained most of my self-respect. Now you come along from God knows where and make it possible to win the big one, but only if I compromise my values."

Parker's eyes strayed upward, as if searching for help from above.

"It's only because of Susan that I'm going to give you another chance. If I kick you off the team, I have no leverage to keep you away from my daughter. I have a feeling you want that state championship pretty badly yourself. If I'm right, you'll stay away from Susan for a chance to get it."

"I like Susan a lot, a whole lot," Stormy replied. "After last night, I know it doesn't look that way, but it's true."

"Good. If that's the truth, you'll leave her alone. Think about it. Honest-to-God, think about it. You'll be leaving soon. Don't confuse her or hurt her any more." Demanding eyes nailed Stormy to the wall. "Clean up your act or you're gone. Stay away from my daughter or you're gone. And that'll be the least of your problems. Got it?"

Stormy pressed his knuckles together until his flesh turned white. No coach had ever talked to him like this.

"Got it," Stormy said softly.

Cotton's shoulders relaxed, and he propped his feet on the desk.

"Son, life has thrown me a curve or two the last couple of years. Sometimes pain makes people bitter, and other times it teaches them compassion. In my case, I hope the latter is true. I don't like to see people hurt, especially my daughter."

He sat upright again, and Stormy flinched inside, fearing another assault. But Cotton's voice remained gentle.

"Big un, I don't know who you are or where you're from. Heck, I can't find any records that you ever existed before."

Stormy's eyes expanded, and his rear shuffled nervously in his chair.

Parker lowered his chin for emphasis. "You're way too streetwise for these kids, especially my daughter, and I don't want these kids to face the ugly side of life one day sooner than they have to." Cotton rubbed his palm across his chin. "You know I was raised a Southern Baptist, became a sociology teacher and a coach—so you're gonna have to sit tight while I preach a little." Cotton's eyes floated in space. "A man, after he has brushed off the dust and chips of his life, will have left only the hard, clean questions: was it good or evil? Have I done well or ill?"

Cotton Parker's penetrating eyes returned to his subject and he paused momentarily.

"I wish I could remember who said that. Big un, you're one of those few that can make a difference. But what an honor! What a responsibility. So far, I'm afraid you're blowing it."

So that's where Susan gets it, Stormy thought.

Cotton refocused on the newspaper that lay on his desk and remorsefully shook his head. "I guess Stormy's at the bottom of that lake somewhere. He's from this high school, you know. You could make it like him. You've got the talent."

Stormy's eyebrows shot upward.

"He worked hard to make it to the top of his profession. He had nothing else to prove." Cotton's stare latched onto the picture of a large truck towing Stormy's Porsche from the water.

"That's nice to know," Stormy replied, barely recognizing the sound of his own voice.

Bam! The notion hit Stormy like a giant slab of cerebral concrete. Coach was right. What did he have left to prove?

Cotton's eyes inflated, the volume of his voice grew. "Hey, Stormy's car looks just like yours!"

Stormy wasn't listening, his mind already pondering a new game plan.

Woodrow's halls percolated with excitement brewed by the upcoming trip south to Austin, Texas for the state play-offs. Susan Parker, the one exception to the festive atmosphere, watched with hollow eyes. Without warning, Cal Lucas pulled her into an isolated dark corner of the old school. His hands firmly grasped the top of her forearms as if to prevent her escape. Susan's long, dark hair framed her sorrow as much as her smooth face in the dim light of the hallway.

He spoke in a rapid clip. "I've only got a second. I promised your dad I'd stay away."

"Good. Keep your promise," Susan said, her body rigid and her voice cold.

"I know I let you down, but you can't control that. Don't punish yourself."

"I thought you were like my dad." Susan's voice cracked a little when she said dad. "The signs were there, but I believed what I wanted. You're a fraud, a cheat."

"I'm sorry. I don't deserve the right to ask, but...can we at least be friends?" Stormy asked, his eyes pleading.

Susan jerked her arms free from his grasp. A flick of her eyes managed to convey total disgust.

"Yeah, right. We can be friends," Susan said. "Just not good friends."

Stormy watched her disappear into a mass of bobbing heads. This recycling program was beginning to unravel.

Busy with her knitting, Norma sat on the opposite end of her couch from Stormy. Stormy sat quietly, lost in space, staring through the chatter of a television game show.

"You seem preoccupied," Norma said.

His empty gaze remained on the television.

"Me? Oh, I'm just thinking."

Norma dropped the knitting on her lap.

"Is there a problem?"

Stormy was down, and it showed. With no energy left to talk Norma through another crisis over the missing ex-Yankee center fielder, he had hidden the newspaper photo of the tow truck hoisting his old car from the water.

"Let's just say my method of operation has met a little resistance lately." He managed a weak tight-lipped smile.

"Maybe you should change your methods."

Stormy faced his mother. Surely, a man could ask his mother for advice, even if she didn't know he was her son.

"Can people change? I mean really change for the better?"

Hesitating, Norma's thoughts fixed on something private. "I have to believe they can," she finally answered.

"Really?"

"Really."

Neither spoke for the next few minutes providing the silence needed for Stormy to hear an internal alarm. Mac had been staying away: why? Mac had duped him somehow. The joke was on Stormy, but what was the punch line? A piece of the puzzle was missing and it was a doozy.

Mac's voice echoed in Stormy's mind and he repeated the words just loud enough for Norma to hear, "We're a lot alike; we'll both take an unfair advantage."

"What? Did you say something?"

"Oh nothing." Stormy felt dumber than management after signing a washed up ballplayer.

Chapter Twenty-Five
FORGIVENESS

Less than an hour remained to game time; Josh Howard stood by his locker, buttoning his white Boston Red Sox home jersey, when he heard his phone page. Who would call before a game? He leisurely strolled across the plush dressing room carpet to the wall phone dangling in midair; curiosity overloaded his grizzly face.

"Hello...you got him." Josh's eyes gradually expanded with disbelief as he listened to the other end of the line. "Let me get this straight, kid. You want me and Roger Jackson to come to Dallas and give a few pointers to your high school baseball team on Tuesday!" Josh listened further, rolling his eyes in astonishment. "Not you, just your teammates. Pardon me, kid, there must be something wrong with the phone." Josh tapped the phone firmly against the wall before returning it to his ear.

Only the uniqueness of the kid's request prevented him from hanging up. Josh spoke in a hard, clipped, sarcastic voice.

"I can appreciate your team going to the state play-offs and needing some help. But we're in the middle of a minor excursion called a pennant race, and I don't think my employer is going to be real thrilled about our top pitcher and me taking a day off for a little instructional seminar, even if it's in the great Lone Star State!"

He paused to take a breath, which gave the caller an opening for a reply. Josh grimaced with frustration.

"I'd like to know your name. Just in case I meet you, I want to run in the opposite direction. And furthermore, I know we have an off-day Tuesday, but we can't come. Good bye!" Josh slammed the phone to the receiver and walked away mumbling, "Crazy kid!"

Almost instantly, the phone rang and on the second ring, another Red Sox player answered. "Clubhouse. Yeah, hold on." The player placed the phone to his heart and called, "Wilson, telephone!"

Josh raked his fingers through thin strands of dark hair which only partially covered his balding head. "Who is it?"

His teammate returned the phone to his ear and listened. "He says he just talked to you, but if you don't want to talk, that's okay." Boston's young player stayed on the line, barely able to control his laughter. "Hey, Josh, he says he knows your home telephone number. He thought your wife would be interested about your nights out with Stormy Weathers in New York."

With panic on his leathery mug, Josh darted to the phone, slipping once in the process.

"Who the hell are you?" Josh asked, and then listened with disbelieving ears. "Shit! That is my home number!" Josh flinched and shut his eyes. The kid knew everything. "Stormy told you all that?" But then a good thought came to the catcher, his face brightening with hope. "Hey, kid, is Stormy alive?" After the kid's reply, confusion revisited Josh's face. "What do you mean, sorta? Yeah, maybe so."

Now more befuddled than angry, Josh gently returned the phone to the receiver. He stood there thoughtfully kneading his full cheeks with his thick fingers before yelling across the dressing room. "Hey, Jackson, forget that golf game Tuesday. We're going to Texas."

Rubber shuffled loose gravel before Stormy's car finally skidded to a halt in front of the United Gospel Mission. Stormy left the Porsche as if it were on fire and took the steps two at a time. Once inside, his eyes latched onto a man with a face as round as the rest of him. The man wore a pastor's white collar and a wrinkled dark shirt with faded blue jeans. A braided gray ponytail hung past his collar; a bushy, white mustache concealed part of his red face. It was the partial metamorphosis from hippie to preacher, or vice versa.

"May I help you, young man?" The man smiled warmly.

Stormy felt uncomfortable. The place was a zoo. To one side people slept; on the other side a few children darted about in an apparent game of tag. Other people ate, while some simply sat in portable chairs, seemingly comatose. Most dressed scruffy; the pungent smell suggested many of the residents needed a bath. The place gave him the creeps.

"Uh, yes, sir, I was wondering where I might find Susan Parker?"

The gentleman motioned with his eyes to the back of the room. "You might find her in the back office, but I'm not sure she wants to see you, Mr. Lucas."

Stormy flinched. "You know me?"

"I know of you. Susan's discussed her relationship with you to me.

Reverend Al's the name. I run the mission." The man extended his hand to Stormy and the two shook.

"Susan's talked to you about me?"

"I've counseled her. I've worked with Susan since she became involved with our mission." Reverend Al moved closer; the man spoke in a lower volume, raising his eyebrows. "She told me about the other night with your other lady friend. I expect you're concerned and feel remorse, or you wouldn't be here, but I must tell you that's the most upset I've seen her since her mom died."

To his surprise, Stormy found it easy to confide in Reverend Al.

"Sir, I do feel bad about the other night. I tried to apologize a couple of days ago, but she was still too upset. I'd sure feel better if I could have another shot at it. I promised her dad I'd stay away, and besides I'm gonna be leaving right after the state play-offs." Stormy raised his shoulders. "I don't know where else to talk to her."

Reverend Al placed a hand on Stormy's shoulder. "Follow me." They walked side by side. "Susan's quite a lady. In some ways she's as innocent as a child, in others, she's mature beyond her years. Right now, she's working on our budget."

Stormy noticed the paint peeling from the worn walls. "Yea, it looks like you could use a paint job."

"Paint job!" Reverend Al threw his hands up in despair. "I wish that's all we needed. Summer's coming; we have no air conditioning. We need more showers so these people can bathe, not to mention the usual needs for linen, food and clothing. You name it, we could use it. We're in the people-helping business, and unfortunately, business is booming."

The two arrived at a closed door.

"How much money do you need for the showers and the A.C.?" Stormy asked, immediately wondering if someone was speaking for him.

The man's head tilted upward evidently creating a calculator in his mind. "We can do much of the work ourselves. I figure twenty-five thousand would do it."

"I'll get you the money," Stormy heard himself say, "but don't tell Susan."

Reverend Al's thick left paw rested on the doorknob.

"Cal, did you come by this money honestly?" Concern lined the man's face.

"Yes, sir."

"To use terminology that I'm sure you'll relate to, these people have had a bad hop in the game of life. They could use a break any place they can get it." Reverend Al extended his hand to Stormy, and the two shook. "Mr. Lucas, we will kindly accept your generosity."

"Before you open that door, could I ask just exactly what happened to Susan's mother?"

Reverend Al's eyes cut around the room, and he sighed heavily.

"She was a caterer and would always take her left over food to this one underpass where a lot of homeless would camp out. It was one of those miserable August days and the food line was long. Tempers flared." Reverend Al gulped audibly. "One guy had a gun," said Reverend Al, his voice teetering. "He was trying to shoot one of the other guys. Susan's mom got caught in the cross fire…"

Stormy held up his hand in the gesture for stop. Reverend Al opened the door.

"I'll let you two have a few minutes alone."

Stormy entered the small office with the caution of entering a minefield. Susan sat behind a cheap Formica desk in a dilapidated, vinyl-covered, swivel chair. Two metal folding chairs faced the desk. The walls were totally bare. The late afternoon sun peeked through the lone window to shine directly on Susan.

She looked more radiant than ever. A simple white sundress exposed her shoulders. Stormy moved slowly until he stood in front of the desk and faced her melancholy but penetrating eyes. Hands at his side, Stormy managed a timid wave. Susan only hinted at a smile.

"Mind if I sit down?" asked Stormy, relieved that his voice didn't waiver. When she failed to answer, he lowered himself into one of the chairs.

"I've never seen you in a dress before. You look great. I mean, you always look great, but you look especially great today."

Come on, stay cool.

Susan's face softened.

"Thanks. I'm going to meet dad at the church at six."

Susan's hands remained folded in her lap.

Stormy motioned to the door.

"That Reverend Al, he's quite a character." His nervous grin failed to lighten the mood. "How did you meet him?"

"After we lost my mother, dad and I both went into one of those special outreach programs for people who have lost family members." Susan's eyes alternated between Stormy and the desktop. "The counselor said the best way to overcome grief was to help others, so I began to do volunteer work here."

She shrugged. "Eventually I started spending a lot of my free time here."

"Why...here?"

Susan shrugged again.

"Why not? Dad says it's sort of like climbing back on the horse that threw you off."

Staring directly into the young girl's somber eyes, Stormy shuffled his feet and cleared his throat.

"I'm sorry about your mom. If I'd known, I'd..."

"What?" Susan's reluctance flamed into anger. "You never would have brought that girl to your place?"

"I didn't bring her."

"Small technicality."

"Susan." Stormy exhaled enough air to dry an infield. "We'll be going to Austin in a couple of days for the state tournament. I won't come back for graduation." Their eyes locked. "I'll go straight into some club's farm system. I may never see you again." Stormy clasped his hands together so tightly he felt his circulation cutting off. "I don't deserve it, but all I can ask for is your forgiveness."

Stormy had never asked for forgiveness in his life and it felt good, like an exorcism. A tear welled out of Susan's eyes and slowly traveled down her cheek.

After a heavy silence, she said, "It's okay, Cal, I've forgiven somebody for something a lot worse than what you did." She forced a weak chuckle. "You did me a favor. You saved my virginity for Mr. Wonderful, whoever that is. I couldn't have competed with that girl, anyway."

Without his consent, Stormy's body rose from the chair, and he moved around the desk to stand beside her. She reluctantly turned her chair to face him.

"You don't know how wrong you are."

She stood slowly. Only inches separated their bodies. Except for the sound of each other's breath, the room was silent. Stormy tenderly pulled her to him until not even air separated them and Susan's face nestled against his shoulder. Her sniffles became a gentle sob.

She spoke through the tears. "Don't flatter yourself. These tears aren't all about you."

"I hope not. I feel bad enough already." Stormy's voice stayed strong, but he was relieved she couldn't see his glassy eyes. "Susan, you're gonna make some guy the luckiest man on earth some day. I promise you that."

Susan's tears now came rapidly; she clutched Stormy tightly. Her voice cracked with emotion.

"I feel so selfish sometimes. These people at the mission, they're the ones with real problems, but now and then I miss my mom so bad, I don't think I can go another day."

Stormy soothingly stroked the back of her head. Her silky hair smelled as fresh as spring showers. He could relate. After his mother had abandoned him, especially in the early years, he and loneliness became tighter than a good double play combo.

"It's okay, Susan. Time heals all wounds. Sort of." Stormy's voice was just above a whisper.

Stormy and Susan stood as one, silhouetted by the sun filtering into the small, drab office. He consoled Susan, but she had no idea how comforting her embrace soothed him.

She removed her head from Stormy's shoulders and stared directly into his face. "Cal," she said. "Where are your parents? You've never mentioned them."

"Parents?" said Stormy, as if recalled from another galaxy. His eyes darted uncomfortably to the bright circle on the floor created by the sun's haze. "I don't know," he mumbled. "I'm an orphan." *Only a half-lie,* he thought.

Two men in a brown sedan focused intensely on the young man walking down the steps of the mission. Stormy, entrenched in thought, entered his car. Almost immediately the engine roared and the Porsche streaked away, leaving behind two parallel black scars on the asphalt. Both men wore Blues Brother hats and identical dark suits. Matching horn-rimmed dark glasses concealed their eyes. With one man's head towering above the steering wheel and the other barely peeking above the dash, they passed for non-identical twins. With the strides of purpose, they left their car and entered the mission.

Chapter Twenty-Six
WHO'S SWING DOES THAT REMIND YOU OF?

The weather outside Coach Cotton Parker's office matched his sunny disposition. Practice equipment littered the office floor. A small radio on his desk played an oldie-but-goodie rocker from the sixties, "I See The Light," by Dallas' own Five Americans. Coach Parker hummed along with the high-voltage tune as he donned his practice uniform.

"You tried to fool me, but I got wise
Now I won't listen to any of your lies
But it's all right, it's all right,
it's all right."

Nearby, a pencil-thin student equipment manager, sporting greasy hair and an epidemic of pimples on his gaunt face, struggled to heave the bat bag on his shoulders.

"You got it, Richie?" The coach asked, referring to the bats and not the music's lively beat. Cotton tapped his feet to the music's rhythm.

"Yes, sir," the youngster replied, stumbling from the office with the equipment bag draping his narrow shoulders.

Alone, Cotton belted it out good while lacing his shoes.

"From now on, baby, I'm gonna beware
I may be sorry, baby, but I don't care
Cause it's all right, I see the liiiiiiight!"

The final exaggerated sound of the bass drum brought the music to an abrupt halt. Cotton stood, ready for practice when Cal poked his head into the office.

"Hey, Coach."

"Hey, big 'un."

"Sir, I'm expecting a Josh Howard and Roger Jackson to be at practice today. When they show up, would you mind sending them to the practice field?"

Cotton inspected Cal's face. The kid looked and sounded sincere. Maybe the rock n' roll had affected Cotton's ears. Did Cal say Josh Howard and Roger Jackson?

"The Red Sox?" Cotton's eyes squinted suspiciously, his head cocked sideways.

"Yes, sir. Sure are," his center fielder answered matter-of-factly.

"May I ask why a couple of major leaguers are coming to our practice?"

"To help us get ready for the state tournament. Coach, these guys are the best; they can do us some good."

"Well, big un, that explains it." The good coach forced a smile. "Cal, I messed up. I've already asked Babe Ruth and Ty Cobb if they could help us today."

"Coach, my guys will help us more. Babe and Cobb are dead."

"Well, if your men show up, I'll point them in the right direction."

"Thanks, Coach." The face presumably left with his body for practice.

Cotton retrieved his ball bag. Cotton couldn't put his finger on it, but the kid seemed different. Maybe their talk really did some good.

"Coach Parker?"

He looked up to see stars. The husky one in need of a shave and a wad of tobacco in his mouth spoke. Beside him stood a man of slighter build, but a head taller.

"My name's Josh Howard, and this is Roger Jackson. Cal Lucas asked us to help you out. Is there any place we can change?"

Stunned by the visit of two honest-to-goodness, bona fide, major leaguers, Coach Parker forgot to turn off his radio. A news bulletin darted across the airwaves of the deserted office.

"KLIF radio today learned that local authorities have received their first significant lead in the disappearance of former baseball star, Stormy Weathers. A long-haul trucker informed police he provided transportation to a water-soaked teenage hitchhiker near the area of Mr. Weather's submerged Porsche automobile. The hitchhiker told the trucker his own car, also a Porsche, had accidentally entered the water. The incident happened about forty-eight hours before the ex-ballplayer was reported missing. The FBI is reportedly initiating its own efforts to locate the mysterious hitchhiker."

With legs spread in a reverse V and his hands clasped behind his back, a mesmerized Coach Parker drank in the practice session. Standing near home plate, Cotton listened to every word and committed to memory every technique the major league catcher was currently teaching Po Po. Josh, wearing bright red shin guards, darted to his feet from his position behind home. The big leaguer ripped off his mask and tossed it out of harm's way. He snagged an imaginary throw from midair and dropped to both knees, creating a human roadblock that denied passage to the coveted plate. The two catchers exchanged places; Po Po repeated the exercise like an instant replay.

Despite Josh's darker hair, the two catchers could have passed for brothers. Both were burly, rough, and balding, though Josh was much further along in that process. Their jaws were packed—Po Po's with Double Bubble instead of the chewing tobacco that bloated Josh's left cheek.

Josh patted his student on the shoulder. He studied the frenzied expression on Po Po's face.

"You've got the right temperament for the position; I can see that. What did you say your names was?"

"Po Po, friends call me sh…"

"Lawrence!" Parker sternly interrupted, his arms folded and chin lowered.

"Yes, sir, Coach," Po Po said, the perennial mischievous gleam glowing in his eye.

Josh's crooked smile exposed tobacco stained teeth. "You know why they call that home?" He pointed to the white rubber diamond buried in red dirt. "Cause that's your home and anybody gets by you is trying to break in. We can't have any intruders, can we?"

Po Po readily agreed. His veins started to rise.

"Only a wuss wouldn't protect his home would he, uh, Po Po?" The more Josh tried to stifle his grin, the harder it tried to escape.

"No, sir!"

Josh placed a big-brotherly arm around the kid's shoulders. "Kid, you protect that plate. It's a code of honor among us catchers."

God help whoever tried to break in Po Po's home.

On the pitcher's mound, the Red Sox southpaw continued to instruct Smitty on the proper leg kick. Roger's toothpick frame and long smooth face enabled him to appear almost as young as his student. His intense eyes bore down on the imaginary batter; the pitcher followed through with a kick of his right leg so high his right foot concealed his face. His windup culminated with a blast-off from the rubber with his left foot; Jackson's release turned the ball into a whistling blur.

"Wow!" Smitty said.

"Remember, you get just as much power from your legs as your arm."

"Yes, sir."

While he shagged fly balls with the other outfielders, Stormy kept an eye on the infield. From his catcher's position, Josh leapt to his feet. With a rapid, compact, powerful motion, the pro delivered a low, rifle throw to the second baseman covering the bag. Josh's entire body recoiled with the force of a cannon firing.

Stormy's eyes shifted to the mound. Roger snapped his left wrist with authority. The star hurler was showing Smitty the proper grip and motion for a major league curveball. To be sure, Smitty needed a miracle lesson for the Wildcats to compete.

The shrill sound of Coach's whistle meant time for batting practice. A few minutes later, Josh occupied the batters box. Cotton and the entire team stood close by, with Roger perched on the mound. Once again, Cotton blew his whistle to quiet his excited troops.

"Okay, guys, Josh is going to give us a few pointers with the bat. Let's all pipe down and listen up!"

The squad gradually hushed. Stormy heard a panicked whisper in his ear, "The bat's gone."

Stormy's eyes remained on Josh. "Don't sweat it," he answered Po Po softly.

The look of anguish on Po Po's face suggested sweat and lots of it.

Josh's shiny black baseball shoes glistened in the orange sun. His spikes rearranged the dirt until he firmly entrenched himself in the batter's box. He demonstrated as he spoke loudly. "Men, there's no given way to stand. You need to be comfortable at the plate; that's the most important thing." He took a couple of fluid practice swings and then he assumed a batter's stance; the weight of his body shifted backward but only slightly.

"I like to keep my weight on my back foot as long as possible. I keep my back elbow up, parallel with the ground, my arms above the strike zone." Josh now stood primed and ready, as if posing for a magazine cover. "Stay relaxed, men. Don't commit until the last instant—then swing. When you move your body weight forward, pretend you're steppin' on a bug with that big front toe." Josh swung, causing the air to whistle around him.

"Yogi Berra always said if he could get a good look at a pitch, it was hittable. If you can't see the pitch, chances are it's a bad pitch. Sounds simple, but it works; shift that weight forward and swing."

Josh swung again, but this time in slow motion; he emphasized the body movement from back to front as he followed through with his swing. His front foot, the one closest to the mound, barely lifted in the air during the swing. As it touched the surface, he lightly ground his big toe in the dirt, squashing the phantom bug. Stormy smiled to himself. Josh was a good teacher, better than he expected.

"Hey, Roger, goose one up here."

Roger lobbed a ball to the plate and Josh drove it deep to the outfield. He pounded another with similar results.

"Now, one of you guys try it." Josh's glance searched the players huddled together. "Hey, Lucas, step up here."

Stormy expected as much. Throughout the practice, he noticed Josh staring at him. Probably the big catcher was trying to learn more about Cal Lucas. Stormy knew something few people outside baseball would believe. Josh might guess Cal's identity from watching him hit. If Mickey Mantle were reincarnated as a grandmother, Stormy would know after a few swings of grandma's bat. Stranger than fiction, but true.

Exchanging places with Josh, Stormy avoided eye contact with his old adversary. He felt the sting of Josh's glare. Stormy stepped to the plate.

Roger's first pitch was a balloon ball, and Stormy drilled the ball deep, really deep. The ball stopped approximately the same distance from home plate as Josh's best shot. Josh and Roger's eyebrows lifted in mild approval; the ho-hum looks on the other Wildcats faces plainly indicated the regularity of the smash.

Roger's next pitch arrived quicker, but still far from big league heat. A loud, crisp crack of the bat followed and the ball eventually landed just beyond the previous poke and rolled another ten feet. The gallery cheered as if an unknown kid had just outdriven Jack Nicklaus in a long drive contest.

Josh approached Roger at the mound. Josh's craggy, lined face and slits for eyes formed a picture of curiosity. His front teeth clattered together in the manner of someone in deep thought.

"Put some smoke on this one."

Roger went into his windup and delivered a pea. The drastic change in tempo surprised Stormy; he let the ball pass without swinging, and it popped loudly in Po Po's glove. A hint of satisfaction briefly surfaced on the face of both Red Sox players.

From below, Po Po growled to Stormy, "Hey, fifty, the big boys don't like you showin' 'em up."

The practice field quieted. Could Woodrow's best meet the challenge? If so, could his out-manned teammates do the same in Austin?

"Mr. Jackson, if you don't mind, let's see that pitch again. This time, all you got." Eddie Haskell could not have asked more politely.

Roger glanced to Josh who stood beside him, then bent over to pick up the resin bag. He bounced it three times gently off the top of his hand, and finally let it fall to the ground. Looking irritated, he prepared to deliver. Just before releasing the ball, he grumbled loudly, "Cocky shit!"

The fastball left a trail of white air on its path to Po Po's mitt. With the determination of Zeus, Stormy swung. The ball left the infield on a low line-drive trajectory, gradually climbing until it seemed to dart in and out through the clouds. All but Stormy stood with mouths ajar. Necks twisted to follow the ball's majestic flight. Roger flashed a grin, turned to face the veteran catcher, and shrugged. Josh smiled back. Ballplayers respect other ballplayers; Cal Lucas was a player.

"Whose swing does that remind you of?" Josh said.

"No kiddin'!" Roger said.

"Hey, do you think?" Josh's eyes found Cal, who was receiving congratulations from his excited teammates. Josh inspected every inch of the kid. He was built similar to Stormy, and that was Stormy's swing! Josh's heart soared with hope. He had bad knees, and catchers don't last much past his age. Of course! A miracle doctor had fixed Stormy's bad knee and performed one hell of a plastic surgery job, and now Stormy was prepared to share the secret.

Josh blinked hard, as though awakened from a dream. "Aw, no way," he said to no one.

"Are you okay?" Roger asked.

"Yeah," Josh replied, laughing nervously at the absurdity of his dumb idea. He quickly frowned. Cal Lucas owed Josh some answers; if the youngster refused to cooperate, Josh would tell the police this kid might know about Stormy's whereabouts. So what if Cal squealed about his nights with Stormy? Josh's wife was so ugly she wasn't going anywhere. And if she did, who cares? She spent too much money, anyway.

Coach Parker's players surrounded him at home plate. Josh and Roger stayed to one side. The air was heavy with excitement.

"Okay, men, pipe down!" Cotton signaled for silence with his hands. "I want to take a second to thank our guests for making this a day we will always remember."

Cotton glanced to the two professionals and began to clap his hands. The Woodrow players followed his lead. Josh and Roger nodded in appreciation, a false smile fixed on Josh's face.

"I've preached to you guys that baseball is a game of integrity and tradition. A commitment to excellence, the game deserves that," Cotton preached.

"When the best in the business visit our school and help us learn the right way, that's something special." He paused. "I don't know how Cal got you here, but we're glad he did."

Cal's stomach leapt an uneasy notch. Coach might consider a bribe the wrong way to accomplish anything.

Cotton extended his right hand waist-high and the Wildcats huddled around him, stacking their hands pancake style on top of the other. In unison, all yelled, "Wildcats!" With the day's work complete, the team scattered quicker than a covey of quail.

"Hey, Lucas, wait a minute."

Stormy stopped to face Josh, casually loping toward him.

"Nice practice, kid," Josh said, partially winded.

"Thanks."

"I'd say you got a future in the game."

Stormy avoided Josh's eyes.

"Listen," Josh said. "Is Stormy okay?"

"Like I said on the phone, he's sorta in hiding."

Josh leaned close enough for Stormy to smell his Skoal breath.

"Listen, Lucas, or whatever your name is," Josh said with sudden anger. "I'm a long way from home on the only day off I have in the next few months. Why did you get me down here? I deserve that much."

Stormy stared at Josh. "Let's just say it was a chance for me to do something right for a change."

"Aw, wolf shit, kid! You're making no sense!"

"Look, I know I've inconvenienced you and Roger, but I needed some help. These are good kids. I want to help them fire their best shot in the play-offs. I gotta go now."

Stormy turned and walked quickly away.

Roger arrived at his bewildered teammate's side. They watched Stormy's loping stride until he disappeared into the dressing room.

"I get blackmailed into coming here, and he won't tell me squat." Josh cupped a hand around his chin; burdened with serious thought, his eyes became thin slits.

Chapter Twenty-Seven
SOMETIMES PRO'S CAN
LEARN FROM AMATEURS

Steam from the showers invaded the dressing area, which already buzzed like a swarm of frenetic bees. Josh and Roger's surprise visit had contributed to the festive atmosphere, but the bustle was primarily about the state tournament. Tomorrow, Woodrow Wilson would journey south on Interstate 35 to Austin for their first state play-off since the days of Ivan "Stormy" Weathers. Stormy sat by his locker, dressing slowly. Even in a high school locker room, he was still the last to leave.

"Tita."

Stormy glanced up to see the smirking puss of Po Po, his thick frame wrapped in extra large overalls. He wore his thin wet hair swept straight back, spotlighting his receding hairline. Throw in Po Po's ankle-high hiking boots and the catcher could have easily passed for Paul Bunyan's baby boy.

Po Po planted his right hand on his idol's shoulder. "Fifty, my one and only hero. How did you get those guys here?"

"No big deal."

Po Po moved close enough to whisper, but spoke in a normal volume. "Speaking of big deals, where's the magic wand?"

"I got rid of it."

Stormy had hidden the trick bat in the last place anyone would look, a closet crammed full of junk in Parker's office.

"Noooooo!" cried Po Po, glaring at his center fielder as if he suffered from an oxygen shortage to the brain.

"You don't need it. It's in your mind." Stormy's voice turned firm, his tone flat. "I was trying to make you think you had an advantage. It's all bullshit."

Like an old man, Po Po lowered himself wearily to the wooden bench running alongside the lockers. He tossed out a half-laugh, half-sigh.

"Great! State play-offs coming up and you go straight."

Stormy flashed a humorless smile.

"I can't take the credit for it. It was your buddy's idea first. He's not using the jelly anymore."

"Oh, man!" Po Po threw his hands above his head in frustration. "We're gonna get beat like a bunch of stepchildren." He buried his head in the palms of his hands and spoke to the floor. "We were so close. I can't believe it. Smitty's an amateur. Cripes! How did he talk you into this?"

"Sometimes the pros can learn from the amateurs."

Stormy's own words triggered an internal explosion which caused a mild body tremor. It all added up. Stormy had tried to show his new friends his way. Instead, he'd become the student. Baseball was just like life, he realized. Tainted victories come with an asterisk. And if everybody broke the rules, blocking "the right way" the way Josh blocked home plate, nobody wins.

So he really did possess a "new engine under the hood" but only because of a new soul, its growth enhanced by a bunch of amateurs. The two players sat together silently until Coach Parker's crisp bark snapped them to attention.

"Lucas!"

Parker and two men in dark suits stood beside them, all wearing severe frowns. During the last couple of days, Stormy thought he'd seen Coach Parker at his highest intensity level. Not so.

"My office. Five minutes!"

The three men walked purposefully from the dressing room.

Smitty approached his two friends.

"Hey, Cal, if those are more scouts, I wouldn't sign with their team. Those boys look mean!"

Cotton sat rigidly at his desk and digested written words that made him gasp. Cal Lucas was under investigation in the disappearance of Stormy Weathers! Authorities thought the school should know, especially since the teenager's guardian was nowhere to be found. It would be his decision to turn Cal over to juvenile authorities or keep him under his protective watch. The guys in the dark suits had granted him that much.

The coach's eyes drifted back to the report. His heart began to pound; his saliva tasted bitter, and his face went pale. The report stated Cal had recently visited the mission, thus violating Cotton's order. Was Cal stalking his daughter?

Cotton stared at the pages, buried in thought. Who was Cal Lucas? Cotton had contacted the New York school board, but no records of Cal existed. Stormy and Cal came from New York. Did they know each other? If so, as friends or enemies?

Parker's elbows sunk into his desktop; he buried his head in his hands. This felt like the day his wife died: one minute life was fine, but the next minute, things changed quicker than the Texas weather. A tentative knock on the office door caused his head to snap upright.

Stormy entered at the coach's command. Parker sounded down—defeated—and his complexion was like a TV that lost its color. He looked smaller and old. What could be wrong?

"Sit down," Cotton spoke in a coarse monotone.

Stormy took the seat in front of Coach Parker's desk. Parker's eyes darted to some papers on the desk.

"Cal, those two men were investigators with the FBI."

"What's to investigate?"

Cotton's hand went to his chin.

"For starters, they'd like to know how you came up with enough cash for a Porsche. The dealership contacted the police."

Stormy moved uneasily in his seat. He took small consolation in the fact that Parker appeared more worried than angry.

"Starters? There's more?"

"They're interested about a ride you might have had with a truck driver. He claims someone matching your description was soaking wet when he picked him up close to where Stormy's car was found in the lake." Parker wrapped his chin in his left hand and repeatedly tapped his index finger across his lips. "Cal, he says the hitchhiker told him he'd just put his car in the water."

A crack of thunder crashed inside Stormy's head. *This would be a first*, Stormy thought. A man's wanted for offing himself. His mind swirled out of control. He was mad, mad as hell at Mac—but also scared. Scared was ahead in the count.

"I guess it doesn't sound too good," Stormy said while clasping his hands together and staring contemplatively at his knuckles.

"Nope, big un, it doesn't sound very good, at all." Cotton's face became stern but uncertainty showed in his stare. "Furthermore, your Red Sox buddies just told the investigators that you must know something about Stormy's disappearance." The coach ran his hand across his face. "Stormy made a large cash withdrawal a few days before he disappeared. You pay cash for that high-dollar car. A car exactly like Stormy's car. You even told Reverend Al you're going to pay for his improvements at the mission."

Even the priest was turning him in, Stormy thought.

"Don't be too hard on Reverend Al," Cotton said. "I'm sure those FBI boys scared the water out of him."

Cotton shook his head.

"You're going to have to give the authorities some fingerprints and answer a few questions. If your prints are on the car and Stormy's body is in the lake, they'll have a strong case against you for murder or kidnapping or something."

Stormy shuddered at the thought of a prison sentence. *Think, man, think! You're good under pressure.* But Stormy's mind was frozen, his breath sporadic.

Cotton's sturdy frame leaned toward his humbled center fielder. "Are they going to find a body in that lake?"

"No, sir." Not Stormy Weathers' body, anyway.

"Would you care to shed a ray of light on the subject?" Cotton asked.

Cotton stared intently at Stormy and Stormy felt like he was being appraised.

"I wish I could, but my hands are kinda tied," Stormy replied, his voice less convincing than his eyes. "Coach, would you believe me if I said I know for a fact that Stormy's alive and well?"

"For some reason, I think I do—but where the heck is he?"

"He's incognito," Stormy said sheepishly.

"Incognito!" The coach came alive. "Is he in trouble with the law?"

"Not at all. He just wanted to start a new life."

"That makes no sense. Where did the money for your car come from?"

"I earned that money."

Cotton leaned back in his chair. He rubbed both hands firmly across the top of his flat top as if pushing back hair that clouded a view into the future.

"You didn't take the money from Stormy?"

"No, sir! Coach, believe me, Stormy's the last person I would hurt in any way."

"Big un, if you know where Stormy is, you better ask him to make an appearance. You also need to find your guardian, uh, what's his name?"

Coach Parker's eyes searched the report.

"Mac, Mac Swindell," Stormy said.

"Yea, well, have Mr. Swindell contact me. The authorities want him to know what's going on."

"Yes sir." An easy thing to say, but not so easy to do. Would Mac ever resurface, or would he just leave him stranded in this mess?

Parker stood, re-establishing his customary erect posture. The broadness of his shoulders and thick neck brought back his previous, commanding self. He walked around the desk to Cal.

"Come on, let's go. We gotta go to the police station so you can give them some prints. They're trying to locate Stormy's fingerprints, but so far, no luck finding any. You're my responsibility until further notice. I have to keep you in my sight, so you'll spend the night at my house. Is this going to come back to haunt me?"

"No way, Coach. Just make sure they let me play in the state play-offs," Stormy said. His legs were far less sturdy than his tone.

They started for the door but then Cotton stopped abruptly and turned to Cal. "We'll see about the play-offs, but with your current situation I think it's even more important you stay away from Susan."

"Yes, sir."

His heart was in his throat, and his mind raced. The investigation would uncover Stormy's fingerprints. In his early professional days, Boston police had taken his fingerprints after a barroom brawl. Would his old and new prints match? He stood beside Parker wondering what direction his life would take.

Coach Parker placed a fatherly arm around him and his warm touch raised Stormy's hopes. Maybe Woodrow could still win state. Then he could return to the big show. If he could only first slip out of Texas without going to jail.

Chapter Twenty-Eight
THE MOMENT OF TRUTH

Norma sat on her sofa, her bare feet curled under her. Studying the newspaper, she could no longer fool herself: Stormy was dead and there would be no chance for redemption. Stormy's disappearance, his large cash withdrawal, the car found in the lake—all confirmed her worst suspicions.

Norma lowered the newspaper. Why would Stormy come to Texas? Did he know where she lived and decide to visit? But only Mac would know that.

She read further: The *Dallas Morning News* has learned that local authorities are investigating a local teenager who may be linked to the baffling disappearance of ex-baseball star Stormy Weathers." The story went on to tell of the truck driver and the wet teenage hitchhiker. Norma peeled back the layers of memory: the day they met, Cal's hair was wet and his clothes a muddy mess.

The doorbell rang. Her heart pounded rapidly and her chest began to ache. As she approached the door, her thoughts began to crystallize. Mac really was back, having sucked Cal into his treacherous game: another young soul ruined by someone who dealt out more false promises than a lotto salesman. She had chosen badly before, but not this time, whatever the consequences. Her life and probably Stormy's were lost, but she still might save Cal. Norma opened the door.

"Can I come in?" Cal asked.

"I've been wanting to talk to you," Norma said.

She walked mechanically to her living area. Stormy shut the front door and followed. Norma sunk into the sofa.

"You keep saying Stormy's okay, but I don't think so. The newspaper stories don't sound good," she said, scarcely louder than a murmur.

Stormy sat beside her and noticed the newspaper on the couch. She must have been reading about his disappearance. So far, Cal's name had not appeared in the media. The procedures at the police station had pleasantly surprised him: local police had fingerprinted him with no questioning at all.

"I've only got a few minutes. I'm spending the night at Coach's house. We're going to Austin tomorrow morning for the state play-offs."

Stormy neglected to mention Coach Parker gave him one hour to pack his things and return, or Parker would notify proper channels that he was missing. He sighed heavily.

"Norma, Stormy's okay. Don't believe everything you read."

"You're involved in this somehow."

Norma wasn't buying this time. She clasped her hands together violently; her face was as pale as a new baseball.

"I feel it. It has something to do with that man, doesn't it?" Norma asked, trembling slightly as if her nerves were stretched to the center field wall.

"Who?" Stormy raised a quizzical eyebrow.

"Mac, that's who," came Norma's crisp pronouncement.

Nailed! Stormy's eyes widened and his jaw dropped. The words tumbled from his mouth, his voice choked.

"How did you know his name?"

"You really want to know?"

"Yes!"

"A long time ago, when I was very young, I got pregnant." Norma spoke slowly, as if by prolonging the confession she might inflict more punishment on herself. "I went to a home for unwed girls and had the baby."

"Who was the father?" Stormy asked, his voice weak, his eyes glued to the dark television across the room.

"Truthfully…" She paused. "I don't know. I hit a wild streak, too grown up for my own good." Norma sounded deeply ashamed. She sighed apologetically and raised her fragile shoulders.

"Anyway, the plan was to put the baby up for adoption, but…" Norma hesitated to compose herself. A tear slid down her cheek, dragging blush along for the ride.

Stormy desperately wanted to comfort her, but his body, refusing to cooperate, stayed put.

"After I gave birth and saw the baby, no way could I give him up." She spoke through tears. "But later, that's exactly what I did. I gave him up."

"Why?"

Stormy knew he asked the question only because he heard his voice. His throat felt hollow.

"He got sick, really sick."

"What was wrong?"

"Polio. The doctors thought he might die. At least be a cripple." Norma fought back more tears. "He had just turned six."

"You didn't get the child vaccinated?" Stormy struggled to comprehend. Surely a six-year-old would remember a bout with polio.

"I was so young and naive. I didn't have a clue." Norma bowed her head in shame. "I guess I never did. Anyway, Mac, seemed like such a nice guy. He said I would never have to worry about money, that he'd guarantee my little boy would get well." She hesitated again, and her voice lowered to a bitter pitch. "There was one catch. I had to give my child to an orphanage."

Stormy flinched and shut his eyes. His mind went blank; the incredible story confused him too much to think.

"Sounds really bad, huh? I remember telling Mac it didn't seem right." Norma threw her hands high in the air, like it was thirty-five years ago and she was pleading her case. "He told me not to worry. He said my God was forgiving, that God wouldn't mind. Old Mac was smooth." Her tone turned cynical. "He could sell ice to an Eskimo." Norma swallowed. "I was just a stupid kid."

Stormy grimaced with enough vigor to distort the muscles in his face. The serene rhythm of the ceiling fan provided the only noise in the room.

"How did you meet Mac?" Stormy finally asked.

"I can't remember." Norma looked guilty. "He was just one of several guys hanging around at that point in my life."

"So what happened?"

"I gave up my child, and he got well. At first, I thought I did the right thing, but I've been miserable ever since. Funny, Mac was so interested in our well-being." Norma hesitated. "But after my little boy was placed in the orphanage, Mac vanished. It was like he'd never existed, like I'd never had a child, like a bad dream, until…"

Norma's tired voice trailed off to nothing. Mother and son gazed at one another, neither sure what to say or do next.

"Why didn't you try to get your child back?"

"Oh, God, you don't know how many times I tried," Norma said, her voice eggshell fragile. "They wouldn't even let me see him. No telling what lies Mac told the orphanage about me. I just know they thought I was an unfit mother." Norma's head bent in disapproval. "He is one powerful and evil man; I'll tell you that."

How could he have so many different feelings at once? Stormy wondered.

Relief. Pity. Outrage. Gratitude. Confusion.

Poor thing, she'd lived in misery most of his life. But would he have been happier with his mother, even as a cripple? The idea horrified him: no big league ball. No baseball at all.

Mac had wrecked Norma's life, but had healed Stormy once, and now he'd given him a young strong body to replace the one he'd worn out. Why had Mac helped him, but hurt Norma? And why in the hell did he have to live in an orphanage to get well?

And why was she telling him all this? "Why are you telling me all this?"

Suddenly, Norma's eyes and tone suggested the intensity of someone fondling the switch to a nuclear arsenal. "Because if you're mixed up with him, he'll ruin your life. Do you hear me?"

Stormy snapped to attention. "Yes, ma'am."

"There's more," Norma said, her voice calm but her face dry and pale. "My child was Stormy Weathers, and Mac said if I ever told anybody that I would die."

Chapter Twenty-Nine
I'M BACK!

Norma lay on her sofa, her slight frame wrapped inside a blanket as dark as her disposition; her sad eyes locked on the wall that immortalized her son's baseball career. Though Cal had adamantly said otherwise, she knew Stormy was dead. Norma no longer feared death, even welcomed it as an escape from the guilt that had tormented her so long.

Norma hoped only to live long enough to know that Cal had eluded Mac's grasp. She knew too well the difficulty of severing ties with Mac Swindell.

The sound of the front door opening startled her. Cal? The bright glare of the full moon beamed on the guest in her doorway. Mac Swindell stepped from the dim light; the world's first male Chauvinist pig had returned to complete his business with Norma Weathers. Norma's belly rumbled, her heart fluttered and her lungs pleaded for air. Mac looked vicious. Maniacal.

His rumpled, baggy khaki's and puke-green round-collared shirt clashed magnificently with his two-tone brown and white wingtip shoes. He moved briskly into the living room to face Norma. His arms shot forth and he dropped to one knee, offering his best Al Jolson impression.

"I'm baaaaack!" he sang.

Norma sat up so fast it made her dizzy. One hand covered her mouth and the other fiercely gripped the edge of the couch. Jumping to her feet, the blanket fell to the floor; she raced to her bedroom, dove into her bed, and pulled the covers over her head. After what seemed an eternity, she slowly peeled back the bedspread. Mac sat on the bed beside her, grinning widely. A panicked scream erupted from Norma. She dove back under the covers.

"Hello, Norma," Mac said kindly, touching her shoulder.

"What do you want?" From under covers that moved from her trembles, her muffled voice sounded like it came from the bottom of a well.

"We made a deal. You've reneged. Now you have to pay the price," Mac said. "Your life."

150

He stretched out on the bed and laid beside her, crossing his legs and clasping his hands behind his head. His laughter imitated the Wicked Witch of the West.

"You made the wrong choice." More laughter. "Again."

Norma peeked out from under the bedspread.

"You knew I'd tell sooner or later."

"Yep."

"That's why you brought Cal here, next door. You knew he'd remind me of Stormy. That I'd fall for the kid and try to protect him."

"Yep."

"Why me? Why destroy my whole life?"

"Don't flatter yourself, Norma. Stormy's the one we wanted."

Norma raised her head to stare at him. Stormy was the object? What about her?

"Aw, I'll give credit where it's due," Mac said grudgingly. "You had that fabulous body and you were a damn good athlete yourself. Hard traits to find in a female in those days," he said, with slight respect. "But, if you hadn't strayed from the original plan, you would have saved yourself some grief."

"I, I don't understand," she stuttered.

"You were supposed to give the baby up at birth, remember?"

Norma stared from empty eyes, too scared to think.

"You still can't put the pieces together, can you?"

Paralyzed, Norma continued to stare.

"Women!" Mac dipped his chin and by rolling his eyes delivered a package of total and complete disdain. "Well, after you backed out on the adoption, I decided to study the kid for a while. But by the time he was five, we knew the kid had it. We wanted his soul, and we wanted to keep him around as long as possible." Mac smirked. "The public thinks he's a hero, but he's just another self-serving, egotistical bastard."

"Just like you!" Norma blurted angrily.

"Yep," he sneered. "Just like me. I picked you to breed an athlete. But how could I know you'd sleep around and jeopardize everything?"

Norma drew a deep breath. He'd sure had her number all those years ago. Strong body, weak spirit. She'd been okay till she met him, but he'd brought out all her weaknesses.

"I wish I'd just let the doctors do their best with his polio."

"What polio?" Mac said, dryly. "You brought that on the kid when you decided not to put him up for adoption. I needed him in a place that would prepare him for my purpose."

Norma sat rigidly. What was he saying?

"Actually, that might have been better for us." Mac stroked his chin. "Stormy remembers you. Remembers being thrown away, Norma. If we'd taken him at birth, he might not have felt so worthless." Mac laughed. "Stormy's determination to win at all costs is even greater this way. Thanks a lot, Norma. You really helped us out!"

She shook her head again, unable to take in what he was telling her.

"He wasn't even sick?" she asked numbly.

"Nope."

"Phony doctor's reports?"

"You're quick." Mac pushed his index finger against Norma's chest. "Only took you thirty-five years to figure it out! He didn't even have polio symptoms."

"What kind of person are you?" Norma asked. "Why would you do such a thing?"

"What kind of guy am I? I tell you truly, I sometimes lie," Mac answered smugly, his smile intact.

Screaming, Norma pounded Mac's chest.

"You bastard! You absolute, evil bastard!"

Laughing, Mac handcuffed Norma's wrists with his hands and stopped the attack.

"You probably did this with Hitler!" Norma said. "Charles Manson must be one of your pets!"

"Prince of a fellow, Chuckie. And Hitler—things would have worked even better but he threw a gasket and decided he was a field general." Slight remorse surfaced in Mac's sadistic tone.

Mac vanished, leaving behind the smell of cheap cologne. Norma's limbs briefly dangled in midair. Her pulse fluttered like a hummingbird wings and her mind retreated to a distant spring day. The sunny Saturday had started like many, with Norma and her small son playing baseball in her tiny front yard. Several men, including Mac, often strolled by to find Norma, usually clad in a tight skirt and v-neck cotton sweater that showcased her round rump and full breasts.

Stormy stood in the makeshift batter's box scuffing the dirt with his hightop black and white tennis shoes. Norma gingerly pitched a baseball, and Stormy swung his tiny bat like Babe, driving the ball to the base of a short wooden fence in the front yard. With the hurried agility of a two-legged deer, Norma ran to the dilapidated fence.

"You're hitting better every day!" she cried.

"Momma, I'm gonna play for the New York Yankees when I grow up, ain't I?"

Stormy stood, bat by his side, admiring his blast.

"You sure are, angel," Norma said, her tender eyes a clear gauge of her love.

"Momma, I'm gonna pitch to you now, okay?"

"Sure."

The two traded places, and the boy went into a perfect imitation of a major league pitcher. High-leg kick and all, young Stormy delivered his best fastball. Norma wanted desperately to laugh at the sight of her intense little man, but even at age six, Ivan Weathers considered playing baseball serious business.

Norma ripped the miniature bat at the offering; her swing foreshadowed the power and coordination that would later show in Stormy's swing. The ball soared past the giant pecan tree that shaded the front yard, and landed in the street, where it rolled under a rusty sedan.

"Wow!" Stormy blurted. "That was your best hit ever!"

Sprinting after the ball, he quickly dropped to the grass like a young soldier felled by sniper fire.

"My leg! My leg!" Stormy clutched his leg, writhing in pain. "Momma, help!"

Panicked, Norma dashed to her child and nestled him snugly to her body.

The peculiar hospital's stark gray waiting room was poorly lit, the walls bare as an outfield wall. Waiting for Mac's return, Norma sat dejectedly on the dark couch. Stormy's head lay in her lap. She stroked his somber face and murmured reassurance. His ball cap was still on his head. The room was heavy with the aroma of disinfectant but still, as if short of air.

Norma fought back tears. Mac had been in front of the house. He'd heard Stormy's cry and hurried them both to the closest hospital. After running their tests, the doctors had regretfully but emphatically said her son would never walk again. He might even die! The worst case of polio ever—how could this be? But Mac knew of a special place where they could make him well, but not without a terrible price.

Stormy gazed up at his mother's worried face, each exchanging tortured looks.

Norma trembled inside. He already worshipped the game of baseball. She would accept this strange place's even stranger offer. If the boy couldn't walk, in his mind, he would be the same as dead.

Mac entered the gloomy room. "You're all set," he said kindly. "He's been approved."

Norma's green eyes met Mac's briefly and then cut to the cold, gray floor. "Thank you. I guess."

Norma snapped to, returning from her journey to the past. She rolled onto her stomach and buried her face in the thick pillow. Norma often dreamed of that terrible day. When she first awakened, consciousness would temporarily bring relief to her, the nightmare over. But after the cobwebs cleared, it was no dream and her closest companion, depression, would return.

Mac had sentenced her to die. The heck with it—bring the Grim Reaper on.

Chapter Thirty
MAGNOLIA

Cotton scanned the evening newspaper from the oversized reclining chair in the center of his den. Pictures of his family covered much of the den's wood paneled walls. Susan led cheers wearing a red and gray Wildcat uniform cut above the knees. A younger Cotton Parker, dressed in his formal Marine uniform, stared at the camera hard enough to shatter the lens. There were photos of both sets of Susan's grandparents. Framed in dark walnut, a large color photograph of Cotton, his thick arms wrapped around his daughter and wife, hung above the pink brick fireplace; all three wore smiles as splendid as their Sunday duds. The branches of a huge oak hovered over them, dissecting the bright sun into separate streaks of orange; White Rock Lake's calm brown water loomed peacefully in the background.

Reminders of his wife's creativity also flourished on the den walls. Sewn in red pink letters and framed in narrow red wood was the promise: "Next week we've got to get organized." A small oil painting of an extended black family watching a country lake baptism hung to the right of the fireplace. Set against a rich blue backdrop, his wife had also painted a picture of Mary caressing a nude baby Jesus, with six men in bright colored robes kneeling at her feet. Another embroidered message in a patterned silver frame read, "A friend loveth at all times." Some days Cotton's eyes or mind or both would play tricks on him. Images of that hot, fatal day would trample his wife's artworks and march through his mind like his own battalion in Nam.

Susan and her long legs took up most of the peppermint stripped cotton sofa. An Andy Griffith rerun on TV held her entranced. Cotton expected his daughter identified with Sheriff Taylor's family, since no mother lived in that household, either.

Cotton's eyes, tapered and tight from strain, returned to the sports page. He felt a brief surge of pride as he read about his team's journey to Austin for the state tournament. No one gave Woodrow a chance; Houston Jefferson, returning to defend its state crown, had won three of the last five state tournaments. The school was overloaded with talented players; several would receive college scholarships. Cal could run circles around them all but he was only one player. Cotton shrugged. He'd pick Jefferson, too.

Another headline jarred the coach's entire nervous system: "Local High Schooler Under Investigation In Weathers' Disappearance." The front-page story in the Metropolitan section did not mention Cal's name. Cotton's heart sank. Where was Cal? He should have finished packing by now. If Cal went AWOL, not only would Cotton catch hell for letting the kid out of his sight, but Jefferson would bury his Wildcats like landfill waste.

Susan's bare feet streaked across the hardwood floor. Her dad, deeply absorbed in the newspaper, failed to hear the doorbell ring. *Please, Lord,* she begged, *let it be Cal!* She had forgiven him; besides, he'd never promised her a thing. What right did she have to be mad about another woman? What a mess! She wondered if her mother had ever seen her dad with another woman. Not likely. *Get a grip, girl*, she thought, grasping the doorknob. *It doesn't matter!* After the tournament, the pros would offer him a contract. He'd leave town—the best thing for her, and probably for him, too.

Susan ran a hand down her beige silk robe and fluffed her hair before she opened the door.

God! Cal looked as if he'd seen death itself! Eyes as sad as a hound's! His clothes were soiled and wrinkled, his hair poking out at odd angles. Staring, Susan now understood that she was in love.

"Dad said you were spending the night."

Seeing Susan's face was better than basking in a whirlpool after a perfect day at the plate. Stormy caught the fragrance of a fresh shower and sweet perfume. She was an angel: one from Heaven, not from the California ball team.

"Big un, is that you?"

Coach Parker's voice warned Stormy that he wasn't in heaven; if anything, the day had been from hell. Parker filled the doorway, standing next to his daughter.

"Come in this house. It's late." He sounded relieved.

Stormy followed the two into the den, where the family portrait hung above the fireplace. No problem in determining where Susan had inherited her looks; and it wasn't Coach Parker. The family looked happy, full of love. *Man, life can change on you in a hurry,* Stormy thought.

Parker cleared his throat and pointed to the couch.

"You'll sleep here." He turned to his daughter. "Susan Magnolia, time for bed. There's something I need to talk to Cal about."

Stormy fired a rapid muddled glance at Susan. She flashed back the brief, mischievous grin of a kid caught playing instead of doing her homework. Had Coach said "Susan Magnolia?"

"Something wrong?" Cotton asked, noticing Cal's confusion.

"Uh, no, Coach, I, uh, was just thinking—maybe I forgot my toothpaste."

"We've got plenty of toothpaste." Coach Parker approached his daughter and hugged her. On tiptoes, she kissed him on the forehead.

"See you in the morning," he said as she left the room.

"Have a seat, Cal." Coach Parker plopped onto the couch and Cal sat lightly beside him.

"Cal." Cotton tugged at his chin. "You can go to the play-offs if I'm responsible for you. It didn't hurt that your guardian clarified where the cash came from for your car."

They'd found Mac! Outwardly, Stormy remained composed, but his mind was aflame. *Think, man, think*! You can whip Mac and for good measure take on Houston Jefferson, then return to the big show. You can do it—maybe.

Parker put his warm hand on Stormy's arm.

"Why didn't you say it was an inheritance? Your guardian gave them documents to prove everything."

He studied Cal.

"You okay?"

"Sure, Coach. It's just been a hard day."

"It sure has."

"Uh, Coach, do you remember when you said you felt like a loser at times?"

"I do."

"Could you tell me when you most felt that way?"

Cotton exhaled strong enough to stir a breeze, then said, "You really want to know?"

"Yes."

"It was in Vietnam. My platoon was just a bunch of kids not much older than you. We're out on patrol one day and I needed a volunteer to go check out point. This kid steps forward who's eager to please because the day before I chewed him out good for doing nothing more than acting like a kid. Cuttin' up with his buddies, things like that. Anyway, he takes off down this dirt path."

Cotton gulped. Dew clouded his eyes.

"Machine-gun fire cut him up in little pieces."

No one moved or spoke. A chime clock finally shattered the thick silence. After eleven chimes, Stormy heard himself ask, "What'd you do?"

"I charged the nest. Knocked it out." Cotton's voice sounded too flat to pass for bragging; more like acceptance of a situation gone bad. "But you know what? Every time somebody else died that day, I felt like my won-lost record kept getting worse." Cotton took a deep breath. His eyes honed in on Stormy like radar. "I wouldn't have told just any kid that but you're sure as heck just not any kid."

Cotton stood, pointing to a pillow and a folded blanket at the other end of the sofa.

"Get some sleep, big un. See you in the morning."

Cotton turned off the overhead light as he left the den. In darkness, Stormy punched up his pillow and then stretched out on his makeshift bed. He pulled the blanket to his chin, clasped his hands behind his head, and stared at the dark ceiling in an attempt to recap his "hard day." Coach didn't know the half of it.

If not for Coach, he'd be in some juvenile center, held for questioning in his own disappearance. Stormy wanted to confide in the man, but how could he? He imagined the bewildered look on Parker's square face as he recounted his story of Mac's flaming thumb, a torn-down stadium in the sky, his recycled body, his long-lost mother and the death threat that hung over her. Even if he disregarded his future and told everything, he'd only wind up in an insane asylum.

Norma! What would happen to Norma? Stormy closed his eyes so tightly that white flashes danced before them. He had pleaded with Norma to go to Austin so he could keep an eye on her. But Norma had refused, as if she'd accepted defeat. Mac had gotten to her big time.

What a scumbag! The thought of Mac's words, "We're a lot alike," made Stormy's stomach cramp. He'd take any "unfair advantage" possible to defeat Mac Swindell. And without telling the secret, so he could stay young.

Stormy's mind craved rest but he fought off sleep the way he fought off a curveball on a 0-2 count. He struggled to control his feelings for Susan. A teenager! Parker would have a cow if he knew Stormy was closer to his age than his daughter's. Coach called her "Susan Magnolia." Were he and Susan poking fun at Stormy's long-abandoned search for Magnolia? Too tired to think, Stormy tumbled end over end through a dark opening in his mind and landed into a vision of his first encounter with his landlady. She'd said that Mac reserved the apartment in Cal's name last summer, months before Cal had met him. The bastard had planned the entire mess, setting him and Norma up! Stormy told himself to remember this when he awakened. Only in his dreams could Stormy admit that fear was creeping into his brain like an intruder into the night.

Cotton sat on the edge of his daughter's bed, tucking her under the covers as if she were still ten years old. Susan would leave for college soon. Oh, how he would miss her! The thought ate at the lining of his stomach, leaving a hollow feeling.

Cotton pulled the covers to her chin; he would relish every moment these last few months she lived at home.

"He won't hurt me, Dad," she said sleepily.

"Who? Cal?" His head motioned to the adjacent den. "Of course not! I wouldn't let him stay here if I thought otherwise."

"Daddy! That's not what I meant."

"Well, what did you mean?" Cotton stroked her soft brown hair.

"I mean, you know..." Her soft eyes avoided his. "My feelings, what I'm feeling inside."

Cotton had never discussed romantic love with her. After her late night visit to Cal's place, he had simply, but firmly told Susan to stay away; that Cal knew too much about life for her. But she obviously cared for him. Hell, despite everything, Cotton liked the youngster too.

"I know he's leaving soon," Susan said. "I just wanted you to know everything's okay."

"Sugar, we've already agreed his leaving was the best thing." Cotton continued to stroke her hair. "I mean, the kid's a hell of a ballplayer, but I'm not ready to take him in as a son-in-law." He paused for effect, grinning slightly. "Especially since his eligibility is almost up."

"Daddy!" She playfully pushed away her father's hand. "Seriously, I think he's changed. Did you see the look on his face tonight? He's worried, and it's not about Jefferson. I think something else happened today."

"Nope, it's not Jefferson." Cotton hesitated to catch his thought. "Susan, they think he knows something about Stormy Weathers's disappearance, and I do, too."

"It's more than that."

"You think so?" Cotton tilted his body toward her. "Like what?"

"I don't know," she replied slowly, her eyes small in thought. "But I think today he found out what's hurting him."

Cotton leaned back and sat upright. Susan was no longer a child; she was becoming a woman rich in wisdom and thoughtfulness. He bent forward and pulled her into a close embrace.

"I guess that makes him even with us," he whispered.

The remote control of Stormy's dream switched channels from Mac to J.J. singing a slow serenade.

"Whippoorwill singing, soft summer breeze
Makes me think of my baby
I left down in New Orleans
I left down in New Orleans."

Stormy heard the music, but saw no picture.
"Magnolia, you sweet dream, you drivin' me mad
Got to get back to you, babe,
You're the best I ever had."

The picture faded in: Susan Parker peered down with the presence of an angel, wearing the same robe she'd had on earlier in the evening.
"Whisper good morning so gently in my ear.
I'll come back to you, babe, so we can be near."

The stunning vision knelt down hopefully to whisper in his ear, hovering so near he could smell her pure feminine aroma. Their faces now close enough to touch Stormy inhaled her warm sweet breath.

"Cal," she whispered.

Holy shit! Stormy shot straight up. The music stopped. This dream seemed so real it was scary. His breath came in quick intervals. He blinked rapidly, almost violently, hoping the fog would clear from within. Susan sat beside him on the couch.

"I didn't mean to scare you. Are you okay?" she whispered.

Stormy lay still. His lips parted in an attempt to answer, but only air came out. He nodded slowly, staring hard.

Susan retrieved something from the floor and dangled it before Stormy's eyes.

"Headphones," she said. "I thought you might want to hear your favorite song for good luck before the big tournament." She motioned to a small jam box on the floor beside his bed. "I bought the tape. It's my middle name, Magnolia."

Slowly the haze lifted from Stormy's rattled mind. He had been listening to his favorite song under headphones. He glanced at his bare chest. At least he still had his pants on.

"I guess you're wondering why I didn't tell you Magnolia was my name?" Kneeling on the floor beside him, Susan rested her elbows on the sofa.

"It crossed my mind." Stormy's voice was husky.

"Dad always says to save your ammo for when you need it." Susan shrugged. "Tonight seems like a good night to tell you. No big deal, I guess, just a name, but after that day in your car, I thought you might find it interesting." She caught her breath. "Mom thought it was a corny name, but dad loved it."

Stormy ran his hand through his hair. It seemed like he and the coach had more in common all the time.

"What time is it?" Stormy asked, his heart finally starting to beat at a more comfortable pace.

"One AM." Susan's glance darted toward her father's bedroom. "Let's not wake Dad."

"Let's not."

Susan's chin rested on her clasped hands, and her upper body extended onto the couch. She looked up at Stormy with inviting eyes...so young, so innocent. If she really knew him, she wouldn't have spit to do with him. Susan Magnolia deserved a better man than he.

Doing the right thing could wear a man down, Stormy thought. He wanted to kiss Susan Magnolia Parker the way Elvis kissed his leading lady, but she was off limits. He sat rigid as a statue, not daring to move closer.

"I never thought I would see this day, you sleeping in our house." Susan turned her face to him, sounding amused. "I've got to admit, though, you look terrible."

"It hasn't been one of my better days."

"Dad says they're investigating you for some heavy stuff. He said something's not adding up, but he can't believe that you've hurt anybody on purpose."

"That's obvious or I wouldn't be in this house."

"That's just what he said." Susan smiled. "Boy how did you get those major leaguers to practice? It meant a lot to Dad."

Stormy coughed to hide a dry laugh. "Let's say I called in a favor."

"Dad thought you two were making progress, and now more trouble pops up. What's that baseball player's car doing in the lake?"

"I put it there." The reply was so quick it surprised even Stormy.

"I am him, and he is me, and we are both together," Stormy sang in his best imitation of John Lennon. "I am the Walrus." Susan leaned further onto the sofa and punched his stomach. "You're making fun of me," she said, frowning.

Stormy resisted temptation no longer. He dropped onto his stomach and tilted close to Susan. Her dark hair fell to her shoulders, framing her cover-girl face. *Say something, man!* Parker would pound his head with a stick of Hillerich and Bradsby if he saw them so close together.

"How's the mission doing?" It was all he could think to say.

Susan sat straight up, frowning more deeply. Stormy immediately regretted changing the subject to something so sobering to Susan.

"A new man came by this week." She sighed. "He was all bent, with an old beat-up hat and raggedy clothes. Unshaven, and so dirty I could smell him ten feet away. I wonder if he was ever young and happy?" she said wistfully. "Did he ever run and play in the park with friends? Do you ever think about things like that?"

Stormy shook his head. Of course not. For the last twenty years, all he'd cared about was whipping the Josh Howards of the world.

"He looked so broken and sad." Susan glanced up at the family portrait, barely visible in the dark. "I don't know if I'll ever make a difference, but I'd sure like to." Her tone barely supported the weight of her words. "Are you really going to be leaving soon?"

"I gotta feelin' I'm not gonna have much choice."

Stormy turned himself onto his side and rested his chin in his hand. Susan moved so close he could feel her heart beat. He looked and smelled like Josh after a day-night doubleheader, but here she was, nestled next to him. Susan cared for him, and for the life of him, Stormy couldn't understand why.

With Susan gazing so desirously into his eyes, Stormy could hardly focus on the problems at hand. He needed to find Mac but what would he do to the twerp after he found him? How long did Norma have? What if he failed to remain under the watchful eye of his coach? With his luck, the men in the dark suits would toss him in jail with some crazed pervert.

Susan moved even closer, and the touch of her lips startled him. His eyes widened, his head flinched. She slowly moved her arms until she gently held him close. Stormy's arms rose slowly to return the embrace, but he resisted the urge. No more broken promises to Coach Parker.

But, Lordy, did he want this girl! So beautiful, but so tough. Maybe if he'd met someone like her sooner, he wouldn't be in such a mess now.

Susan took the decision out of his hands. Kissing him, she moved onto the couch to lay beside him. Stormy wrapped her in his arms and drank deeply of her kisses, but they would only touch and kiss this night. Stormy would make sure of that. For once, he would do the right thing. He was in love.

Chapter Thirty-One
PRE-GAME

From high in the announcer's booth, television broadcaster Chuck Hansen's bushy head of silver hair waved incessantly. The high winds posed little problem to the hairless dome of Chuck's broadcast partner, Dale Murray.

Today's state tile game was televised throughout the state. The University of Texas in Austin provided their team's diamond for the tournament site. U.T.'s single-deck facility resembled an old minor league park; it seated close to eight thousand, with wooden seats extending well beyond both baselines. As at Reverchon, an overhang covered only the seats around home plate. Irregular bursts of wind pushed the smoky smell of hamburgers and hot dogs across the packed stands.

The old ballpark was unique in one way; it had no outfield fence. Austin is in the Hill Country, and a long embankment formed the outfield barrier. If an outfielder could climb the berm to catch a ball, more power to him. Fans often sat at the top of this grassy mound; only Babe Ruth's most prodigious shot could clear the natural obstacle, which was fifteen feet high at some points.

Norma still lay on her stomach on her living room couch, listlessly watching the television broadcast of the big game. A blue, cotton robe hung loosely to her body. Her hair was stringy. Her body reeked. Dark half-circles lay beneath her bloodshot eyes. She hadn't bathed or eaten since Cal left three days ago. Norma suspected it was the bottom of the ninth for her. Hansen and Murray emphatically stated that the strange weather posed a greater threat to Houston Jefferson than the upstart Woodrow Wildcats. Blustery winds and dark clouds existed solely near the baseball stadium. The rest of the city enjoyed a beautiful late spring day. Norma feared the worst. Mac must be at the ballpark spoiling even its weather.

As Hansen and Murray critiqued the participants' strengths and weaknesses, the cameras scanned the playing field and stands. Jefferson's and

Woodrow's bands performed along the first and third base sides, adding to the electric atmosphere. Norma managed a vacant, detached smile at the sight of Susan and the other cheerleaders enthusiastically conducting cheers to the vocal Woodrow supporters. The commentator's next words made her head spin.

"Today's drama is intensified by the rumor that Cal Lucas, Woodrow Wilson's spectacular star player, is currently under investigation in the disappearance of the ex-major leaguer, Stormy Weathers," said Chuck Hansen in his distinctive baritone voice. "Lucas, a transfer from New York, has no record of having played high school ball, which makes the situation even more bizarre."

The weight of Hansen's words pressed Norma's head heavily to the sofa.

Cotton sat anxiously in Woodrow's third base dugout jotting down his lineup. He stopped scribbling and gazed up at the black sky. What strange weather: one minute windy as hell, and the next, the air's frozen. The peculiar conditions increased the game's tension, which suited him fine; a moment like this might never come his way again.

He wanted to lead his players well today. He wanted to stand victorious and with honor after this season, a sensation he'd never felt in his life.

Cotton stared across the park and watched the Jefferson players warm up. Bigger and stronger than the Wildcats, they wore serious expressions: not intimated, as he suspected some of his players were, but all business. Hell, even Jefferson's duds were intimidating. Accompanied by dark, high-crowned wool hats, Houston's white with black pinstripe threads fit like fine imported suits. By comparison, Woodrow's uniforms, seemingly supersized, dwarfed Cotton's players.

Cotton smiled proudly as his players went through their own warmup. Most played catch. A few participated in pepper, a pre-game ritual in which a batter tapped the ball lightly to three or four fielders. Smitty's uniform swallowed him whole; the wear and tear of pitching all season had probably caused him to shrink, reasoned Cotton. A tear in the butt of Po Po's pants exposed red gym shorts. Only Cal's uniform fit impeccably.

Cotton's eyes darted to the first base side, honing in on two Jefferson players: Pete "Sluggo" Williams and Jose "Speedy" Gonzalez. Built like an oversized fire hydrant, Sluggo stood tall in shallow right field taking powerful practice swings with a bat the size of a tree trunk. Nearby, his lean, wispy teammate stretched his rapid legs.

Woodrow needed to keep the ball in the park when Sluggo batted who had the power of Mantle but the speed of a wounded turtle; if Woodrow kept Sluggo to the base paths, only a homer would score him. Speedy was just the opposite: even Josh would have a hard time keeping Speedy from stealing. Woodrow had to keep Speedy *off* the bases—a difficult task, since his on-base percentage was higher than Po Po after his night on the town.

Could Woodrow win? An army of ants would receive better odds on dragging a loaf of bread uphill. Still, he had Cal. Playing like his life was on the line, Cal had won the three previous qualifying state-tournament games almost unaided. Woodrow had a chance. Coach Parker felt it in his soul.

Stormy stood by the Wildcat's dugout mildly fanning the air with practice swings. The desire to win burned as much as ever, but he also felt the sobriety of his last day as a Yankee. He would return to the big leagues as a youngster with promise, or he could go to prison for the disappearance of himself.

If only he could figure out a way to save Norma! He'd called her last night, but her voice was weak, as if she spoke from the bottom of a well. An unpleasant idea jolted Stormy so severely, he hit himself in the back with the baseball bat. Whatever happened—whether he was in pro ball or in jail or back in his old body—life with Susan Magnolia would cease to exist. "Big un, are you okay?"

In his trance, Stormy had failed to notice Coach Parker's approach.

"Yes, sir. I'm fine."

After a moment, Cotton leaned close.

"My daughter thinks you have more problems than we know, as if what we're aware of isn't enough. Is that true?"

Stormy's eyes found Susan who led cheers near home plate. Man, this girl could see through mud. Whoever married her had better not stray; she'd read the unfaithfulness on his face easier than a pitcher reads the catcher's signal.

"Yes, sir."

"Is there anything I can do?"

"No, sir."

Parker's hand rested reassuringly on Stormy's shoulder. "Few monsters warrant our fear we have of them," he said. "A French writer said that a long time ago. Big un, best I can tell, it still applies." Woodrow's sociology teacher walked away to inspect the rest of his troops preparing for battle.

"Hello, Cal." Mac's voice came without notice and carried a tone that Stormy hadn't heard before. "Or do you prefer Stormy?"

Stormy felt a cold frost suddenly ushering itself into the ballpark. Mac stood on the opposite side of the railing that separated the playing field from the stands. He wore a brown tweed suit with a starched, white, round-collared shirt and a derby hat. Stormy walked toward him until only the divider separated them. Nuclear darts had replaced Mac's eyes and his deceptive grin had become a sneer.

"Why, Stormy, you look rather upset," he said derisively. "You should be thankful I helped you out with the matter of your car. It's keeping the authorities off your back long enough to play in this tournament." Brushing an imaginary speck off his lapel, he fixed Stormy with a malignant glare. "Wait till they run down a set of your old fingerprints. That'll throw the investigation into a tizzy!"

Mac's laughter perfectly replicated machine-gun tatter. Stormy's face flushed in anger.

"Scumbag!" he barked.

"I take it you've had a chat with Norma. Nasty consequences for her, you know." Mock sorrow poisoned Mac's voice.

"Fifty! Mr. Swindell!"

Po Po eagerly lumbered toward them with a bat in his hand. How did Po Po know Mac? Stormy wondered.

"Hey, fifty! Mr. Swindell gave me back the bat!" Po Po happily waved the magic wand. "Can you believe it? Just in time, huh?"

"Just your basic unfair advantage." Mac shrugged. His old, affable smirk stretched across his face.

Stormy turned on him.

"We're gonna talk about this after the game!"

Po Po backed away in shock as Stormy jerked the bat from his hands and stormed into the Wildcat's dugout. Po Po followed. "What's the matter, fifty? You look royally pissed off!"

With one violent swing, Stormy smashed the illegal bat on the concrete dugout floor. Splintered wood and cork exploded from the bat like candy from a piñata.

Cotton and the rest of the team rushed to the scene. Po Po stared in silence as Stormy held what remained of the bat. His eyes searched for Mac, but he had vanished quicker than a magician's stagehand.

"Clean this mess up." Cotton waved to his equipment manager while he stared intently at the debris on the dugout floor.

Cotton then made the trek toward home plate, where the umpires waited for the starting lineups. The rest of the team dispersed; only Smitty and Po Po stood beside Cal.

"Smitty, old buddy, old pal." Po Po broke the awkward silence, tugging at his gray ball pants. He thrust his chest outward. "I was just telling my good friend Cal how I wished we would get rid of that bat once and for all."

Minutes later, Coach Parker's players huddled around him, tense and eager. Cotton removed his Wildcat ball cap and ran his hand through his stubbled hair. He rubbed the back of his neck. Though his eyes showed the moment's seriousness, their expression was warm and comforting.

"Men, I've never gotten this close, either, so my stomach is tied in knots just like yours. Just give it your best shot. Don't worry about losing, or you'll play like crap. If we give a hundred percent, we win no matter what the score. Win or lose, it's a great day in our lives. Relish it, savor every second, taste it like a fine meal. It might never happen again."

Stormy took a mental snapshot of every face in the huddle. They were focused beyond even his expectations. Coach Parker extended his right hand, palm down, to the center of the huddle. "When the game's over, I want you to leave everything you've got on the field. That's all I ask. Let's have some fun and kick some tail!"

Sixteen hands immediately piled onto Coach Parker's in unison; the players let out a yell loud enough to rattle bats in the dugout.

Stormy was pleased with the results of Coach's short speech, although he wasn't sure why Coach threw in the part about the "fine meal." A fine meal to these guys meant a hamburger at The Lakewood Cafe, a twenty-four-hour greasy spoon that had opened shortly after Texas' war with Mexico.

Chapter Thirty-Two
THE GAME

Po Po stood defiantly at home plate, this defiance camouflaging the doubt leaking from the corner of his eyes. He rolled his tongue around the corners of his mouth and coiled his bat high above his head as if holding a conduit to heaven and divine assistance. He'd played before football crowds almost this large, but burying his helmet in the opponent's mid-section a few times would bury the jitters as well. But he couldn't hit anyone now, only the ball—and even that, not very well. Po Po had produced only one swinging bunt in the three previous play-off games.

Teeth clenched, Po Po ripped at the pitch but only fanned a breeze for the ump and opposing catcher. It hardly seemed fair, Cal changing the rules in the middle of the game. What was so wrong with a trick bat? Shoot, everybody scrambled for an advantage, didn't they?

The sound of cowhide meeting wood shocked him back to attention, but it was only a weak pop-up to short, the last out of the first inning. With his head hanging as low as his confidence, Po Po retreated to the dugout. Strapping on his shin guards, he mumbled cuss words toward the bat rack, as if the missing bat was his roadmap to big league stardom.

"Stay up, bro," Cal said, patting Po Po's rear. His tone was as intense as his eyes. "It's still zip zip. We're gonna need you before this game's over."

Po Po gave a short respectful nod and watched Cal gallop to his position. With a play-off performance so embarrassing, Po Po thought he might as well die. Cal seemed focused as never before, a human hand grenade certified combat ready. Po Po hoped he would not let his hero down.

Smitty leaned down from the pitcher's mound in search of Po Po's signal. After two singles and a walk, Jefferson had the bases loaded. Though all eyes in the packed stadium were locked on him, Smitty still felt more alone than an abandoned child. To make matters worse, the crowd was so loud he could barely hear himself think. As he stretched into his windup, a gust of wind nearly

169

blew him off the mound. Times like this made Smitty wish that he'd shit-canned sports and focused on his studies and position as class president.

Whack! The ball raced past Smitty's head, nearly taking one of his ears along for the ride. Jefferson's runner on third loped toward home; waving both arms in the air, he took in the scene in the manner of a haughty conqueror.

Okay, Smitty thought. *So the bastard's scoring the first run of the game. Big deal! But don't gloat about it.*

Stormy charged the low line drive, scooped the ball on one brief hop, and rifled it toward home. The ball zoomed, soared, darted and arrived on the third base side of the plate.

Po Po raced up the third base line and punched air with his round mitt to snag the throw. He slap-tagged the unsuspecting runner with enough force to knock him to the ground and then dropped to his knees, obstructing passage to home plate; Woodrow's catcher braced himself for the human fireplug barreling toward him. The runner dove head first but Po Po denied passage the way a windshield denies a bug for the third out. Woodrow supporters in the third base stands erupted into a wild sea of joy as Jefferson fans on the opposite side gasped in stunned disbelief. Jefferson's shell-shocked runners dejectedly walked toward their dugout, avoiding their teammates' eyes.

Coach Parker sprinted to home plate and embraced Po Po. Jefferson still had not scored after two and a half-innings. Making his way to the dugout, Stormy smiled for the first time since the tournament began.

By the top of the fourth, Woodrow led one to nothing, courtesy of Cal's monster home run, but the lead was in more jeopardy than Po Po's high school diploma. After Speedy Gonzalez legged out an infield hit, Sluggo Williams prepared to take the batter's box.

Smitty took a deep breath and the smell of diamond dust stirred an unsettling thought in his mind. If he pitched around Sluggo, Speedy would steal second, then third. If he pitched close to the plate, the big slugger might knock it past the grassy knoll.

Smitty was sweating hardballs, and over half the contest remained. Could he last? His heart told him yes, but his head said otherwise. His next pitch meandered slow as cane syrup to home plate. Sluggo, his neck and forearms corded with muscle, ripped at the pitch.

Splat!

Stormy drifted under the towering fly ball. Perched on first base, Speedy prepared to tag. Stormy pulled his glove back, and the ball crashed to earth, practically burying itself in the thick grass. Stormy rapidly retrieved the ball and fired it to second. Now forced to advance, a wide-eyed Gonzales sped toward the base, but the second sacker met him with the ball. In disgust, Speedy kicked up a cloud of dust. Spitting out specs of ruffled dirt from his mouth and wrinkling his nose, he made the long, embarrassing journey to the dugout.

Stormy smiled for the second time. Sluggo, the lead foot, stood on first.

Before the crowd noise died down, the next Jefferson batter blasted a shot directly at Smitty. The ball smashed Smitty's right big toe and then trickled toward second base. Smitty's toe went numb, but he managed to hobble off the mound and in one sweeping motion, shovel the ball to second with his bare hand; the toss forced Sluggo for the third out.

"Where did you learn that play?" Smitty asked from his seat beside Stormy in the dugout. "I thought Gonzalez was gonna bust out crying!"

Grinning, Stormy shrugged.

Smitty cackled as if someone passed a silent joke. "Don't tell me. Hanging out at Yankee Stadium." Smitty laughed louder than before. "You sure fooled him. I'll bet he'll never make that mistake again!"

"Don't bet on it," Stormy replied. "If Gonzalez is on base next time the big boy bats, throw him a couple of fastballs outside the strike zone. Then goose one over the plate so slow it looks like a balloon."

"Huh?"

"Sluggo's over-swinging. A major league pitcher in the forties used the balloon ball a couple of times to take advantage of overeager hitters. It won't work but a time or two. Besides…" Stormy paused, allowing his proposal time to simmer amid the tension, then continued, "You got any better ideas?"

"Okay. I'll do it."

From the top of his dugout steps, Parker peeked up at the rolling dark clouds which had taken over the sky. In mid-afternoon, a groundskeeper had already turned on the stadium lights, which cast long shadows across the outfield grass. An increasingly urgent wind stirred school pennants and swayed the lights, threatening a storm. Nearby, the city of Austin still basked in sunshine.

The umpire's shout, "ball four!" jarred Cotton's attention back to the game. Smitty had walked Gonzalez; the fleet runner made his way to first base, all but licking his lips like the fox who'd found a chicken farm.

"No foolin' him again," Cotton mumbled to nobody.

"Stick a fork in 'im. He's done," a Jefferson player yelled from his dugout in reference to Smitty.

171

With the score tied at one each in the top of the sixth, Cotton closely examined his tenacious, young pitcher. He limped from the earlier line drive, and sweat drenched his forehead. Smitty was running on fumes. Sluggo Williams approached the plate and Cotton feared the worst.

Jefferson's power hitter pawed his cleats into the batter's box. Ball one, outside. Cotton buried his hands in his back pockets. Jefferson had pounded the ball hard all day, but Woodrow's one hit had been Cal's homer. Only superlative defensive play, mostly by Cal, had kept the game close. Ball two in the dirt.

Parker's eyes widened as Smitty delivered a rainbow pitch so slow it was a wonder it reached home plate at all. Sluggo attacked the pitch with enough force to screw himself into the soft dirt at home plate. Whack!

Cal stood as still as the outfield monuments in Yankee Stadium. He folded his arms at his chest while his eyes locked on Gonzalez who was taking root on first base. The ball descended lazily from the now motionless sky, a perfect white against black, but Cal didn't seem to care.

Apparently reconsidering the situation, Gonzalez suddenly broke for second with mercurial speed. Speedy reached the bag safely and thrust his chest proudly forward. Cal extended his glove and snagged the ball just before it could touch the ground. Gonzalez gasped for air, threw it in reverse and hurried back toward first base. Cal's throw beat Gonzalez by a step to complete the double play and the third out. Gonzalez dropped limply to the ground and held his head in his hands.

Gloom fell over the Jefferson crowd while the Woodrow fans roared. Woodrow's center fielder smiled for the third time.

"Where the hell did he learn that?" Cotton said.

Smitty's head tilted back against the concrete dugout wall. Po Po and Stormy flanked him.

Smitty's forehead looked like he'd been rooting with pigs; his sweat housed a deluge of infield dirt, leaving a reddish paste on his face and neck. His breath arrived in weary intervals.

Po Po resembled an unmade bed. His sweaty, soiled jersey hung loosely on his heavy frame. One shoelace was untied. A huge wad of gum rolled furiously in his thick jaws. He held his cap in his lap, exposing thin hair that pointed in every direction.

Even Cal displayed signs of strain, but only in his most intense eyes, which now watched the playing field.

"Hey, fifty?" Po Po snorted in Smitty's direction.

"What?"

"How long we been friends?"

"Since kindergarten." Smitty's eyes looked off and he felt a surge of nostalgia from Po Po's question. "Long time." He sighed heavily, and smiled. "Long time."

"Long enough to know we're in trouble if you don't use the KY I've got in my bag," Po Po said louder than Smitty would have liked. Po Po leaned close to Smitty, to keep him from avoiding eye contact and lowered his voice an octave. "Lather that sucker up. Fifty, you got nothin'! Only a few minor miracles have kept us in the game."

The veins in Po Po's neck started to rise, and he dimpled Smitty's chest firmly with his index finger. His words came as fast as explosive bursts of fire from a burp gun.

"Grease it down, man, three up and three down." Po Po demonstrated with his fingers, applying imaginary goop to an imaginary ball. "Cal gets us a run in the bottom half. Game's over, we're done, out of here, we get scholarships. State champs. What do you think?"

Smitty gulped. He was the weak link, the stumbling block to the coveted title. No doubt. Boy it'd be nice for that sinker to dance the jitterbug the last inning. What's the big deal with a little jelly?

But Coach Parker's words, often repeated, came crashing in like giant waves assaulting a beach. "If you'll cheat on the little things in life, you'll cheat on the big ones." Smitty drew away from Po Po as if his deceitfulness was contagious and sighed heavily. Feeling more irritated than tempted by such a misguided request, he pitched his lips into a thin line of resolve.

"No," Smitty said after an eternal pause.

Po Po pursed his mouth and rotated his lips as if swishing mouthwash. He snorted a stiff gust of air through his nostrils.

"No, of course not," he said, jamming his cap on his head so fiercely that it hid his eyes and his ears stuck out like Dumbo's. "I was just kidding. You got these guys just where you want 'em." Shoulders slumped he scowled at the floor.

The Woodrow batter grounded out for the last out of the sixth inning. Wrestling with self-doubt, Stormy had almost suggested Smitty take the advantage but had resisted the temptation. Just the other day Coach Parker had said, "So much of the sports world has become a world of hedged values, lack of commitment, and short cuts." Stormy stood. Change had to start somewhere.

"Let's get 'em, guys," he said and headed toward center field.

Woodrow needed only one more round of miracles in the field. In the bottom of the seventh, he'd hit another homer to win the state title that Cotton Parker deserved, the state title he blew over twenty years ago with a sissy slide. He assumed his position in center field, but a painful pressure pierced his chest. Hitting the homer was the easy part. Mac presented the real test.

Susan Magnolia sat in the first-row bleachers directly behind the Wildcats' dugout. She was falling more helplessly in love with Cal the more spectacularly he performed and she felt guilty about it. Did she love him because Cal might deliver something so important to her father, or because she suspected they shared the same type of pain, a similar loss? She feared more than fear itself that she might never learn the whole truth about him. Immediately after the tournament, he would leave Woodrow. Her dad already prepared her for that.

Chapter Thirty-Three
THE FINAL INNING

Stormy surveyed his precarious situation: men on first and second, courtesy of two walks. Restlessness preoccupied the base runners—too restless in fact; their eyes keyed on the base paths below them, as if they contained valuable secrets. Stormy broke rapidly toward the infield.

"They're going!" he yelled, sensing the double steal. *Dumb strategy,* he thought, considering Smitty's effectiveness was fading faster than a cheap shirt.

Smitty heard Stormy's warning during his windup and, thinking quick as a class president, pitched out to Po Po. The catcher leaped to his feet and fired a no arc strike to third so hard that his catcher's mask flew off. The knee-high throw arrived in time for Twiggy to nab the headfirst slide of the Jefferson base runner. Pumping his fist, Po Po flashed a warrior's victorious smile. One out. With a rooster's strut, Po Po approached the mound and faced his battery mate.

"How'd you do that?" Smitty yelled over the deafening crowd noise. "That's the best throw you've ever made."

Po Po's eyes scanned the stands. The fans were standing, hollering at the top of their lungs. Riding the high of his last peg, Po Po loved the attention and it showed.

"I pretended I was Josh Howard," he confessed.

"Whatever, the guy's coaching must've worked," Smitty said. He wore the look of a child who longed for his parents.

"Well, I'm just your coachable kind of guy." Po Po sounded cockier with every word. His eyes scaled Smitty from hat to shoes. "You look like shit."

Smitty removed his ball cap and wiped his crimson sleeve across his forehead; sweat saturated the cotton material, turning it dark red.

"I'm trying to use my professional pitching lesson, too, but right now I'm having trouble remembering everything."

Po Po glanced at the Jefferson runner on second base. "Yeah. Well, try to remember, 'cause there's only one out and a man on second. You're throwing grapefruits and they been knockin' the snot out of the ball all day."

Suddenly, Coach Parker arrived at the mound; his breath came in mini-puffs.

"If you think it looks bad from over there, Coach." Po Po motioned to the Woodrow dugout with his look. "You oughta be out here."

Smitty rolled his eyes in frustration.

"Look, Smitty, give it all you've got. That's all anybody can ask." Cotton patted his pitcher on the rear, then faced Po Po. "Nice play back there Po, uh, Lawrence," he said.

As if Po Po needed to burp, Cotton slapped his catcher firmly on the shoulder.

While Smitty's heart pounded with anxiety, he watched Cotton retreat to his dugout and Po Po lumber back to home.

Smitty pitched the next ball with such effort he stumbled off the mound. The crack of the bat hurt like a broken bone. Smitty looked up to see the ball dart into the outfield at warp speed. *No way anybody's going to get that ball,* he thought. It's outta here. Like me.

Stormy broke instantly for the soaring shot in left center field. Ordinarily, he would never reach the ball in time, but he'd shaded toward left field, fully aware that a right-handed hitter would pull Smitty's tired fastball.

Stormy had the field to himself; the left fielder, Henderson, was nowhere near. As if vaulted by a hidden trampoline, Stormy soared into space. Successfully lunging at the ball with his bare hand, his deflection caused it to hang in midair. Stormy fell on his side with such a heavy thud, it briefly knocked the breath out of him. Undaunted, he reached up and snagged the ball in time.

The crowd hushed, not sure what they had witnessed. Stormy lay motionless; his face pointed to the midnight black sky. Slowly his glove hand rose to the clouds, triumphantly waving his mitt for all to see. Woodrow's crowd exploded with joy, while the Jefferson fans stifled gasps.

The teams exchanged sides and Woodrow's first two hitters made outs so quickly, Stormy barely had time to grab his bat from the bat rack. Strolling from the on-deck circle to home plate, he battled invading desperation. Woodrow was down to their last out unless the game went into extra innings, a decided advantage for Jefferson. Houston had another pitcher as good as the starter prepared to take the game as far as necessary. Woodrow Wilson had only Smitty, and Smitty was toast.

Short of the batter's box, Stormy noticed Mac at the top of the stands, towering above the crowd. He looked ten feet tall, with ice in his eyes. Stormy started to avoid Mac's evil gaze, but changed his mind: he would back down to Mac the way he would back down to an inside fastball which is to say not at all. The two exchanged smiles as false as a starlet's bosom and Stormy stepped to the plate.

The first offering drifted so far outside that Stormy doubted the Jefferson catcher could even slow down the pitch, much less catch it. The sight of the catcher standing beside home plate with the ball briefly stunned Stormy. Where was his head? With no runner on first base, of course, Jefferson would walk him! Po Po batted next, and he couldn't hit with a sack full of bats. The second pitch arrived, also far outside, for ball two. *Think, man, think!*

Stormy let ball three pass while he held the bat low at his side; his posture clearly suggested no reason to prepare for the pitch. He couldn't remember if it was Willie Mays, Ted Williams, or who, but somebody had once successfully lunged at a pitch out.

Houston's hurler delivered and Stormy knew his strategy had succeeded. The sight of Stormy, his bat uncocked, had lulled the pitcher into complacency. Ball four strayed outside the strike zone, but not far enough. Stormy coiled his bat and lunged at the pitch with a ferocious swing. From the sound alone, Stormy thought he'd hit the hardest ball of his life. When it sailed far over the green berm, his suspicion become fact.

The air had been still, but suddenly the wind roared to life stronger than ever, its howl hanging over the field. The ball slowly returned into play. Stormy's blast stopped in midair and dropped harmlessly to the turf in shallow center field. Disbelief flowed off Stormy's face as he arrived safely at second base.

His angry eyes found Mac, who still loomed at the top of the stands. Mac fired a scornful glance. Stormy delivered the game winner, but had Mac used the wind to return the ball in play? Why would Mac care who won the game?

An uneasy feeling spread through the stadium. The wind and the crowd became equally still.

Po Po trudged toward the plate feeling a crushing burden. Cal had hit a sure homer. The game should be over, but now it was all on him.

"Hey, Poophead."

Po Po's head shot around to see Smitty, who had limped out of the dugout to the on-deck circle.

"You wanna hit for me?" Po Po asked sheepishly.

"Shoot, no!" Smitty said. "You can do it. Remember what that Red Sox player said: if you can see the ball, it must be a good pitch to hit. If you can't see it, don't swing."

"Smitty, if it's that easy, how come you're hittin' a buck twenty for the year?"

"Hell, I don't know," he blurted. "Just shut your eyes and swing."

Smitty retreated to his dugout in the knick of time. The umpire's impatient glare said more than any words.

"Play Ball!"

The heck with it, Po Po thought. Like Coach said, they gave it their best shot. Who wanted to go to college, anyway? He and Smitty would work at the Dr. Pepper plant on Mockingbird. At lunch, they'd walk across the street to Campisi's for the best pizza in Dallas. Life wouldn't be so bad.

Stormy took a big lead off second base. If by some miracle Po Po delivered a base hit, he could score. Strangely, Stormy felt nervous. His anxiety was not for himself, but for Po Po, Smitty and, especially, Coach Parker. As he slipped further and further off second base, a thought slipped into his mind: Who was his dad? Was he anything like Cotton Parker?

Stormy crouched low enough to touch dirt with both hands. His forearms rested on his thighs and his fingers jiggled fast enough to play the boogie woogie.

"Come on, Po Po!" he yelled.

Jefferson's second baseman stared at Stormy like his fly was open.

"Friends can call him shit for short," Stormy explained, his tone not cynical but totally deadpan.

The first pitch traveled to home plate. Stormy gawked in shocked disbelief as Po Po swung with his eyes closed. At the crack of the bat, Stormy dashed forward, heading for home.

The soft Texas leaguer drifted barely beyond the second baseman's outstretched glove and fell safely in shallow center field. Coach Parker furiously waved Stormy home from the third base coach's box. As Stormy's foot caught the inner portion of third base and he thundered toward home, Parker turned his back to the plate.

Houston's catcher, a formidable hunk of granite, blocked the plate and prepared for a violent collision. Everyone in the stadium knew Cal Lucas would not shy from contact at the plate, and Stormy knew from his own scouting that this catcher appreciated a little contact himself. Stormy also understood that the Jefferson center fielder possessed a stronger arm than any he'd met in high school; the incoming throw would probably beat him to the plate. The ball bounced once and landed in the oversized catcher's mitt. The catcher's eyes bulged wildly as Stormy blazed on a path for his chest with the ferocity of a runaway train. And then it happened. Stormy dropped gracefully to the dirt on his right side, expertly curled his body, and executed a textbook hook slide. Specks of dust fluttered in the air around home plate. Stormy's left foot barely touched the outer part of the plate. There was no contact at all!

"Safe!" The umpire's nose hovered less than two inches from Stormy's outstretched shoe, his arms spread wide in baseball's favorite signal for the base runner.

At that precise instant, a peaceful shower started to fall from the sky. The players froze and looked to the sky, a small band of ball-cap bills catching light raindrops. Black clouds opened to reveal a beautiful rainbow stretching from left to right field.

Coach Parker wore the expression of a terminal patient who'd just received a clean bill of health. Then the Woodrow players rushed wildly to the infield and piled on home plate. From underneath, Stormy managed a grin. Jefferson's players stood together in shocked disappointment observing the festivities.

The sight pierced Stormy to the heart. "How can you laugh when you know I'm down?" The tune played in his head—like his last game at Yankee Stadium. But he was the winner now, redeemed from his only athletic failure. What did he have to feel bad about? He was on his way back to the majors! Peering out from under the pile, Stormy searched the stadium in vain for Mac.

He crawled undetected from under the celebrating heap. His eyes finally found Mac who watched, expressionless, from high atop the stands. Mac slowly back-pedaled, but he never took his eyes off Stormy. Stormy hopped the railing and began to vault the stadium steps three and four at a time.

"Cal! Cal Lucas!"

Stormy never hesitated. The familiar voice could only be a delusion.

"Lucas! Stop!"

Shit! It was no hallucination! Stormy wheeled to face a sight he could not believe. Doc Rivers, the old Yankee clubhouse man, enthusiastically moved toward him.

"Doc? What are you doing here?" Stormy wanted to kiss him. "I'm a Yankee scout." Doc said, panting hard enough to sail a boat. Still dressed in solid white, Doc didn't look like a scout; he looked like a clubhouse manager. "Used to be a clubhouse manager with the Yankees, but the damn music in the locker room drove me crazy." Doc abruptly stopped talking and his face wrinkled in suspicion. He pulled the ever-present cigar butt from his mouth. "Hey, how did you know my name?"

"It's a long story. Sorry, Doc, I gotta go," Stormy said, and took off after Mac. He stopped when Doc called after him once more.

"Hey, kid, I hear you may know something about what happened to Stormy." Stormy gave no answer. "Okay, kid, just tell me this. Is he okay? He was a friend of mine, and I miss the crusty buzzard."

"He's okay, Doc," Stormy answered, while he pivoted for a quick exit.

"You know, Stormy Weathers was out on darn near the same play in his state championship game," Doc offered.

"Yeah, I know," said Stormy. "It was a shitty slide."

And Stormy took off, sprinting up the stadium steps.

In seconds, Stormy reached the top of the stadium. Mac back-pedaled in short, tentative steps.

The thought and action happened simultaneously. Stormy dove for Mac's foot. Stormy and Mac tumbled to the concrete floor directly beneath a concession stand. A large plastic container of mustard burst on impact with the pavement, and the fresh scent of mustard wafted through the air. Passing spectators stopped paralyzed in their tracks to see Woodrow's star player wrestling with the strangely dressed man.

Stormy quickly and easily straddled Mac's chest. Mac offered little resistance, but flashed a poisonous smile. Stormy drew his powerful right fist back; his nostrils flared with a prizefighter's fury. Mac would probably vanish before taking much punishment. In the interim, Stormy might deliver a few choice pops.

With his clenched fist on a downward spiral for Mac's skull, Stormy pulled his punch. The events of the last few months had produced a divide in Stormy's inner self. The break was unrepairable, center field-wide, preventing Stormy from returning to the other side. Only minutes before, he had bypassed the opportunity to blast the Jefferson catcher and now he was doing the same with Mac.

"Why me? Why? Why Norma?" Stormy said, stammering with frustration.

Mac's smile broadened, as if mocking the questions.

"I've already explained this to your mother," he said, his eyes and tone cold as opening day in Chicago.

"Leave her alone."

Mac shrugged. "She knew the rules."

"You knew Cal would remind her of me," Stormy said.

"Yep."

"To protect Cal from you, she'd eventually tell."

"Yep."

"I hope you don't mind, Stormy, going back to your hometown," Stormy said, mimicking Mac's tone. His voice hardened. "It was a setup, all part of your plan to ruin our lives."

"If you say so. Norma's not important, just a domino. But why get technical at this point in the game?"

"Why did you stop my home run? What did that have to do with anything?" The thwarted homer confused Stormy more than anything else. By Mac's own admission, Stormy's success enhanced Mac's cause. "What an asshole."

"That's no way to talk to your father," Mac said.

A pained expression overtook Stormy as if clubbed from behind. His mind raced toward panic faster than he raced around the bases.

"Okay, so best I can tell, it's about a one-in-four chance," Mac continued flippantly. "One for four won't win any batting title, but it's still better odds than that peter-pulling idiot teammate of yours had of driving in the winning run, and look what he did."

Stormy's body teetered on the edge of convulsions. Stormy thought of opposing catchers who had tried to rile him with negative chatter, hoping to sucker him into swinging at a bad pitch. *Control yourself. Don't swing at a bad pitch.*

Stormy studied Mac. A wide smirk consumed Mac's now confident face. A bolt of lighting in Stormy's head revealed the missing piece of the puzzle.

"You didn't stop that home run. You don't have control of me anymore," he announced.

Mac's smirk collapsed, terminating the gleam in his eyes. His body shrank. The grin of a man who just delivered the game-winning hit covered Stormy's face.

"Asshole," Stormy said. "I think you and I may be able to cut a deal."

It was the first time that Mac had looked at Stormy with anything resembling fear. He squirmed and kicked, but Stormy held him down. Sighing heavily, Mac finally shut his eyes and lay still, a technique evidently borrowed from little children playing hide-n-seek.

Jefferson's coach, Billy McCarthy, a tiny man with a considerable reputation, approached Cotton. McCarthy's large ears perfectly matched his huge nose. On this disappointing day, he still moved with the boundless energy of a man much younger than his fifty years.

"Coach Parker!" The Jefferson coach's voice sounded so deep Cotton wondered how it came from such a small man. "Nice job," McCarthy said, extending his hand for the congratulatory handshake.

"Thank you, Coach," Cotton replied, dew forming in his eyes.

Cotton felt he should apologize for his players gloating. Po Po first lay on his side and ran in circles while slapping his face in a Three-Stooges imitation and uttering indecipherable sounds.

"Don't worry about it," said McCarthy, recognizing Cotton's concern. "Your kids deserve it. Besides, some of my guys can learn from this." McCarthy glanced to his team. "Bad as I hate to say it, it's time my bunch experienced the downside. Life's not always so kind. The real winners in this world often are the ones who learn how to bounce back from defeat."

Emotion so overwhelmed Cotton he could only nod.

"I just have one question," McCarthy said with narrowed eyes. He spoke slowly while tugging on his chin. "Who in the hell is that kid you got in center field?"

Cotton Parker's heart suddenly sank to his toes; he saw the two dark suited investigators approaching, and they looked serious.

"Coach, where's Lucas?" one said. "We found some of Stormy Weather's fingerprints."

"Yeah. Hold onto your shorts," the other added. "They match Lucas's."

The announcement sent shock waves through Cotton's body. He shook his head, more in frustration than anything else. How could Cal and Stormy have the same prints?

Where in the world was Cal? He wondered, scanning the area. And where was Susan?

Chapter Thirty-Four
CAL'S LAST RIDE

Stormy skated out of control in the stadium parking lot. Metal baseball cleats served well for a natural surface, but not for asphalt during a light rain. He frantically attempted to enter several parked cars, but all were locked.

Everybody in the parking lot recognized him and, thanks to the media, many knew of the investigation, too. One of the Jefferson fans would probably call the cops.

"Cal, what's wrong?"

Stormy slammed on the brakes but skidded several feet before stopping, leaving behind a trail of tiny electric sparks. Susan, her face the shade of red in her cheerleading uniform, raced toward him; her breath came in heavy surges.

"I need to get to Dallas in a hurry," Stormy said. "Do you have your car?"

"Sure. Let's go."

Susan sped north on Interstate 35 at seventy miles per hour. Cal still had not uttered one word. His anxiety clouded the car's interior, his concern far too conspicuous to hide by mere silence.

"Cal, what on earth's going on?" she asked, unable to further endure the thick silence. "You haven't allowed yourself to enjoy the victory for one minute!"

"Norma's sick, and I need to check on her."

She glanced away from the road to see his fists clenched; worry beaded his brow. *Cal didn't have a soul in the world to count on,* she thought. *Life must be scary for him.*

"Cal, do you believe in God?"

"Don't know. Hadn't thought about it much. Do you?"

"I must."

"Why's that?"

"Because every time I need help or get worried about something, I pray."

"Just like that, you pray for help?"

"Uh, huh. I prayed for Po Po to get that hit, too."

"You're kiddin," Stormy said. "You're something. I'll tell you that for sure." Stormy paused for a moment. "Susan Magnolia."

She turned to him, smiling. Cal had used her middle name, his favorite. It sounded great.

"If you don't mind, why don't you just pray to your God that Norma's okay?"

"Of course," Susan answered gently. It was the last words spoken for several minutes.

"Cal! Earth to Cal!"

Stormy was looking away with a stare vacant enough to trap his mind in a dark hole.

"Cal!"

He jolted to attention like a kid caught daydreaming in class.

"Mac's not really your legal guardian, is he?"

Stormy did not reply, but she saw the answer plainly inscribed on his face.

"Cal, I know you have your reasons for not telling me everything, and that's okay. But you're not going to jail. The truth will come out. You didn't harm Stormy Weathers."

Susan Magnolia hesitated, and her eyes clouded.

"You're going to leave us, though, aren't you? You're going to play pro ball, and I'll never see you again. Why do you think I disobeyed my dad and gave you a ride? Four hours alone with you is all I'll ever have!"

Stormy, now staring at road stripes, stayed mute.

In Waco, Susan stopped for gas and both used the restroom. Cal already sat front seat shotgun when Susan returned and started the engine. The car eased onto the interstate.

Their relationship reminded Susan of a lit fuse, rapidly burning to an end. Her dread of losing him fought her fear of never learning the truth.

"Cal, I wasn't sure about your reasons for getting back to Dallas, but you look so concerned, I believe you now. Dad's right; you've really changed."

Susan turned to Cal, hoping to change his dark mood. She saw a change far more significant.

An older man with a ruggedly handsome face now occupied front seat shotgun! Grey ran thru his thick head of hair like white lightening in a dark cloud. He needed a shave; specs of white there too. Incredibly, he wore a

Woodrow Wilson Wildcat baseball uniform. Though squinting slightly, the man stared calmly ahead. Susan slammed on the brakes, and the car fish-tailed along the empty highway until it lurched to a halt, smothered in its own exhaust.

Stormy expected the time of reckoning had arrived when the road signs started to blur. The shrill noise from Susan's mouth reinforced that suspicion. It sounded like a night animal startled by the Texas sun.

Susan looked catatonic behind the wheel. He touched his knee; the son-of-a-bitch ached. He leaned slowly toward the rear-view mirror to avoid startling Susan and checked himself out.

Stormy, not Cal, stared back. He tilted his head upward. Even the gray nose hair was back and, yep, a few strands of hair sprouted from his ears. Hell, no wonder Susan was in shock.

"Well, you said yourself I was changing," he said, smiling. The smile came easily, naturally. Ever since Stormy cut the deal with Mac, when and if this moment came, he wondered how he'd react. To his great surprise, he felt more like a winner than any time in his life.

But the truth soon beaned Stormy squarely between the eyes. He was old, or at least too old for Susan. His heart sank below his injured knee. Just when he thought he'd turned the corner, life had jumped up and bit him in the ass.

"Susan Magnolia, this is going to take a little explaining."

The incredible tale seeped slowly into Susans' dazed mind. This man had Cal's same mannerisms and inflections in his voice. Stormy Weather and Cal Lucas were the same! The middle-aged man spoke kindly, but directly; he said sadly that their age difference must end their brief relationship. Susan accepted the news calmly but hidden tears trickled down the inside of her face, dragging her youth along for company.

Chapter Thirty-Five
WHO ARE YOU?

After three rings, Norma still had not answered her doorbell. From outside her door, Stormy and Susan could hear only a muffled TV news broadcast of another nightly crisis. Norma's yellow Volkswagen was in the parking lot, quiet and still as a monument on wheels. She must be home.

Stormy kicked the door open to see Norma lying motionless, her face pressed sideways against the living room floor and her mouth half-open. Stormy darted to her side, dropped to the floor, and laid her head in his lap. Susan stood beside them, shaking from concern.

"Norma! Norma!" Stormy cried. "Wake up!" If Mac had double-crossed him, Stormy vowed revenge.

Norma's eyes barely opened, revealing thin slices of shame. "Susan? Is that you?" she asked, her words barely audible as if working her tongue was as hard as knowing that Mac once duped her into abandoning her son.

"Who are you?" Norma asked Stormy, her eyes piercing, but not judgmental.

Stormy's glance flew around the room before landing on the wall that served as a shrine to himself.

"Uh, would you believe I'm the guy whose pictures are plastered on your wall?"

Norma glared briefly at him. She turned to Susan.

"Is this a joke?" she demanded. "Susan, where's Cal? Is he all right?"

"It's me, Stormy." He almost added "your son," but his jaws locked against the words.

Norma cocked her head, squinting one eye toward Stormy. Though her face remained intense, her look suddenly turned maternal. Norma's expression revealed more than she could ever say or think or feel about missing her son. She stared long enough for Stormy to bat twice in the same inning. No one spoke. Finally, her hand reached out to cup the back of Stormy's head and gently pull it down to rest on her bosom. Tenderness was the blanket that covered the room. At first, Norma sobbed softly, but then her tears rushed like the Guadalupe River after a hard rain. She cried and cried, then cried some more because she held her son for the first time in thirty-five years.

Susan watched the emotional reunion with both sadness and joy. In this mother and child reunion, Norma's gain was Susan's loss.

The three sat on Norma's couch talking and laughing, ignoring the TV news. Stormy, still wearing his baseball uniform, was sandwiched between the two most important females in his life. Only hours ago, life's burdens weighed on his spirit, but now he felt as if he were floating.

Tomorrow he would address the darker side of his current predicament such as his nonexistent baseball career and his impossible love for Susan Magnolia Parker. Also he would leave behind the people he'd learned from and grown attached to, his new and only family.

Susan's voice shattered his brief trance. "You should have seen Cal, uh, Stormy-whoever-chasing that man. The guy wanted no part of Stormy!" Susan spoke rapidly, except her mouth hiccupped every time she said, "Stormy."

"Mac? Nooo! How wonderful!" Norma cried. "But how did you talk him out of my uh, sentence?"

"Easy," said Stormy, eyeing both of his listeners. "I figured he couldn't use me in his so-called recycle program anymore. He no longer had control over me and I wasn't doing him any good. You see." Stormy paused for effect. "Primarily, Mac's a businessman, and businessmen cut their losses and move on. So," Stormy hesitated again, "I just offered him a trade. My youth for your pardon."

Stormy looked at his folded hands. Norma picked at her wrinkled clothes and at her tousled hair. Susan cleared her throat.

"You gave up your chance for all that fame and fortune for someone who deserted you." Norma's voice was distant. "Why?"

"By telling Cal what happened, you had sacrificed your life. You didn't know it was me; you were just trying to save some kid. You showed me how to do something that's so often not easy—the right thing; I decided to do the same."

No one moved; no one spoke. With no place to go, all eyes stared at the television. Then Stormy's picture appeared on the screen, riveting their attention to the newscast.

"Dallas Woodrow Wilson defeated Houston Jefferson earlier today in Austin for the school's first-ever state baseball title. Woodrow's victory was clouded, however, by the disappearance of Cal Lucas, who is currently under investigation in the disappearance of the ex-Yankee Star, Stormy Weathers. Ironically Weathers, a Woodrow alum, was a member of the only other Woodrow state finalist team. That Wildcat team lost to—you guessed it— Houston Jefferson."

Before anyone in the room could comment, the doorbell rang. It was an ominous ring, worrisome in tone.

Norma went to the door. "Who is it?" she called.

"FBI. Can we visit with you for just a minute?"

Stormy hurriedly left the room. Norma cracked open the door and saw two stoic-looking, flat-topped gentlemen in matching dark suits. Though the sun had set hours ago, the men wore sunglasses. "May I help you?"

"Ma'am, we're looking for your neighbor, Cal Lucas. Have you seen him?" said the larger of the two.

Stormy cringed. No problem to show himself, but how the hell could he produce Cal now? *Don't swing at a bad pitch; stay calm.*

"The last time I saw Cal was a few days ago, the night before he left for Austin to play in the state tournament. Is he in any trouble?" Norma asked. Her false concern managed to muffle the alarm in her voice.

A loud crash, followed by Stormy's "Ouch!" came from the bedroom.

Everyone bolted to attention, their eyes round.

"Ma'am, I'm going to have to ask if we can look around," the smaller man said stiffly.

"That won't be necessary," Stormy announced; he hobbled into full view but now wore only a pair of blue gym shorts and a Yankee T-shirt. He approached the two baffled investigators still standing in the doorway.

"I forgot about this bad knee," he blurted.

The son-of-a-bitchin' knee had deflated on him like a punctured tire. No problem going down, but getting up was another matter altogether.

"Are—are you Stormy Weathers?" asked the bigger investigator.

"Yeah. Who are you?"

Looking at the duo, Stormy's initial thought of "Dragnet" quickly yielded to Laurel and Hardy.

"I'm Special Agent Crandall and this is Special Agent Adcock," said the smaller man. "You're not dead?"

"Not that I can tell. Come in, guys. Sit down."

The men entered. After the proper introductions, everyone except Norma sat down. Another matter concerned Stormy's mother. On the bedroom floor, partly visible from the living area, lay Stormy's Woodrow Wilson jersey. She stood in the doorway between the two rooms trying to hide it.

Susan occupied a chair beside the sofa, where the three men sat. Noticing Norma's mission, she valiantly attempted to mask her alarm.

Stormy broke the silence for the befuddled men.

"I'm gonna make this quick and simple." His voice took on the presence of a top government official. "The kid's a friend of mine from New York; he hung around the stadium a lot. I had some unfinished business here," he said, his eyes shading to Norma. "He came along with me. Helluva ballplayer, huh? Taught him everything he knows."

Stormy smiled internally at the irony of it all. For he had learned from Cal and at least, Cal had the good sense to learn from somebody.

"Anyway, we put my car in the water and the rest is history."

"Why did you disappear?" Crandall asked.

"My career was over. No other skills; worse yet, no other interests. I felt like a nobody, invisible. When the car accidentally dumped in the water, I told Cal to go on, that I would just lay low for awhile." Stormy stared down both men. "You guys leaned on him so much, I had to resurface and bail him out."

"Where is he now?"

"Does it matter? He's done nothing illegal; you've found me. So why don't you guys go tell whoever is in charge here to forget it. No harm, no foul. Otherwise, I'll hire the kid a lawyer. I think we have one hell of a harassment case."

"Eventually, we're going to need to talk to him," Crandall said damn near apologetically.

"Eventually, maybe you can."

"But what about the fingerprints?" Adcock inquired nervously. "Yours and Cal's matched."

Magnolia and Norma's heads both involuntarily flinched. Stormy crossed his arms and propped his feet on the coffee table. "Maybe you should tell your superiors that you've solved the case. That Cal and I are the same." Stormy smiled.

Susan's face flushed and she expelled air with a soft hiss. Norma still stood to conceal the jersey, but her legs wobbled as though nudged from behind.

The investigators reserved such a reverent focus on Stormy that they failed to notice Norma and Susan. Crandall stood first, and Adcock followed.

"Yeah, I think this baby's over," said Crandall.

Adcock exhaled heavily and tugged on his belt buckle.

(Susan Magnolia wondered if Crandall's bullet was safely secure in his front shirt pocket.)

Crandall slowly walked toward the jersey.

"What's that?"

Stormy, Susan and Norma fired panicky glances at each other.

Abruptly, Crandall stopped and stared at the wall that displayed Stormy's athletic accomplishments.

"Nice career," he said, his hands clasped behind his back. "My boy's in the third grade. It'd make his day if I brought home an autograph."

Crandall withdrew a pad from his hip pocket and looked at Stormy. Stormy took the pad.

"What's his name?"

"Ben."

"Your son probably wants a younger player's autograph, but here it is, anyway." Stormy scribbled on the paper and returned the pad to Crandall.

Some avid fans would always appreciate his athletic deeds, Stormy thought, as he had with Dimaggio or Williams or Musial, but most would move on to the new phenom. Far better to gain his self-worth from a family of some sort, than from the superficial attention of fans.

The men thanked him and left. Norma and Susan breathed a heavy sigh. Stormy flashed the warmest smile of his life.

"Best defense is a good offense," he announced triumphantly.

Chapter Thirty-Six
GOODBYE

Cotton Parker peered out at all his players except one. Dressed in casual school clothing, the team huddled together on the first two rows of the gymnasium stands. Woodrow's victory had cast away the monkey of defeat from Parker to torment some other undeserving soul but one of those spooky Austin clouds must have followed the Wildcats back to Dallas.

The main spoke in the wheel had fallen off. Sometimes Cotton wondered if he'd dreamed everything about Cal. Repeated efforts to uncover Cal's school records had come up empty. Today, Cal proved equally invisible.

Cotton found it not only peculiar, but also sad that Cal left before saying goodbye to his coach and team. The rejection stung Cotton like one of those jungle insects from Nam; surely, the team had felt the same way. Parker struggled most with this: no reason existed for Cal to skip town. Stormy Weathers was okay, his appearance was the talk of the morning KLIF Radio sports segment. Cotton Parker cleared his throat.

"Men." His voice rattled in the near empty gym. "Other than my marriage and the birth of my daughter, this is the proudest day of my life." Cotton rocked on the balls of his feet; he kept his hands clasped together behind his back. "We've accomplished something no other team in the history of this proud school has ever done." Cotton paused. Truth was, he'd have given Custer better odds at Little Big Horn.

Cotton tugged on his shirt collar. Inside the non air-conditioned gym, the warm air barely moved. "I wish I could tell you more about Cal, but…"

Cotton suddenly felt his team's eyes staring right through him. He wheeled around to see a middle-aged man. Wire-rim glasses rested on top of his moderately pointed nose; he wore a neatly pressed sport shirt and slacks.

"May I help you?" Cotton asked.

The broad-shouldered visitor carried his weight as effortlessly as if carrying a warmup jacket. Although he walked with a slight hobble, he managed to move with a dancer's grace. A jock or ex-jock. A drift of cologne hinted of a fresh shave.

"Yes, sir, my name's Stormy Weathers. Cal Lucas asked me to stop by."

At first, Cotton stared right through Stormy. Then his deadpan expression turned all smiles.

"I heard this morning you were alive. Uh, I mean in town."

"Do you mind if I say a few words to the team on Cal's behalf?" Stormy's smile, though warm, seemed uncertain.

"Of course! Be my guest." Cotton stepped aside, relinquishing center stage. His spirits lifted. Cal hadn't forgotten them.

Stormy gazed at his ex-teammates. Smitty and Po Po sat together and Stormy wanted to join them, but he forced that notion aside. It seemed like he'd known these people longer than a few months: more like a lifetime. In a way, this was true; he had known them for all of Cal's lifetime.

"Cal asked me to say goodbye to you guys."

Stormy gulped. From the forlorn look on the player's faces, this revelation was as difficult for them as it was for him.

"He's doing great, so don't worry. He's going back north." Stormy took a deep breath. "Cal learned a lot from me over the years, and I just wanted to say most of it was crap."

The unexpected remark jolted his audience like a rock-n-roll band in church. Stormy caught Cotton's eyes and gave the coach a reassuring look.

"Let me tell you the real scoop on baseball," Stormy said, struggling to control his emotions. "The real players play for the respect of their teammates and their opponents. The real players have no respect for the cheaters. Hitters that use juiced-up bats, the pitchers that doctor the ball. The guys that intentionally try to hurt another player. There are too many bean balls. If a pitcher can't get a guy out with his best stuff, he shouldn't be in the game."

Afraid of making a fool of himself Stormy skeptically watched the team's reaction, but no one's mouth moved or eyes blinked. He decided to take his lesson to the next level.

"I didn't teach Cal any better when it came to women. Treat them like you want to be treated, and you'll be okay."

Stormy wasn't sure how or why he'd fallen short with women, but he knew this: he wouldn't want his daughter dating a Stormy Weathers. At least, not in his previous incarnation.

"Cal also wanted me to tell you guys how much he enjoyed the camaraderie and the purity of the competition, the unity that it brings."

Stormy looked directly at Smitty and Po Po. He wanted them to remember Cal as their friend. Both looked up, their eyebrows furrowed with confusion. Po Po and Smitty were one step closer to manhood, thought Stormy, forced to recognize that life was not perfect nor always understandable.

"The state title isn't the proof of a successful season. The commitment to excellence; that's what it's all about," he added.

Coach Parker nodded.

"Someone's got to lose, but that doesn't make him a loser. Only the ones that don't try are the losers." Stormy's voice strengthened slightly as if building to a crescendo. "This is no dress rehearsal, on or off the field. There's no promise of a wake-up call in this world, so always give it your best shot."

He paused again, analyzing the silent faces in front of him. They were listening. He could influence young people, even teach them. Like Parker. Stormy abruptly knew what he would do with the rest of his life. He would coach.

"Thanks for the time," Stormy said solemnly. "See you around."

Parker's applause broke the thick silence but he clapped in an unusually slow and mechanical rhythm. Gradually his applause took on a more normal cadence until all the players followed, and applause filled the gym. Mist filled Stormy's eyes as he studied his audience. This sounded as good as any ovation he had ever received in a major league stadium.

He quickly approached Coach Parker.

"Coach, uh, you know Cal didn't know his dad, but he told me he sure would have been proud to have had one like you."

Before the startled coach could respond, Stormy hobbled away. Smitty and Po Po huddled together near the bleachers.

"Hey, guys, you must be Smitty and Po Po," Stormy said. Both boys grinned as if they'd just won college scholarships.

"Smitty Pierce." Smitty and Stormy shook hands.

"Po Po Bonkers," announced Po Po, offering his hand. "Friends can call me shit for short."

"I guess graduation is in a few days," Stormy said, feeling better already. The boys nodded.

"Is Cal coming back for graduation?" Smitty asked hopefully.

Stormy shook his head. "I'm afraid his attitude toward school is another bad habit he picked up from me."

"We're sure gonna miss him," Smitty said.

"Are your college plans rounding into shape?" Stormy asked.

"No, sir," Smitty answered. "No college for us. Our parents are busted. We're planning on applying for jobs at the Dr. Pepper plant."

"E," Po Po grunted.

"That means yes," Smitty added.

"I know," Stormy said automatically. "Listen, think positive. Maybe those scholarships will come through."

"I doubt it, sir," Smitty said. "Neither one of us exactly sizzled in Austin. Cal's the only reason we won."

"E," grunted Po Po.

Stormy jabbed Smitty firmly in the chest with his index finger and repeated the gesture with Po Po. "Start getting ready for college boys; the scholarships will come." He strode out of the gym, leaving the two boys bewildered.

He stopped suddenly in the doorway, almost colliding with Susan Magnolia Parker. The two looked deep into each other's eyes, both seeing a gaze riddled with misery. Stormy's head told him to flee, but his heart and eyes wanted to stay and stare at her beautiful face for eternity. *Get out of here, man, before you make a fool of yourself!* He offered a smile weaker than the swing of a number nine batter and trudged out the gymnasium door.

Stormy opened the driver's door of the black Porsche parked in front of Woodrow Wilson. A distressed voice called his name and he turned to see Susan Magnolia sprinting toward him. Her brown hair bounced around her face, concealing her expression. Stormy knew what her expression was anyway. But nothing could interfere with her radiance, not even the sadness that ravaged her heart and mind.

"I know it's you," Susan said, her head practically touching Stormy's chin. "I can feel it inside."

Stormy's eyes darted to the front entrance of the red brick school. What if Parker had followed his daughter? How would Stormy explain that only tiny pockets of air separated them?

"I know it was hard, giving up your youth," Susan continued. "That's why Mac picked you. He never thought you'd do it. But you did the right thing. Don't you see? Come back for me, please."

But how could that be the right thing?—to come back for a teenager, lamented Stormy.

"You're too young." Stormy stared at the ground, unable to look into her eyes.

"Not for long," Susan said desperately.

"I'll die before you're fifty. Then what?" If he didn't leave soon, he might die of heartache right on the spot. "It's just less than perfect circumstances, to say the least," sighed Stormy. He stood rigidly, as if holding his breath.

"My mother was blown away by someone she was trying to help. She died before she was fifty! It's less than a perfect world, wouldn't you say!"

Stormy saw anger in the tears in her eyes.

Susan spoke slowly and deliberately."I'll take the years we can have together. I want to be with you for as long as we can have."

Feeling stranded between the base paths, Stormy's instinct to flee battled desperately the urge to hold Susan. A yellow taxi pulled up beside the Porsche and Stormy motioned to the driver with his eyes. He retrieved a large suitcase from his car and entered the cab.

From the back seat, he gazed sadly through the closed window.

"I'm sorry, Susan Magnolia," he said softly.

She could only read his lips, but she knew what he'd said. The taxi pulled away, leaving his car at the curb. Susan approached it apprehensively, but immediately spotted an envelope with her name scribbled on it taped to the steering wheel. She opened it to find a note wrapped around a key.

"Susan Magnolia, the title's in the glove box," it said. "I didn't want you walking in the rain. You'll probably sell it and give the money to the mission, but that's okay. Stormy."

Susan Magnolia Parker managed a grin of no kin to happiness. She had lost at the game of love and would never feel the same.

Chapter Thirty-Seven
LIFE APART

The cabin air smelled of processed food. Over the headphones, some aging rock group was assassinating an old Beatles tune, but Stormy felt too weary to change the channel. From his window seat, the Texas sunlight glowed brightly enough to make him squint. Thinking of Susan, his insides felt as empty as the desolate prairie below. Stormy's rookie season in the game of romantic love was a bummer Stormy decided, generating all the satisfaction of a last place finish.

At JFK, Stormy, quickly recognized, easily caught a cab and arrived home less than an hour after his plane arrived. Nothing had changed except the weather; he had left a cold New York City, but now beads of sweat marked his forehead and arms. Was it possible he'd been gone for only a few months, just one school semester? The months felt like years.

The doorbell rang before Stormy could unpack his suitcase. He found Jaynie standing in his entranceway, the steady stream of city traffic grumbling behind her. She looked as hot as the weather. If she wore her black miniskirt one inch shorter…well, why bother to wear one at all? High-heeled sandals raised her face to Stormy's eye level. Her moist lips were pink and enticing. She wore an inviting perfume that made Stormy's heart beat faster.

"You look fabulous," Stormy said sincerely.

"You look different," Jaynie answered. She smiled a close-lipped, symmetrical smile. "I mean, you look great, but you look different." (Jaynie's hungry green eyes traveled the entire length of his strong body. *Slacks instead of blue jeans?* thought Jaynie. *No sandpaper beard? Shiny new Cordovan loafers vs. tennis shoes?* A peaceful acceptance glowed in Stormy's brown eyes, replacing the quiet, controlled fury of before. What's next—Stormy in Sunday school?)

"It's all over the news that you're alive. At least you could have called to say you were all right," she said, a blend of hurt and irritation in her voice.

"It's kind of a long story," Stormy replied while lifting his shoulders.

"If you ask me in, you can tell me about it," said Jaynie, her hopeful glance darting to the interior of Stormy's dwelling.

Stormy cleared his throat. "I don't think you should come in."

Stormy's words drove Jaynie back like an inside fastball. "Is it another woman?"

"Hmmm," Stormy pondered a second then answered, "No." "Not a woman. A girl," he said internally.

A blind man could see the hurt on Jaynie's face. It was his legacy to present and past friends, Stormy decided.

"You want me to leave?"

"Not really." Stormy buried his hands in his back pockets. "It's just best that you do. Look, Jaynie, I'm a rounder, always have been, always will be I guess." He placed both hands on her shoulders and looked her straight in the eye. "You're a beautiful young woman in your prime. Don't waste any more time on me," Stormy said, his tone and eyes displaying good intentions. "It's just not right."

"Since when did you become so concerned with doing what's right?"

Stormy didn't know the answer. After a moment, she turned away.

"Good luck," she said with clearly false sincerity.

She turned and dejectedly walked away. The flawless shape of her small but muscular buns gyrated in perfect rhythm. Doing the right thing sure could be tough on a man.

On the stage, a tiny man wearing a tux rambled incessantly, extolling the virtues of higher education. Susan, sitting between Smitty and Po Po, managed a warm smile, loaded with memories of their twelve years together. Smitty seemed to listen to the graduation ceremony but boredom smothered Po Po's face. Since Cal's disappearance, the boys had put up a brave front, but Cal's silence miffed them both. Smitty had told Susan that it was as if Cal had never existed, and the friendship never happened. She vowed that some day she would tell them the truth, the whole truth, so help her God.

Two weeks had passed since Stormy left, with misery replacing him as her companion. She longed for Stormy but couldn't tell a living soul. How do you explain you're madly in love with an older man you've met only once?

From her front-row seat along the third base line, Norma proudly watched her son receive one gift after another. Stormy stood in street clothes at home

plate of the near-packed Yankee Stadium. A giant scoreboard in center field
flashed "Stormy Weathers Appreciation Day." The infield resembled a
department store, with various merchandise sprinkled across the diamond. The
Yankee's organization gave the most unique gift—his-and-her prize cows.
Norma almost bit her tongue when she overheard one of his ex-teammates
comment, "the livestock's a joke; Stormy never spends any time in Texas."

Stormy waved to the crowd, displaying his best-forced smile. At times,
Stormy seemed to withdraw into himself, indifferent to his surroundings.
Norma had recognized it two days ago when he picked her up at the airport.
She knew the problem, but no discernible solution came to mind.

Susan Magnolia ignored the confident glance of the Nordic hulk sitting
beside her in broadcasting class. Rays of sunlight slanted through a classroom
window, spotlighting the red, All-American football patch on one sleeve of his
blue letter sweater. His square jaw, lavender eyes, and long, strong nose made
the perfect advertisement for the Aryan race. The jaw was as smooth as a
baby's.

Susan's full academic scholarship to SMU in Dallas allowed her to stay
close to her dad. Though her dorm room phone rang constantly with requests
for dates, all male suitors had struck out miserably. Often these suitors
followed her across campus, hoping for any sign of encouragement.

Susan had received a welcome call from Smitty and Po Po a few nights ago.
The two roomed together at Texas Tech in Lubbock, where both had
unexpectedly received full scholarships: Smitty's for academics, and Po Po's
for baseball. Especially Smitty had expressed disbelief with his scholarship.

"What if it's a mistake? I made C's that last semester! What if the
admissions department discovers the error, dismisses me from school and
sends my parents a bill?" he worried.

On the other hand, Po Po seemed just fine. Through beer-induced burps and
hiccups, Po Po happily reported on his first panty raid.

"As we speak," he'd bragged. "I'm wearing some young darling's panties
on my head. I asked her to marry me."

"Have you heard from Cal?" Smitty had asked wistfully.

"Not a word," she'd said.

The Nordic hulk dropped a note on her desk. It read: "Do you want to go
to the dance with me Saturday night?"

Susan peeked at the football player perched assuredly in his seat across the
aisle. His eyes were focused on the instructor but the leer dangling from the

side of his mouth boldly pointed toward Susan.

Susan scribbled her reply discreetly, and when no one saw, handed her message to the swaggering jock.

"I think you're a child," it said.

Stormy sat at his booth, miserably signing one autograph after another. The card-show circuit was wearing thinner than a summer windbreaker. Spring training would start soon, his first spring without baseball. The Yankees had offered him a coaching position, but he'd frozen at the plate.

"Maybe next season," he told them.

Stormy had too much time on his hands. Maybe he would take a trip to Dallas, visit Norma. No telling who else he might bump into.

Epilogue

- or -

SEVENTH INNING STRETCH

Cellos, violins, bass, and oboes merged to fill the car's interior with rich, classical music. The slow-cruising vehicle resembled a spaceship on wheels. With its built in computers, buttons and gadgets, the dashboard bore a striking similarity to a jet plane's cockpit.

The black auto quietly eased to a stop in front of Woodrow Wilson High. The proud old school had not changed in the least though the neighborhood had aged more like people favorable to greasy-spoon diners and all-night roller-skating rinks. Paint peeled from the modest frame houses. Weeds infiltrated the grass in the front yards, where unsupervised kids played among aging cars.

From under a thick growth of white hair, Stormy stared admirably at the three-story dinosaur sparkling beneath the late afternoon sun.

"Some things never change," he said.

He looked over to the lady sitting shotgun. Streaks of silver raced through dark hair that now stopped short of her shoulders. Sporting lively eyes and skin as smooth as an infield, she possessed that rare gene that enabled her to age more gracefully than other women.

A warm fall breeze sent leaves skipping, mimicking the sound of soft raindrops kissing the pavement. Through tortoise shell glasses, Stormy peered to the practice field, where a handful of grade school kids played baseball.

When the ball met one of those god-awful metal bats, the old man's shoulders recoiled at the hollow sound. The pure sweet sound of timber spanking cowhide; now, that was classical music to his ears! *Praise the Lord,* he thought, *pros only used wooden bats.*

Only minutes ago, the drive through Lakewood had revealed another progress scar. Years ago E.C. Harrell had reluctantly sold his pharmacy to a national drug chain, and soon after his death the blue tower had burned to the ground. Led by the present principal of Woodrow Wilson, the citizens of Lakewood had pressured the property owner to duplicate the landmark in Harrell's memory. Still, the sight of the newer tower had pricked Stormy's heart like a splintered bat.

"I'll watch these kids play for a while." He motioned to the practice field. "That'll give you a little time to explain things to the honorable principal." He spoke in a voice so warm, all ears would know how much he loved his front seat passenger.

"You will come inside in a few minutes?" the lady asked in an equally caring tone. "I could use some help on this, you know."

Stormy could hear the smile in her voice. "Sure will, Magnolia," he said. He hadn't called her Susan since her twenty-first birthday, the day of their marriage.

Magnolia Weathers left the auto and started for the school's main entrance. A kid playing ball glanced in the direction of Stormy's car.

"Wow, look!" cried the youngster. "Let's get an autograph."

All the children immediately dropped their equipment and sprinted toward the vehicle. They streaked past Stormy's car as if it wasn't there.

"Ms. Weathers!" yelled the same kid that originally spotted her. "Can we have your autograph?"

Stormy watched with pride when Magnolia stopped to sign autographs and chat with the children. Still transported by elegant legs, she resumed her path toward the front door; her lively pace generated a perfect bounce and swing of her hair. Magnolia disappeared into the halls of Woodrow Wilson, and the kids migrated back to the ball diamond.

Stormy spoke to his high-tech music box. "Hey, Babe," Stormy said gently. But the music machine remained silent, leaving its owner slightly miffed. "Babe Ruth!"

"Sorry, Stormy," a groggy voice replied in an automated computer tone. "I was taking a little snooze."

"It's okay, bro," said Stormy. "She's gone. How about some real music, something appropriate for the occasion?"

"You got it, bro," replied Babe, the twenty-first century's most modern musical invention.

But the music Babe played was J.J.'s version of "Precious Memories." Watching the kids' inept efforts at baseball, a rushing stream of nostalgia flooded his mind.

"As I travel on life's pathway
Know not what the year may hold
As I ponder, all grows fonder
Precious memories flood my soul
Precious memories how they linger
How they ever flood my soul."

Tranquil steel guitars guided the gentle cadence, spiritual and soothing as a country choir. J.J.'s voice sounded scratchy, even muffled, yet comforting as wind chimes. Stormy tilted his head backward and reflected on his life. With closed eyes, he inhaled deeply, drinking in the smells and sounds of the ball field.

"In the stillness of the twilight,
Precious sacred scenes unfold.
Precious memories, Hallelujah!
How they ever flood my soul.
In the stillness of the twilight,
Precious sacred scenes unfold."

A weak grounder rolled between the small fielder's legs. A waterfall of clear thick mucous flowed from the child's nose, contributing to his fielding woes. Evidently undecided whether to wipe the river of snot or fetch the ball, the youngster hovered over the ball. Chided by his friends to "quit holding up the game," he finally bent over to retrieve the scuffed ball.

"You guys need another player?"

The youngster peered up to see an old man towering above him, displaying a likable smile.

Though the receptionist in the school's main office had not yet surrendered to old age, the raising of the white flag seemed imminent. She seemed baffled with Susan's inquiry, but Susan suspected the elderly lady and confusion hung out on a regular basis. What was Susan thinking, asking for Smitty in the first place.

"Please ask the principal if he has a minute to see Susan Weathers," she said rephrasing the question.

The perplexity on the receptionist's face suddenly transformed to a huge splash of sunshine. Susan wondered if the disoriented woman recognized her or simply felt relieved at the ease of her request. In either event, the lady shuffled in small skittish steps through a door marked "Principal."

Susan found the office as comfortable as her favorite nightgown. Little had changed since she'd graduated forty years ago. The old, dark wood desks and original countertops from the 1920's remained in place, carefully maintained. Numerous pictures still hung on the beige plaster walls, even some that Susan remembered from high school.

One picture tugged on Susan like it was a nuclear-powered mini-vac. Of course, the school principal would showcase the team picture of Woodrow's only state championship baseball team!

Cal stood between Smitty and Po Po in the middle of the first row. Her father stood to the side, but his eyes drifted toward Cal, as if already concerned about his center fielder's high-spirited behavior.

But it was Cal's confident smile that she locked onto, a smile warm enough to protect her from the chilly side of life for four decades. The only cold spell had been Norma's death. Norma had never left the Lakewood area, often trading visits with her son and daughter-in-law. Norma Weathers died in her sleep twelve years ago from an overdose of contentment.

"Now why would the country's most famous new anchor visit old Woodrow Wilson High?"

Susan spun around to see Smitty, now thicker, thank goodness, but not too thick. His face was fuller and ridges lined the area around his eyes. White mostly ruled Smitty's once-red hair but at least he still had hair. (Po Po's head was now shiny as a new marble.) Susan hugged Smitty the way relatives do at family reunions. He ushered her into his office quicker than Cal Lucas had disappeared forty years ago.

Smitty dropped into his chocolate leather chair, then propped his feet on his desk as Coach Parker used to do, and clasped his hands behind his head.

"You and Stormy been married for what…"

"Thirty-seven years."

Smitty shook his head in friendly disbelief. "It doesn't seem that long ago."

Susan sat in a sturdy wooden chair normally reserved for students sent to visit the principal. *Probably the same one from 40 years ago,* she thought.

"It's been a blur," she said.

"I read that your daughter's retiring from the tennis tour to take a job as a head pro in some plush private club."

"Martha," Susan said, nodding. "Her little boy's eight, and she wanted to quit traveling." Susan's voice rose. "Now little Stormy: He's the next baseball player in our family."

"Good coaching, I bet."

"His granddad needed somebody to toss the ball around with."

"How's your son doing?"

"Fine. He's teaching creative writing at Northwestern."

"He never showed any interest in baseball?"

"Nope. Kind of amazing really." She was glad, and she suspected Stormy was, too. "Stormy II" was no life for a kid.

"I'll tell you what else is amazing. You're in the news as much for your charity work as your television specials. You look even better in person than on television."

"Flattery will get you everywhere."

"Is your dad still scouting for the Yankees?"

"Not much. He's eighty-three now, but still going strong. Dad seemed to get over Stormy's and my age difference after Stormy got him that job," Susan said through a youthful laugh.

"Small world, with Stormy coaching Po Po that year in the minors," Smitty said.

Stormy had coached Po Po one season at Albany, New York, but never told Po Po the truth. Stormy suspected Po Po would just grunt "E" and walk away, but he wasn't sure enough to take the risk.

"You know," Smitty said, pushing the tips of his fingers together, as if in deep thought. "Your husband was a successful manager in the majors, but then went back to coaching in the minor leagues. What was that all about?"

"The older he got, the more he decided to do what he enjoyed most—coach the kids, work with them before they develop bad habits."

"Well, Stormy must be one hell of a coach," Smitty enthusiastically offered. "'Cause Po Po made it to the big show."

"And for sixteen years," Susan added proudly. "He never developed into much of a hitter, but he played some great defense. Nobody ever wanted to tangle with him at the plate, that's for sure."

"Why do you think Po Po kept marrying all those strippers?" Susan asked.

"Well, you know what he always said," Smitty replied. "They make great money. You don't have to buy them a lot of clothes."

"How many were there?" Susan asked, grinning.

"Let's see." Smitty's glance searched the room in a contemplative manner. "He divorced what's her name…Foxy Lady after she quit dancing to be a computer programmer. He said she didn't look the same in those straight clothes."

"Didn't his second marriage end when she caught him with another stripper?" Susan asked.

"That would be Chastity, who found him with Brandi, whom he married immediately after the divorce. Then that ended when he discovered Brandi in the sack with another dancer named Honey. I think it kinda hurt his feelings when she didn't want him to join in," Smitty said, his face cracking open a grin.

"Geez, I didn't know all that! I hope he didn't marry Honey."

"Nope. Even Po Po knows three strikes and you're out. I told him to consider a relationship with someone who doesn't take their clothes off in public. It doesn't pass the smell test," Woodrow's principal added with a sly grin knowing that he sounded like his visitor's father.

"Do you remember Sammy Norton? That first baseman who served as a fire hydrant for Po Po after that big fight."

"How could I forget him or that day?" Susan said.

"Well, Norton became a big time Dallas attorney and developed quite a taste for fine restaurants and good champagne."

"Good for him," Susan said but not in an unfriendly tone.

"Maybe. Maybe not. One night, after Norton drank way too much bubbly, things really went to the dogs, so to speak. With one leg suspended, he actually relieved himself on an unsuspecting customer dining at the adjacent table."

"You've got to be kidding," Susan said incredulously. "How do you know all this?"

"It was in the paper. The article said he kept mumbling, 'I can hit a curve. I can hit a curve'."

"Oh, my God!" Susan said, her hands darting to cover her mouth. "I bet those other customers hoped Norton didn't mistake them for a curve."

Both started to laugh so hard, Susan practically hyperventilated and Smitty had to clear his throat.

"How about the game on national television when Po Po's bat broke and all those corks fell out? He told me he did it in memory of Cal," Smitty said, re-igniting the laughter.

"It's a good thing Po Po never had to work a day in his life after he retired from baseball."

"What an incredible time! I'll never forget that last semester. Looking back, so much happened, it seems like it lasted for years," Smitty said.

"I know."

"I think the most baffling thing was my receiving an academic scholarship," Smitty said, his tone turning serious. "I never could figure that one out."

Susan bit her lower lip harder than she intended. Stormy would not approve of what she was about to do.

"You never got a scholarship," she said.

"Huh?"

"Neither did Po Po."

The room went so quiet Susan heard the sound of Smitty's front teeth slowly clacking with one another in a sort of contemplative rhythm.

"Stormy paid for your college, and Po Po's too." Susan offered a kind and confessional smile.

Smitty stared at his hands, appearing more puzzled than if trying to hit his super sinker.

"There's something else, Smitty. Stormy has a heart murmur. The doctors want him to stop coaching," Susan added in a motherly tone. "He's wanted to clear something up with you for a long time. I've convinced him now's the time."

"I don't understand any of this," Smitty blurted.

"Maybe this will help." Susan Magnolia retrieved a picture from her purse and slid it on top of the principal's desk.

Smitty stared noncommittally at the picture. It was the picture taken at the topless club the night Woodrow won city. After a moment, he broke into a massive smile.

"That's the night we got thrown in jail! I remember a photographer selling the picture to Cal."

Smitty's eyes alternated between the snapshot and Susan. "You said you never heard from Cal," he said suspiciously. "How did you get this picture?"

"Stormy's always had the picture," Susan said neutrally.

"Last time I saw it, Cal had it."

"You could say Cal had it, too," Susan said. "Go outside and ask Stormy."

"Now I'm really confused. Is he here?"

"Look." Susan pointed to the window behind Smitty. "He's in the car."

Smitty stood and walked slowly to the window.

"He's not in the car. Looks to me like he's still coaching."

"Okay, bro, get that back elbow parallel with the ground, like I showed you." Stormy stood halfway between home plate and the pitchers' mound, facing the young batter. "Keep your knees bent. Relax and watch the ball."

The youngster followed his instructions diligently. Stormy practically handed the ball to home plate, and the youngster slapped a sharp grounder to shortstop. The kid flashed a victorious grin.

"Attaboy," Stormy yelled, turning to see the baseball roll unhindered between the fielder's legs. Stormy hobbled toward his snot-nosed shortstop who gazed dejectedly downward. Stormy retrieved a handkerchief from the back pocket of his baggy Levis and wiped the kid's runny nose.

Stormy placed a grandfatherly hand on the boy's shoulder. "Just remember to keep in front of the ball and stay down. Keep your eyes on the ball." While holding his back rigid, Stormy bent his knees and lowered his borrowed glove until it touched the ground.

"Worst thing that will happen is the ball will hit your glove or arms," he added. "You still have a chance to throw out the runner."

After limping to the pitcher's mound, he delivered another pitch to his now-accomplished hitter. A lazy fly ball drifted to shallow center field. The outfielder unsteadily circled the fly ball until it plopped to the ground untouched. Stormy crossed the field toward him.

"Son, that's my position you're butchering," he said with friendly concern. "Let me show you a couple of things."

As Stormy attempted to give the child a friendly pat, the skinny kid recoiled, as if Stormy's carried a transmittable disease. The child was skittish as a squirrel, the face hardly visible; an oversize baseball cap was pulled down so snugly, it nearly concealed the child's ears. Stormy leaned in for a closer look. The child's skin looked smooth and soft, almost like a baby's. It was a girl! Her ball cap barely exposed blonde hair bright enough to light a ball diamond.

"What's your name?" Stormy asked cordially.

She shuffled her feet; her remarkable blue eyes avoided Stormy's. The youngster still declined to speak.

"That's my twin sister, Kate!" yelled snot-nose. "She's ten. She's kind of a pain. She wants to learn how to play ball. Everybody knows girls can't play baseball."

"I taught my daughter to play ball, and she could outplay any boy in her high school class. I'm not lying. She would have been the first female in the major leagues, if she hadn't liked tennis better. I taught her, and I can teach you."

A flicker of hope suddenly appeared in the child's shy glance.

"Hit a fly ball!" he yelled toward home plate.

The gimpy-kneed old man gracefully caught up with the fly ball and with equal grace hauled it in. Stormy lobbed the ball back to home plate.

"Kate," he said. "Keep it simple. Just tell yourself that if you don't get to that fly ball before it hits the ground, you're gonna die."

The little girl stared hard at Stormy.

"Okay, okay," he said. "Maybe that's a little harsh, but you get the picture. Success depends on how badly you want it. Hit another one!" he bellowed.

The batter produced a much shorter fly ball; Stormy plunged forward without hesitation. With a desperate last second lunge, Stormy made the catch.

"See what I mean?" he called to Kate. Turning back to home plate, he yelled, "One more!"

By now, Stormy's cheeks looked as if he'd spent too much time in an Alaskan blizzard. The next ball soared far over his head. He wheeled around and ran so hard the wind pushed his hair away from his determined face. He could feel the pace of his heart elevate. As Stormy extended his glove hand for the ball, he felt a chest pain so sharp his legs went numb. Stormy and the ball seemed to fall in slow motion. Stormy rolled on his back and stared upward; the ground felt warm from the afternoon sun. The air above him seemed ill suited for breathing purposes and a galaxy of white stars dominated the sky. Stormy's tongue felt too big for his mouth; his throat felt parched and his view was turning dim, though he hoped it was because of the sun sinking in on the horizon.

Except for the startling high-decibel sound of his own breathing, Stormy's world was now a black and white silent movie. He could now barely see small, concerned faces above him, close as shadows, chattering at seventy-eight RPM among themselves.

Life passed too quick, Stormy decided, like a Nolan Ryan fastball exploding by home plate, past him before he could really learn enough about it. True, life after baseball had been just as rewarding; it was simply a matter of relinquishing the batter's box to the next hitter.

Darkness crept closer and closer until he was engulfed in black. Almost immediately, Stormy was walking along a narrow road but saw a bright light at the end of it. As he passed a giant image of his family on his right, his anxieties released like balloons on opening day. He felt both secure and at ease with the notion of leaving his life. But wait, he desperately needed to hang on long enough to say goodbye to Magnolia. If not with words, with a glance or a flicker of the eye; some action that would let her know everything was all right. Stormy was determined to fight off death the way he once battled a side arm flame thrower.

Susan raced toward the practice field faster than her long legs had ever carried her. Smitty ran beside her, both exchanging fearful expressions. While frantically screaming her husband's name, she thought of her conversation with Stormy in the Porsche that rainy day forty years ago. Did she subconsciously allow him to fulfill his own wish: to die on the ball field?

Her mind retreated a few years. She heard Stormy coughing uncontrollably, obviously struggling for air, while taking a shower. She immediately dashed to his rescue but found him smiling. Water had located an unwelcome opening in his throat, but he was all right, a false alarm. In that very instant, she understood how incredibly empty she would feel the day it proved for real.

Hopefully, today was another false alarm. Thank goodness! Stormy was moving on the ground. No! Shit! Susan was running on her heels, causing everybody and everything to move with every wild step.

If able, Stormy would remind her to run on her toes not her heels. "You can't catch a fly ball if everything in sight bobs like a boat in a storm!" he would say.

Susan dropped heavily to her knees. She rushed Stormy's head to her bosom, massaging his white mane, as if she stroked it long and hard enough, she might transfer some of her life into him. Her body trembled and a breathtaking pain overpowered her lower abdomen. This was no false alarm.

Smitty, searching for air, stood beside Susan and looked incredibly helpless.

A teacher, also breathing heavily, arrived and whispered into Smitty's ear, "An ambulance is on the way."

Everyone was still. Susan's gentle weeping provided the only sound.

Although Stormy's eyes were closed, if he tried hard enough, he could still vaguely visualize the disturbed crowd above him. He could see Kate and her brother. If only he could speak. "Hey, honey, save those tears for somebody else. Snot nose, be nice to your sister. Remember, keep your bridge down. And, for God's sake, tell your parents to give you something for that cold!"

Stormy located Smitty standing above Magnolia. His eyes were moist enough for a rain delay. "Hey, Smitty, I played with some real pros in my day, but nobody had more balls than you in that state championship game!"

Stormy could feel Magnolia's loving clutch tighten. "Okay, so I shouldn't say balls in front of the kids." He wanted to say, "You're fading away, but I know you're there," but, he could not. Thank goodness Susan made it in time, she'll know everything's okay. An internal rush of air surged to his head, leaving him dizzy. Stormy expected it was his last breath because he felt his veins constrict and his esophagus close.

Magnolia sensed a change in Stormy's breathing. She gently pushed

Stormy from her bosom so she could see his face. Stormy appeared flash frozen; something mightier than the fear of crossing to the other side took command of his face. The mystery left quicker than one of his four baggers left the park because then his mouth pointed north at the corners. His peaceful expression said plenty about his new home.

"I think he's dead, Smitty." Magnolia's voice already possessed a tranquil tone of acceptance.

Smitty positioned himself to listen to Stormy's heart. His somber face reported what his ears did not hear.

A space-aged ambulance sped across the ball field. From Stormy's last black vehicle, Babe broke the quiet, by respectfully playing one last tune for the fallen hero. J.J. mumbled with deliberate slowness,
"When you and I are ready
No longer earthly bound
We'll travel through
The crystal night...starbound"

The ambulance lurched to a harsh stop only a few feet from Stormy, leaving skid marks on the outfield grass. Puffing in its own exhaust, the car sent smoke signals as black as the mood into the blue sky. Two subdued men jumped out, dressed in white, as if they understood only to appear at Woodrow wearing something traditional. They briefly stared at Stormy's body which lay beneath the fading sun, throwing off an exaggerated shadow. As carefully as a mother would handle a newborn, the two men placed Stormy on a stretcher and began to slide him in the back of the ambulance. Second verse, Babe dutifully instructed J.J.
"Heaven holds a mystery
Wrapped inside a sound
Through the eyes of midnight stars
Starbound, you and I"

Smitty helped Susan enter the ambulance. She sat beside Stormy. Her hands lay folded in her lap, her eyes glued to the stretcher.

"Would you like me to go with you?" Smitty asked through his sniffles.

"Thanks, but I think I'd like to be alone with him," Susan whispered. Her face was ashen.

"Susan!" Smitty said, working his voice up a notch. "Look, he's smiling." Sure enough, Stormy, who according to J.J., was no longer earthly bound, grinned as if now aware of great pleasures that mere earthlings knew nothing of.

"I know," Susan tenderly replied, managing a grim smile of her own. "This is the way he wanted it."

The ambulance door shut. Though the siren blared and red lights flashed, Stormy's last ride left at a more hurried than frenetic pace.

"One last verse, J.J.," requested Babe.

"A failing star is what we are
Suspended in space
Homeward bound is all we found
To save the human race"

After all the children migrated back to the ball diamond and resumed play, Smitty slowly started his way back to the school. The burden of a situation he could not comprehend rendered his walk a tad bent. He scrutinized the picture that Susan gave him the way he would study the formula for eternal youth. What in the hell did an old photo have to do with anything? What did Stormy Weathers have to do with his life? Why did Smitty feel so much hurt? Was it because he cared for Susan? No, it was more than that, but what? And what on God's earth had ever happened to Cal?

A prisoner to his own feet, every mechanical step carried him deeper and deeper into a nostalgic trance. Suddenly, Smitty's head snapped back so that he appeared to study the sky. His knees buckled at the thought: the grin on Cal's face in the snapshot was identical to the contented expression on Stormy's face. Either both used the same orthodontist or Cal and Stormy were the same.

"No way," Smitty said, shaking his head in disbelief, but then he said it out loud. "Cal and Stormy were the same?"

Smitty repeated the words over and over. The thought, as outrageous as it may be, brought a hint of relief. Susan's marriage, held at the old Gaston Avenue Baptist Church on Gaston Avenue, would seem less peculiar. To Smitty's recollection, Susan only met Stormy briefly the day he visited Woodrow. A year or so later, while Susan still attended SMU, she announced the date; her twenty-first birthday, he believed.

Cal's hasty departure had haunted Smitty and Po Po like a recurring bad dream for all these years. Wasn't their friendships important enough to warrant a simple goodbye? If Smitty's current suspicion was true, the friendships had proved strong enough for he and Po Po to receive college educations! Smitty racked his brain, searching for clues, determined to bend his thoughts backward. The echoes of Cal's voice played in his mind. The night at Harrell's, Cal had asked, "Does Mr. Harrell still own the store?" Doc mentioned that Stormy used to come in all the time. That night, in jail, Cal said he would explain everything before he died. Was today linked to Cal's promise?

The season Stormy coached Po Po in the minor leagues, Po Po mentioned receiving special attention from Stormy, the kind one would receive from a wiser, older brother. Furthermore, when Po Po quizzed Stormy concerning Cal's whereabouts, Stormy had always replied, "We've lost touch." Cal and Stormy were the same!

No wonder the son-of-a-gun knew so blasted much. We learned a great deal from Cal Lucas or Stormy Weathers or whoever he was, about baseball and life. Smitty felt a sense of elevation, as if riding a fuel-injected elevator. Stormy's farewell in the gym *was* Cal's goodbye. It was a revelation that finally filled a void Smitty carried for so long.

Thomas "Smitty" Pierce, educator of young minds, now stood at Glasgow Avenue, the street that divided the front of Woodrow Wilson High and the practice field. Thinking of his last semester caused him to be overwhelmed by desire to return as a student. Since, evidently, that wasn't possible—evidently, in that Stormy seemingly managed it, Smitty would always find solace in Cal's farewell speech. Stormy Weathers, alias Cal Lucas, even then the old pro, learned plenty from a bunch of amateurs. No doubt, heroes are hard to find.

Kate, age ten, twin sister of snot nose, charged the ball gently descending from the Texas sky. She feared she would not reach the ball before it dropped to the grass. This was not good news. The neat old man had said: "Get to the ball before it hit the ground or you might die!" He hadn't caught up to that last fly ball and look what happened to him.

After the ball vanished into Kate's glove, the other children erupted into tumultuous praise. In majestic triumph, she held the ball out for all to see, as if she just caught the prize-winning fish. All decided the startling catch symbolized a perfect ending to a remarkable afternoon of baseball. How often do you see a gimpy-legged old-timer play center field like an All-Star, then die right on the spot? And with a grin on his face? It was a day to remember in older age, such as high school, a day to rekindle thoughts of childhood.

Kate walked with her head held proudly upright. In a few years she might become the best player in her high school. The old-timer said it was possible. If only he could have stayed around longer to teach her some more. Her brother and the rest walked ahead of her, but at this moment she enjoyed her independence and her solitude.

Without warning, a most ridiculous sight stepped into full view from behind a tree. A man wore a baggy, gray wool uniform with the name "Browns" sewn on the front. (Kate did not recognize the uniform because it was the uniform of the St. Louis Browns, a major league team of dubious distinction that folded in the 1950's.) In the advanced stage of disintegration, a decaying gray ball cap hung sideways on the man's head.

The strange vision approached Kate with a most affable demeanor. "Please allow me to introduce myself," said the man, offering a modest bow to the little girl. "My name is Mac Swindell, young lady," he said, extending his business card. "How would you like to be the first female to play in the major leagues?"

Kate ignored the card. She pinned Mac with a frightful stare; her nostrils flared like a bull hell bent on sighting red. She suddenly assumed the disposition of an executioner on death row, one that enjoyed working weekends.

"Suck a rock, fish face!" Kate answered testily. Translation: "I might be the first woman major leaguer some day, and I don't need your goofy-ass help."

Mac's eyes widened and he gasped the way people gasp after a lung full of tear gas. His hand disappeared into his shirt pocket and he pulled out a cigarette, rapidly flipping it into his mouth. After rummaging through both pant's pockets, he failed to locate a match. Undaunted, Mac relied on his thumb technique, except without success. As daylight surrendered to dusk, the old high school loomed over Mac as if watching his every move. He repeatedly attempted to light the tobacco stick dangling from his wicked mouth.

Mac mumbled in disgust, "Kids these days!"

This ball game's over.

Printed in the United States
22960LVS00006B/1-24

9 781413 716672